VENGEANT

VENGEANT

A NOVEL

ERIC ARTISAN

VENGEANT

www.EricArtisan.com

This is a work of fiction. All of the
characters, organizations, and events portrayed
in this novel are either products of the
author's imagination or are used fictitiously.
The science, however, is real.

Published in the United States of America
Also available as an e-book

ISBN-13: 978-0692762707
ISBN-10: 0692762701

Book Design by Jim Arneson

Song lyrics in Chapter Ten are from
"Spirit in the Sky" © Erik Jacobson

FOR *THIS* YOU

Nothing is more hidden from us than the illusion

which lives with us day to day;

and our greatest illusion is to believe that

we are who we think ourselves to be.

~ Rilke

Happy! So happy!

Charlene has his arm as they wade into the throng, everybody hanging out by their cars and trucks. One of his teammates—Dave!—hands him a cold beer. People patting him on the back, congratulating him—whether for the scholarship or for simply graduating, it doesn't matter. He can feel himself beaming back at them, at all the smiling, happy faces. The whole school must be here!

Some of Charlene's friends go to pull her away, but she hangs on tightly to his hand. This is their night to celebrate, she'd said earlier. Together. Forever. The first night of the rest of their lives, she said.

He can see her face—her beautiful, beautiful face—glowing golden beside him. Her eyes dancing green sparkles; her lips like pillowed candy; the constellation of freckles at her throat. She's wearing that light yellow sundress with the little flowers that she bought for her eighteenth birthday, for their trip to Norman, for him, she said.

He can almost feel her squeeze his hand in hers, hug him, hold him close, stare into his eyes as they would lie together in the grass, legs intertwined . . . The soft curve of her waist, her hip . . . the finest pale hairs beneath his palm . . .

But now she's gone . . .

Where is she?

Where's Charlene?

People moving herky-jerky, like shadowy red demons, around the raging bonfire. The scene strangely silent. He too seemingly moving in fits and starts, drunkenly, scanning the crowd. Even more kids now, from other schools, everybody congregating at the lake for the start of summer.

Ah, there she is . . .

But who's that she's talking to? . . . Oh, yeah, the asshole from that fancy East Coast college—Marni's cousin, the pretty boy. Big money. What are they laughing about? What's so funny?

He stalks over.

His finger in the asshole's face. Strong words. Staring him down.

Then Charlene, pulling at his arm—scolding him, at first, now coaxing, sweet-talking, making him *feel like the asshole instead.*

But . . . she'd had her hand on the asshole's arm . . . standing close, looking up . . . laughing so brightly . . .

Her worried face.

The asshole's smug grin.

Everybody's eyes upon him . . .

And now he's walking away—angry, proud—accepting the proffered joint. Making a show of it.

Don't go, she says. Don't go.

He stops and looks back. She hasn't moved from the asshole's side.

Let's go to the bluff, she says. Their spot. Where they can watch the sunrise, like they planned.

It hurts him, it kills him, it hurts him so bad . . .

But he turns away.

MONDAY, SEPTEMBER 19, 2011   **DAY 1**

CLAY WAKES with tears in his eyes and the smell of garbage in his nose. He makes a face against the stench and harsh light and turns his head into the crook of his arm—the arm he's clearly been using for a pillow. His back hurts. There's a sharp pain in his side from where he must be lying on something, a lump of some sort. Without looking, he reaches beneath him and sweeps whatever it is away—only to start, with a cry, and sit up quickly, staring at his hand—at the deep gash in his first three fingers, already running with blood.

Reflexively, he puts his hand to his mouth and sucks on the wound. Gags at the putrid taste. His hand is filthy! He puts pressure on the wound, instead. He looks for what cut him and finds it on the ground, on the littered cement: the bottom to a broken liquor bottle, its jagged edges upright, ready to strike again.

Cursing, he looks up . . .

. . . at the mouth of an alley . . . from deep inside it, maybe sixty feet in. Two overflowing dumpsters and two tall buildings frame the picture. Garbage bags and cardboard boxes and wooden crates and other assorted junk line the walls toward him to either side. There are more tall gray buildings across the street; flashes of bright color and shiny metal and the discordant hum and honking of vehicles; a steady flow of people walking by, no one once looking his way.

Clay's gaze continues upward, between the high, close walls, and he blinks at the hazy ball of sun directly overhead. It must be noon, he thinks, or close to it.

He looks around him, at the piles of trash; then at himself, at his raggedy, disgusting clothes, bulked up with numerous layers; atop it all a greasy, stained overcoat.

What the . . . ?

He's at a loss: he has no idea where he is, or what he's doing here—or, for that matter, why he's dressed like a bum.

He goes to get up, forgetting his injured hand and pushing himself off the ground with it. The pain makes him wince and he stares down at the red imprint on the ground, grabs a fistful of shirttails to staunch the blood. He feels dizzy, nauseous, but not because of his hand. He staggers back a step, then another.

Something's not right . . . He sways and sidesteps and goes down hard, the refuse beneath him breaking his fall.

He sits there, head bowed, eyes closed, taking slow deep breaths, willing his heart and stomach to relax. Feels stringy bangs hanging down, covering his face; something like wet dirt under the one good hand supporting him—the one that now begins to shake.

He feels sick. Hot and cold at the same time. His thoughts muddled, confused.

Okay, get a grip, get a grip. It'll come to you in a second.

But nothing comes. His mind is a blank. There are only the broken fragments of a nearly forgotten dream . . .

"Charlene . . . ," he whispers.

"Hey, ya stupid fucker, yer bleedin' all over yerself!"

Startled, Clay swings his head up and around toward the voice, off to his right. Catches sight of a man—rail thin, filthy, in a long brown coat—wresting himself from a mound of debris. But the motion's too much and Clay's head spins, his stomach lurches. He retches and throws himself forward, throwing up strings of yellow-green bile, having landed in a sideways crouch, his forehead touching, then retouching the ground.

He feels immediately better afterward, though. Leans on an elbow, wipes his mouth on an already ruined sleeve.

"Way to start the day, huh?" the other man says. "What'dja do, cut yer hand? How the hell'dja do that?"

Clay warily eyes the stranger and scoots back against a rusty drum barrel by the alley wall.

But the guy's paying him no attention now. "We're gonna have to getcha cleaned up," he says to his feet as he kicks at the trash strewn around them. "Yer gonna scare the hell outta everybody, lookin' like that."

Clay looks down to where his hand is clutched in his lap. There's a brown-red circle the size of a dinner plate staining his outer shirt, a once-nice light-blue button-down.

His strange, skeletal companion makes a triumphant sound and, reaching down, picks up a short length of thick metal pipe and raises it high. "Ha! Can't hide from the hider, ya!"

Clay unclenches his hand and holds it to his face. The bleeding has lessened to a thin wet line that starts again when he flexes his fingers. He balls up a section of cloth at his chest and squeezes. It hurts; throbs. He closes his eyes against the pain and his sudden tears—against the unfamiliar nightmare he's found himself in.

Why can't I remember? . . .

What the hell is going on? . . .

Clank! Clank! Clank!

The man's now squatting beside him, hitting his metal pipe on the ground. Up close he has the look of a cadaver, a dead man, his eyes bulging round in their sockets; dirt-lined, sickly pale skin hanging loose over sunken cheeks; suppurating sores on his lips. He smiles wide, revealing sparse, rotten teeth, as something falls out of the end of the pipe.

A small plastic bundle lies on the ground between them, before it's quickly snatched up.

"Ha! Don't worry, my friend. Wiley'll take care of ya. We'll getcha fixed up in no time." The man's googly eyes burn with intensity. His head shifts nervously back and forth, scanning the alley, as he unwraps the package. "Ya didn't think I'd forget aboutcha, didja?" He raises a placating hand. "Yeah, yeah, I know, I shoulda cooked this last night if I had it. But then where would we be now, heh? Later. Wouldn't be fit for society. Ha!" He chuckles and glances up. "Ya sleep all right? Ya were hollerin'."

But Clay doesn't answer, he can only watch in stupefied silence as the man reverently unfolds a red-and-white-checkered piece of wax paper—a fast-food wrapper—and lays it out like an altar cloth, its foreign contents idols and offerings to some lesser god of insanity.

There's a rustling and the sound of a tin can falling and both men are instantly alert, peering down the alley to where it's dark and closed-in.

Then after a sufficient pause, the guy goes back to work. He shuffles closer, muttering, puts his back to the alley's entrance.

Clay doesn't know what to say to this person—this living corpse—so close beside him. He's afraid to say anything, actually. But knows he must, at some point.

The man continues to fiddle, hunched over, with intensifying purpose, his lips moving silently.

"Uh . . . What's going on?" Clay asks, finally, the depth and seriousness of his question lost to even his own ears.

"Ha! What's goin' on is today's the day! It's yer turn to score, my friend. Or didja forget? Ha!" The man twists his head to look up at the thin slice of sky above them. "It's gettin' late. We need to getcha in line. Pronto. Before two." He nods to Clay's bloody hand. "We'll wrap that up, don'tcha worry. Outta sight, outta mind. Ha! They won't letcha in like that. I'll trade shirts with ya before we go. Stupid fucker," he adds with a shake of his head.

Clay pulls his hand away from the sticky cloth. His whole palm is a bloody mess; he can't make out the cut anymore. It should be all right, though, after a while.

"Uh, where . . . ?" he begins, looking around hopelessly. "How'd—?" But what can he ask this stranger who seems to know him so well?

"Yeah?" The guy's holding a lighter to a bottle cap full of cloudy liquid.

"Uh . . . I, uh . . . I don't know what's going on," Clay says. "I, uh . . . I'm not really sure what I'm doing here."

The man just flicks his eyes in Clay's direction, concentrating on the task at hand. Shakes his head. "Well," he says at last. He drops the lighter and adds a tiny piece of white cotton to the boiled liquid. "I don't know what to tell ya, man." He picks up a much-abused hypodermic needle and deftly inserts its tip into the cotton. "But this should straighten ya right out, that's for sure."

"No, I'm serious," Clay says, tensing up, eyeing the needle. "I mean, I have no idea who you are. Or what the heck you're doing with that thing . . . Is that *drugs?*" He can hear the panic in his voice.

The guy just looks at him, deadpan, holding the syringe, point up. Then: "Ha! Yeah, right. Come on, we gotta get goin'." He holds out the needle for Clay to take.

But Clay puts up his hands and uselessly tries to scoot further back. "No, no, I'm okay. You go ahead."

"Huh? Ya stupid fucker. Yer already pukin' yer guts out. Look atcha, man, yer shakin'! In a minute yer gonna be shittin' all over yerself, and then where will we be, heh?" He moves closer. "Ya want me to do it for ya?"

"No! Hell no! I'm not—I don't do this kind of thing . . . Really."

The man sits back on his heels. Cocks his head. "Oh, yeah? So now *I'm* the only one with a problem, huh? Like yer suddenly better than me, or somethin', country boy?" He scoffs.

But then he's staring, hard. Puts his disgusting face even closer. And must see something in Clay's expression. "Look atcher arms," he commands.

Clay can only stare back, horrified. He can feel the trembling in his limbs, the twisting of his insides, getting stronger; the nausea returning even worse than before; the craving in his mind for . . . something . . . something . . .

Sanity, for Chrissakes!

When he still hasn't moved, the man reaches over and yanks up the sleeve of Clay's coat. "Look atcher fucking arms!"

Clay looks. His forearm is a mottled purple and blue along the soft inside, the whole thing riddled with needle marks from wrist to elbow. Some look infected.

He gasps. *Oh my God!* "No way!" he says, stunned.

"Yes way, ya stupid fucker. Now, hurry up. We gotta getcha cleaned up and lookin' presentable. Getcha in line before two."

Despite the revulsion Clay feels, the sick yearning deep inside him is even greater, so he reaches for the syringe. If this is what he needs to put an end to it, then . . .

But how could this have happened to me? he thinks sorrowfully, frantically, as he takes the needle and stares at it in his hand. *How did I end up like this?*

How could I have forgotten who I am?

His hand begins to shake uncontrollably.

"Oh, for the love of Pete!" the guy says. "Here, just let me do it, all right? Get this the fuck over with." He grabs the needle. "What's wrong with ya today?" He reaches out and slaps the side of Clay's neck.

"Hey! What the hell!" Clay raises an arm to block the next blow.

"This is how we gotta do it now, dumb-ass," the man says mock-patiently. "Now, I know ya've gone and lost yer damn mind, but we *really* need to get a move on." He sighs extravagantly. Glances around. "Ya trust me?"

Clay doesn't know; he has no idea. He has no clue who this person even is.

But then something rings a bell . . . Is it something he remembers? . . . He doesn't know.

"Uh . . . Wiley? Is that right?"

The man's grotesque face beams. "Ha! Hey, there ya go! Ya really had me goin' there for a minute. Jeez!" He reaches over and roughly slaps the side of Clay's neck a few more times.

Clay can barely feel the needle enter his skin.

And then, instantly, like a miracle, the nausea is gone; the tremors are gone; the splitting headache he hadn't even realized he had is gone. His thoughts are clear now, untroubled. And . . . and . . . he can remember . . . he remembers something . . .

Charlene . . .

He can see her angelic form—outlined, her long hair flowing, brightly lit from behind, as if at the entrance to a luminous tunnel—hovering, just out of reach. Her arms outstretched.

Clay holds out his hands. "Charlene!"

"Oh, ya stupid, stupid fucker," he can hear his friend say from beside him, from another world, another dimension, far far away. "Charlene's dead, man. She's *dead*. For the last time: *Get over it.*"

A bright moon shimmering across the water. The hypnotic lap of waves upon the shore at his feet. He sits cradling his knees, a warm beer in his hand. A number of empty bottles by his side.

This wasn't the night he had planned—that they had planned—was it?

Was he wrong to be so jealous? Maybe it really was nothing.

But Charlene knows how he gets. He's told her a thousand times.

Still, he needs to find her. Apologize.

A shout, laughter. Come on! his friends call as they run into the water, naked, splashing each other gleefully. He recognizes the guys but not the girls—very shapely girls, he sees.

It looks like fun. And isn't that what he's supposed to be doing? Having fun? Celebrating?

He downs the last of his beer and stands, sways. Hesitates.

Then he's walking back up the path through the trees, increasing his pace as he goes. Determined. Remorseful.

He'll make it right. He's always able to make it right again.

Everything is a flickering orange-red around the fire, much smaller now. Only half as many people as before. But still they want to talk and laugh, hand him a beer.

I'm looking for Charlene, he says. Have you seen her?

Where is she?

Where's Charlene?

She's dancing, says one of her friends. Over there.

But she's not there, either.

She left already, says a girl.

No, she went down to the lake, says another.

Oh, wait, is that her?

From too far away he can see Charlene standing beside a sports car—a Camaro—yellow, like her dress.

He calls to her, calls again. But she doesn't hear.

And then that asshole is there. Beside her. Opening the passenger door.

No!

She's getting inside.

He's running now—but drunkenly, slowly—too slow, too slow . . .

Then they're driving away.

She's driving away . . .

The taillights finally wink out of sight.

DAY 2

CLAY WAKES with a shout—"No!"—his legs kicking.

He lies naked atop the sheets, covered in a sheen of sweat.

A golden-red light fills the room; then is gone; then is back again; pulsing, coming in through the large, open window near the bed. Dark . . . red . . . dark . . . red . . . dark . . . He tries to slow his breathing, match his heartbeat to the same steady rhythm. And in the one-second intervals of blinking light, takes in the dingy room around him: the front door and window to his right; a low dresser with an ancient TV in front of him, at the foot of the bed; a small round table and two chairs to his left, between the bed and the wall; an empty, doorless closet and the bathroom farther left, around the corner, reflected light coming off of the small mirror above the sink.

Brown paper bags and Chinese take-out cartons litter the tabletop; there's a half-full jug of orange juice. A set of clothes on a chair: a red polo shirt over the back, a brown leather jacket over the arm, a pair of jeans. Some things on the dresser, beside the TV.

He lies back to stare at the ceiling as it flashes red.

He doesn't feel fucked up . . . or hungover. He doesn't *feel* like a heroin addict . . .

Thank God! he thinks. It was only a dream.

Clay swings his legs off the bed to stand at the window. It's night. A salty, humid breeze with the tang of industry blows in, doing little to dry his skin. An indecipherable column of Chinese characters attached to the wall outside is the source of the blinking light—red outlined in gold—each at least a foot tall. Similar signs in Chinese are all across and down the street, signifying what must be shops and restaurants, one clearly a liquor store. He's on the second floor of an apartment building or hotel, or over one of the shops, he guesses. The narrow street is empty but for a dog strolling casually down its center.

Whoa! Am I in China? . . . I must be.

He closes his eyes and tries to think . . .

But, *Nope.* Nothing. He has no recollection of where he is or how he got here.

He tries to think of something that happened yesterday . . .

Last week . . .

Oookay. Last month? . . .

Last year? . . .

Oh, this isn't good.

He turns back to the room for some sort of clue, something to jog his memory. But nothing registers.

The light switch is by the door and he flicks it on, illuminating a round, white paper lantern hanging in the center of the ceiling. It's dim but more than adequate and partially dispels the pulsing red.

There's a large wooden cut-out of a leaning, wind-blown tree on the wall over the bed. His wallet (or at least he thinks it's his) and some change are on the dresser. He steps closer—there's also a cell phone, a large key. He stops—and a gun.

Whoa, now. He hesitates. Is it his? It must be. But, why? Is he a cop? A criminal?

The gun's an automatic, tarnished black, its handle well worn. Old. A .44 or .45, he figures, by the size of it. It's huge, like something the Terminator would carry. He picks it up carefully; it's even heavier than he thought. "Colt" it says on the long barrel. He points it at the empty closet but keeps his finger off the trigger. He's fired a few handguns before, of course, for kicks, but his experience is mostly with shotguns, hunting rifles. He peers one-eyed down the sights. "Bang," he says softly. "Bang."

He sets the gun back on the dresser. Doesn't see a holster for it anywhere. Or a badge. So: not a cop, he wagers. It's probably for self defense, a rough neighborhood.

He takes up the phone now, relieved. Everything'll be on the phone. It's slim and wide, like one of those new BlackBerrys, but not a model he recognizes. The screen lights up when he pushes a button, turns blue, with a dashed line and prompt: ENTER PASSWORD.

Huh? . . .

Shit! He tries to think. But how can he enter a password when he doesn't even know what day it is? Or, wait, does he? . . . *Nope,* not a clue. Maybe everything'll come to him later. He sure hopes so.

Does he have amnesia or something? he wonders. He's seen a movie once where that happened to somebody. But when was that? He was a kid, maybe . . .

Absently, Clay steps back and sits on the edge of the bed. Stares at the gun on the dresser, then at his warped reflection in the television screen. He can remember the trailer he grew up in, he and his mom; the Indian reservation nearby. He remembers grade school and his third-grade teacher, Mrs. Barrett. His dog Stormy; their neighbor's horses. All of his childhood friends.

Then moving to Taloga with his mom and her new boyfriend. Junior high. Football. High school. Charlene. Graduation . . .

He recalls the previous nights' dreams and it makes him shudder. That's the last thing he can remember, no matter how hard he tries: Charlene leaving in that asshole's car.

But was it a memory? Or only a dream?

Clay's eyes land on the fat leather wallet on the dresser, and he snaps to attention. Answers. Maybe his wallet will have some answers.

Inside it the first thing he sees is a thick wad of bills—hundreds, fifties, twenties, only a few smaller. *Nice.* There's a single credit card, a gas card, library card—all in his name—but no receipts, no slips of paper, no real clues at all. Just a condom. Then there's his driver's license, of course, in the plastic sleeve; the photo of him . . . but older. Different . . . The date of issue says 4/20/12.

What? No, that can't be. 2012? That's, like, *eight years* since he graduated!

What the hell?!

Looking closer, Clay sees that it's not an Oklahoma license at all but—New Hampshire? Where the heck is New Hampshire?

He pulls out the license, and a piece of paper behind it flutters to the floor. He bends to pick it up. It looks like a business card at first, but . . . Charlene! It's her senior photo, "Class of '04" embossed in gold at the top, its edges frayed. What's he doing with it hidden like that and not proudly displayed? And now that he thinks of it, if it's really eight years later, why doesn't he have something more recent of her?

Where is she now? he wonders.

Wait! They're married! Right? They must be.

Aaargh! Why can't he remember? How could he forget something so important as that?

Clay places the photo and billfold on the dresser and steps to the clothes. He needs to get dressed and get out of here. Get some answers.

A pair of boxer shorts are on the floor beside the bed and he hurriedly puts them on. They're white and covered with colorful little pictures—cats and dogs wearing clothes and sunglasses. *Huh.* Cute. But weird.

He notices a cheap black wristwatch on the table amid a mess of napkins and soy sauce packets and chopsticks, and he puts it on. The hands read 3:15. A little window says that it's the 10th; but what month?

Clay cracks open a fortune cookie sitting there and eats it. He's starving. *The frog in the well knows nothing of the ocean,* reads the slip of paper inside.

Dang. He was kinda hoping it would be some kind of clue, like in a movie; like one of those old *Twilight Zone* episodes.

He lifts the half-full jug of orange juice and gives it a shake, removes the top, and chugs it down . . . and too late is spitting it up. "Blaargh! Aauuggh! Aaack!" *Oh my God! What the hell?!* It's more alcohol than orange juice. He can already feel the drink heating his insides; his eyes are watering. *Hoo wee!* He needs some water, and fast.

In the little bathroom's sink he splashes his face and gulps a few handfuls. Lifts his face and is shocked by what he sees in the mirror . . . It's him, of course, definitely, but . . . *way* older, way more than eight years. He leans closer. Prods his face with disbelieving fingers. His skin is pale and pudgy. There are dark circles under his eyes. Wrinkles! Crow's feet! He really needs a shave. Plus, his hair is a disaster, and much, much longer than he's ever kept it before, almost to his shoulders. Dull and stringy. He reaches up to smooth it down, tugs at it in places. Grimaces. Makes a face. Opens his mouth wide. His once perfect teeth now have numerous fillings; some are even missing in back; and there's, like, a brown-yellow stain to them all; a thick gray coating on his tongue. He has nose hairs sticking out all over the place.

Oh, man . . . This can't be him. There's just no way.

For the first time now, practically forcing himself, Clay looks down at his body. His chest is covered in a mat of curly black hair. He has a belly—a beer belly!—just like he's seen on so many older, out-of-shape guys. Guys he swore he would never become. He'd cry if he wasn't so damn confused. He flexes his once proud biceps, but they're nothing but flab, like a woman's. Worse. And his legs? The powerful pistons that had made him and his team all-state champions are now nothing but pathetic sticks.

His knees sag and he has to catch himself on the tiny sink. It's all too much. It's insane! It can't be real. This has to be a dream—a bad one. Another one. "Wake up!" he says, slapping his face. Then again, harder, louder. "Wake up, damn it!" He punches the mirror with his fist, shattering the glass. Aims a kick at the old-fashioned bathtub with his bare foot—and instantly regrets it.

He just lets himself fall, collapse, draping an arm over the edge of the tub. Rests his forehead against the cool porcelain, rolling it back and forth. Moans in pain. And despair.

This isn't a dream, he knows . . . And maybe his being an addict wasn't a dream, either . . . Maybe he's lost his mind and is some kinda crazy person who can't recall one day to the next . . . He's probably on welfare or something, a ward of the state. A loser. A freakin' nut job.

He thinks of the gun . . . He could be dangerous, even.

But what about all that money in his wallet? If he doesn't have a job . . . No. No, he refuses to accept it; he isn't a criminal; he doesn't have a mean bone in his body.

Clay turns and puts his back to the tub. Looks again at himself, at the parts that he can see: at his arms, his hands, the familiar freckles and scars, the long-ago fractured knuckle; at his legs, the clover-shaped birthmark on his thigh, the same big goofy feet, the swollen big toe that hurts like a bitch and is probably broken. *Shit.* It's him, all right. However the hell it happened.

He sighs. Then resigns himself to doing whatever it takes to figure this shit out and get his life back on track. Whatever the hell he's been doing up to this point, it hasn't been productive, that's for sure.

Clay limps back to the chair with the clothes. Checks the pants' pockets, without much hope, and finds them empty. Then the leather jacket, which produces a near-empty pack of cigarettes and a lighter. *No way!* He doesn't smoke; he'd *never* smoke, not in a million years. Coach would kill him! But, wait . . . Oh, yeah; that was a long time ago, wasn't it. He can only shake his head at such a thing. Cigarettes! *Jeez!* What an idiot. He throws them into the corner, as much as a part of him wants one badly.

The left, inside pocket of the jacket holds a small, spiral notebook and a pen. *Yes! Jackpot!* However, he's quickly disappointed to find that only the top page has any writing on it; and what little there is doesn't make much sense. But it's definitely his, in a tiny, cramped scrawl.

There's an address (he thinks) written across the top: *4 Financial Plaza.* Then some letters and numbers—days and times, obviously—with some notes and numbers beside those:

M	6:15 –	home	
T	12:10 – 2:35	Grill	(3)
W	12:15 – 3:20	Mona's	(4)
R	12:15 – 2:45	Trattoria	(3)
F	3:55 –	?	
M	6:40 –	home	
T	12:05 – 2:20	Grill	(4)
W	12:15 – 3:10	Mona's	(5)
R	12:10 – 2:55	Trattoria	(3)
F	4:10 –	home	
M	6:25 –	home	
T	12:10 – 2:40	Grill	(3)

If the last entry was yesterday, he reasons, then today must be Wednesday. Or, wait . . . Unless today is Tuesday and he's supposed to be at the Grill at 12:10 . . . No, that doesn't make any sense. It's gotta be Wednesday, and he's meeting somebody for lunch there—or at 4 Financial Plaza, more likely.

Huh. Does he work there? he wonders. And if so, what does he do?

Is he meeting Charlene? His heart leaps and he cheers up at the thought. There are just so many questions he needs answered. Like, What the hell is wrong with his memory? for starters.

And what is he doing with that gun?

The jacket holds nothing else, so he tucks the notebook and pen back into the pocket. Thank God for this, at least, he thinks. But . . . What if the list is out of date? What if it doesn't mean anything at all?

"Well," he tells himself, picking up the jeans, "there's only one way to find out."

THE BUILDINGS CONTINUE to blow his mind, even after so many hours of walking among them, beneath them, around them, looking up, gawking at them. So incredible . . . so tall . . . so many! Miles of them! Block after block. The teeming streets packed with cars, trucks, taxis, speeding bicycles, people . . . My God! The *people!* It's all put Clay in a state of shock. In awe. He's never seen anything like it, even remotely close, except for in bits and pieces on television. But that was just make believe. This is *real.* And in his face.

New York City . . . *Wow* . . . He had no idea people actually lived this way. It had taken him an hour in the early morning to walk from Chinatown to the Financial District, getting lost, then getting directions, repeatedly. (The relief he'd felt learning that he wasn't actually in China was enormous!) Since then he's been walking the busy streets, taking it all in, the riotous sights and sounds. The shops, the restaurants, mostly high-end, like nothing he'd ever see in Taloga, or even Oklahoma City.

Earlier, he'd treated himself to a large (and expensive!) breakfast in a small café and had spent a lot of time reading the local newspaper, the *Daily News*. But afterward was just as confused as ever—more so, even. It's as if he's been suddenly, in his sleep, transported to another world, another culture—another time.

It's 2016, for Chrissakes.

Being a time traveler would be pretty cool, Clay thinks, if he could understand what the hell was going on. But the more he learns, the more he realizes how much he doesn't know. He still doesn't have a clue what he's doing here. Or why.

Except for that one scrap of paper in his pocket.

So now he's sitting impatiently in front of 4 Financial Plaza, a massively tall, blue-and-silver, glass-and-steel tower that looks more like a spaceship than a building. He's taken up a post atop a low brick wall, like a bench, surrounding the one lone tree at the plaza's center. A few young people have recently come out from the adjacent buildings to join him, sack lunches in their hands.

Clay looks at his watch: 12:05. Any minute now, he thinks.

But who will it be? Who is he meeting? And why?

Although he'd first thought of Charlene, he doesn't think she would ever want to live in a big city like this. But, then, neither would he. So he must be meeting somebody else. For business or something, probably. Whatever business that might be.

Of course he can't help but think of the gun, tucked securely in his waistband at the small of his back, hidden from view under the leather jacket. He couldn't just leave it at the hotel: What if he's supposed to have it with him for some reason? What if it's a part of his job?

God, what have I become? he thinks for the hundredth time.

And something else has continued to nag at him: It's been twelve years since their high school graduation. Twelve years! Why doesn't he have a more recent photo of Charlene? Of his *wife?* What's happened to her? Is she all right? More than anything else right now, this is what he needs to find out. He needs to at least know that she's okay.

More and more people have been filing out of the buildings now. Most of them dressed in fancy-looking clothes, business attire. Many foreign-looking people, Clay notices. Every shade of white, black, and brown. As many women as men . . . Just amazing . . .

Clay keeps his eyes glued to the revolving doors of building number four, hoping against hope that he'll recognize somebody. He scrutinizes every face that leaves.

12:10. Is it that person? That one? He stands, to make himself more visible to whomever might be looking for him. Steps a little closer to the doors and the crowds streaming out.

He'd been inside, much earlier, in the lobby, with its great expanse of polished black marble and glass, and had gone over the list of names posted there on the wall—mostly business names, corporations. But not one had seemed familiar. And with the gun in his waistband, the sight of a security guard and metal detector had sent him hustling right back out again.

There's an older man, Clay sees now, wearing a long, fuzzy, tan coat, standing off to one side by himself, clutching at a large black briefcase with both hands held before him—as if looking for somebody, waiting. They make eye contact. Clay does his best to smile.

The man steps forward and stops, still some distance away. "You must be Liam," he says amiably enough, reaching into his coat.

"Uh . . ." *Am I?* Clay isn't sure of anything anymore. Does this man know him as Liam? Is he supposed to be Liam?

"The driver?" the man prompts.

"Oh. No, uh . . ." He can't be the driver without a car, right? Was there a car at the hotel? There'd been just the one key . . .

"No, I'm sorry," he says. But the man has already walked away to resume the same position.

Clay quickly looks back to the doors—*Shit!*—afraid that he may have lost his moment. He scans the backs of those who have already gone past in various directions. Sees a pretty yellow dress and golden hair and makes to follow, but, no, that was a long time ago.

He swivels back toward the doors, anxiously looking—and his head snaps back around. There was something in that face . . . the tall guy. He's sure of it. He's seen it just recently.

Clay jogs to catch up, limping painfully on his broken toe. He keeps the bobbing head of wavy light-brown hair in sight, veering off at an angle to get a better view. The man's walking at the head of a few others, tossing a comment over his shoulder to a guy who pulls out a phone and dials. They're moving at a good clip, leaving the plaza, and Clay has to hurry.

He bolts ahead, deciding on a place to stop directly in their path. See if they recognize him. He sure hopes so; he hopes he hasn't set his sights on the wrong person and wasted his chance.

He stops and turns to face them, smiling.

And time slips away . . .

. . . *His finger in the asshole's face . . . Charlene pulling at his arm . . . The asshole's smug grin . . . Opening the door for her . . . Driving away . . .*

Clay's vision tunnels, zooms, and all he can see is the asshole's face, still talking at those with him, coming closer, flanked on both sides. The guy's older but there's no doubt: it's him, the pretty boy, big money, now dressed in a snazzy gray suit and bright orange tie. There's no mistaking the arrogance, the sense of entitlement. The nerve.

And it's then that Clay has the sudden inkling of why he's come, what his purpose here might be.

He's filled with an inexplicable rage, his face growing hotter by the second, flickers of red at the edges of his vision. He doesn't think or care to ask himself why.

He steps to the side and holds up his arm—straight ahead, palm out.

The asshole's head is turned and he runs into Clay's hand before stopping. He looks surprised for a moment, then pissed. Looks to Clay's hand and steps back, just enough.

"Where's Charlene?" Clay asks through gritted teeth.

The burly gorilla to the asshole's right doesn't hesitate but reaches out and swats Clay's arm away. Moves up to stand chest-to-chest with him, forcing him back.

"What do you think you're doing?" The guy's voice is low and dangerously soft. He has some seriously bad breath for somebody so well dressed.

Clay goes to move around him but The Gorilla puts out a meaty hand and shoves him back even further. From five feet away Clay can see the asshole looking back at him, confused, without the slightest bit of recognition.

Clay meets his eye. "Where's Charlene?" he asks again, loudly, over The Gorilla's shoulder.

"Hold on," the asshole tells his friend, who's raised a cocked fist. Then to Clay: "What did you say?"

"I asked you: Where—is—Charlene?"

The man tilts his head, as if pretending to think. "I don't know any Charlene."

"Oh yeah you do. You drove away with her, remember?" Clay can feel his whole body tremble with anger, his hands itching, twitching at his sides, wanting to wrap them around this asshole's throat. There has to be a reason he's reacting this way.

"And just where did I drive away with her *to?*" the asshole smirks.

Then, unless he imagines it, Clay can see the guy's eyes widen a fraction and his cocky expression waver a bit as he *does* remember—as he realizes exactly what they're talking about.

"I don't know," Clay says, his voice strained. "Why don't you tell me. That's what I'm asking."

A heavy pause, laced with consequence. Then: "You've mistaken me for someone else." The asshole signals with his chin, frowning. "Get rid of him, Saul."

It's the command his buddy has been waiting for, for no sooner are the words spoken than Clay feels a powerful grip clamp onto the back of his neck and he's practically lifted off his feet, toes dancing. He's being marched sideways and back. And as furious as Clay is, he's afraid to strike out, lest he be hit back by this goon even harder. Out of the corner of his eye he can see the asshole and the rest of the group walk on. He can hear somebody laughing.

If he was as big as he used to be, Clay thinks ruefully, and in shape, he'd take this guy on. But right now his neck is being crushed in a vice and there's absolutely nothing he can do about it. This mother is *tough!*

They stop, finally, in a section of grass beside a tall metal sculpture, and there's that bad breath again, in his ear. "Are we going to have any further problems out of you, dickwad?"

Clay wants so badly to tell this guy off, but "No" is all that comes out, in a grumble.

"What's that?" Unbelievably, the grip tightens and gives him a shake.

"No! No!"

The vice is gone. "All right, then. Now, get lost." The Gorilla puts a point on it with a shove.

Clay stands there for a minute, rubbing his aching neck. He sees people looking his way with worried faces, some shaking their heads, some smiling, pointing, twittering behind their hands. One young woman about his own age—the age he *was*, that is, that he remembers being—her long blond hair done up in a bun; large round glasses like Charlene used to wear when they'd first started going out, their sophomore year—gives him a pitying glance.

Why just her senior photo? . . .

Why the gun? . . .

Why am I so angry? . . .

It doesn't matter that he can't remember.

He's walking quickly now. Steady, determined, resolved. Catching up. To do what he knows he's come here to do.

"Hey! Asshole!"

The Gorilla is only half the distance away, and he turns back with a crooked smile and a shake of his head when he sees Clay coming toward them. But then dives when Clay stops and draws the large gun from behind his back.

A woman's scream. Some distant yelling.

Clay plants his feet and takes aim, arms straight, both hands gripped tightly together, the sights dead on the asshole's back. He experiences the briefest moment of doubt before pulling the trigger. But nothing happens. He pulls it again. *Shit!* Looks closely at the gun. *Oh yeah*—the safety—he flicks it off and points the gun again.

The asshole has stopped too, now, and is turning to watch all the commotion around him—the running, shouting. His friends are all gone.

Clay aims and pulls the trigger. But again nothing happens. *What the hell?! This is crazy!* He looks at the gun again and immediately realizes the problem. *Shit!* He grabs the top of the gun and pulls back the slide and lets it go, sending a bullet into the chamber.

This time, when he points, Clay's eyes and the asshole's lock, just for an instant, before the asshole is crouching down with his arms over his head and the gun goes off. *BOOM!* Clay adjusts his aim as the asshole scrambles away. *BOOM!* Firing the second shot just as he's hit from the side by a freight train and goes crashing, skidding, to the ground, the train on top of him. An excruciating pain in his wrist. His side. He can't breathe.

And then there's The Gorilla's face in his own, the meanest thing Clay has ever seen, even on the field. And then—

Nothing.

The hum of the road. *Music playing softly on the radio. Ahead, the slightest lightening of a deep purple sky.*

Hey, watch out, his friend Neil says. Cops.

Two girls sit on the seat between them, asleep. A light rap on the back window, another warning from those in the bed of the truck.

It's all right, he says. Relax.

Two black-and-whites on the left, lights flashing, spinning. A nondescript sedan on the right. A red truck farther down.

An officer signaling him to stop.

He slows, pulls over, gravel crunching underneath.

A familiar face at the window. Tragic. Sad. Hey, Clay. Uh . . . Stay here for a minute, will ya? Stay in the car. Somebody's gonna wanna talk to you in a minute, all right? Just stay in the car.

He waits. The strobing red and blue lights putting on a show, lighting up the dense forest around them. Why me? he thinks. Why talk to me?

There must have been an accident, Neil says.

He's taking a leak in the ditch when a car pulls up on the other side of the road. A man and a woman get out and are met by an officer. Then another. A scream, a keening sound, shouts of anger.

He crosses the road, toward but away from the commotion. Nobody stops him.

Police tape flutters between stakes in the ground, the spot within lit by headlights, the strobing colors. The late spring grass is tall. There's a dirty bare foot, a calf. He's drawn closer.

The face is ruined, unrecognizable under a mask of blood. But there's her pretty yellow dress. Her long blond hair . . .

He drops to his knees.

Too shocked, at first, to cry.

TUESDAY, MARCH 2, 2010   **DAY 3**

CLAY WAKES with a jolt.

   "We're here," says the speaker beside him, touching his arm.

His face is pressed to a window, a bunched-up cloth for a pillow. Large cement pillars pass by. Multicolored people. A gigantic, bustling space.

The man beside him—a stranger—is holding out his hand. "Thank you for your service," he says.

Clay hesitates a moment before taking it, unsure of what the man means. The elder's grip is strong, firm, and it takes him by surprise. He has a kind smile, which Clay does his best to return.

"Have a good time," the man says. Then he's up and standing in the aisle, swaying the slightest bit as he retrieves a bag from the bin overhead. There are many other people around them, also preparing to leave the . . . train?

Is this a train? . . .

As he looks again out the window, whatever they're on comes to a full stop. There are the faintest vibrations of things settling, easing, being locked into place.

Where am I? he thinks. It's become a familiar feeling lately.

He closes his eyes and puts a hand to his temple. Gives his head a shake. To dispel that nightmarish dream as much as regain his senses.

The last thing he remembers . . . *Oh my God!* He shot that guy! The asshole. Or did he? . . . He knows he sure tried to . . . *Wow. Jeez* . . . He definitely remembers getting tackled by that big son of a bitch with him.

Clay tentatively touches his face, certain he'll find his cheeks bruised, his nose broken. But everything feels okay. Normal. There isn't the slightest bit of tenderness. Which is impossible, because he expressly remembers that guy's massive fists pummeling him mercilessly, at the end.

Weird. That *was* yesterday, right?

He takes stock of the rest of him. Notices the camo fatigues and shiny black boots; the olive green T-shirt with A*R*M*Y proudly emblazoned across his chest.

Uh . . .

And then the jacket—his former pillow—the same mottled green-and-brown camo as the pants; his name—NEHMAN—sewn over the left chest pocket; a colorful patch on one shoulder, a US flag on the other; stitched black insignias on the lapels. It all looks real. As official as it gets.

Ohhh, shit . . . He is so screwed.

How could this have possibly ever happened?

"Are you all right, sir?" This from a heavyset black woman standing over him, in the aisle. She's rested a large plastic bag and a coat on the seat next to him and is slinging a small carry-on over her shoulder. "You look a little lost."

Clay doesn't know what to say. He *is* lost. "Uh, yeah. I guess you could say that."

"This your first visit to the city?"

He's not sure. He looks out into the train station, at all the people, the commotion. "I think so," he says.

"Well, you'd best hurry if you're gettin' off," she suggests, taking up her plastic bag and coat. "There ain't no tellin' when this train's takin' off again."

"Oh, uh, yeah . . . Right." Clay clutches the jacket to his chest, at first unsure of what to do; then stands, in a daze, begins scooting out.

The woman points with a bejeweled finger. "Don't forget your bag."

There's a small, sand-colored backpack beneath the seat in front of where he'd been sitting. He bends to pick it up. It has the Army logo—a large square with a black star inside it—and the letters "U.S." stenciled underneath. Like the clothes, he has no idea how he's come to possess it.

Or why.

"You on leave?" the woman asks as they make their way down the aisle. "My husband's in the Marines. Second Division. They off in Afghanistan, 'round Kandahar, for that big 'Surge' they be talkin' 'bout. But I don't see what good it gonna do. Even though Obama say he be puttin' an end to all the fightin' over there, like they done in Iraq. But I don't think it happenin' anytime soon. From what my Ronnie say, we ain't *never* leavin' that place. Neither one." She steps off the train and onto the platform. Waits for him with a smile. "You been over there yet? In Afghanistan?"

CLAY LEANS BACK, slouched, in the molded seat, arms in the seat beside him, legs splayed wide. Staring at the vaulted ceiling above.

2010 . . . Somehow he's gone from 2016 to 2010. He wouldn't believe it was true—he wouldn't believe the date posted large over the Amtrak ticket counter; he wouldn't believe the three people he asked, disbelieving; he wouldn't believe the front page of the *New York Post* crumpled in his fist—he'd think it was all an elaborate joke—if he hadn't seen the proof of it in the mirror, in the men's room. He's *at least* six years younger than he was yesterday. And in shape. No doughy gray skin, no pot belly, his chest and arms even bigger than they were in high school.

It's as if that day spent in New York City was a dream or something. A nightmare. A hallucination. Not real at all. Not like *this*.

He looks around him at all the people, all so different, so alive, so *real* . . . walking, talking, reading, eating, laughing . . . The hollering kids running by with their toy planes . . . The flocks of men and women in their business suits and dresses . . . Just like at 4 Financial Plaza.

Just like this . . . It was just as real.

It's like a continuation of the same bad movie: He can't remember anything, except for the past two days—if he can admit to himself, finally, that the first one actually occurred.

And his dreams . . . his horribly disturbing dreams . . .

Or are they actual memories? . . . His last memories . . . He has a sickening feeling they're real too.

The painful image of Charlene's mangled body flashes through his mind, and Clay has to lean forward and put his head in his hands. *No, she can't be dead,* he laments. She's his life! His future! He'd cry if he knew for certain it was true . . . It was bad enough when he had no idea what happened to her, or where she was. But this . . .

No. No, there's no way. For the simple fact that he couldn't have survived this long without her. She has to be somewhere.

But why can't I remember?!

He wants to scream it at the top of his lungs. He wants to hit somebody, break something. *Aaargh!* He sits up and smashes his elbows back into the seats connected to either side, shaking the entire row. He can feel his face growing hot, his pulse pounding, a dull roar in his ears. Red lights flickering at the outskirts of his vision. He sees a number of people staring at him anxiously, some readying themselves to leave.

He's embarrassed now, which only compounds his frustration. He tries a smile, but it just makes the little girl across from him duck behind her mother's legs. The elderly couple to his left quickly look away.

They think I'm crazy, he realizes. And who's to say they're not right?

But he refuses to believe it, himself. He doesn't *feel* crazy. Not *crazy* crazy. He just can't remember anything, that's all.

And believes that he was in 2016 yesterday.

Clay picks up his backpack and leaves hurriedly, weaving his way through the congested rows of seats. He needs to find a place to get his shit together. Come up with some answers. Somewhere with a little privacy, if that's even possible in this crowded city.

THE CONTENTS OF his wallet (red nylon, Velcro): $386 in cash; one Virginia driver's license, with an address in a place called Mount Vernon; two military IDs; two credit cards; a folded, pink carbon copy—LEAVE AUTHORIZATION—signed and saying he's to return (somewhere) on the 5th; and, again, Charlene's senior photo, worn at the edges.

From his jacket pockets: a large orange-and-yellow booklet/brochure—Prospect Group, *Where others see risk, we see opportunity*, a lightning bolt-arrow sort of thing for a logo; an Amtrak ticket folder (Alexandria, VA, to New York City, Penn Station—then back again, open ended); a well-worn, Army camo baseball cap; a pack of breath mints; a pen.

All of these things, including a set of keys and a cell phone found in his cargo pants, are laid out on the table in front of him.

One military ID has nothing but the Army logo, a recent photo (stone-faced, buzz cut), his full name and social security number, and lists his rank as "E6," whatever that means. That's it. A bar code covers the bottom. Another laminated card has a smaller photo, "Fort Belvoir Army Base," and DEFENSE LOGISTICS AGENCY, which sounds pretty cool; another bar code, and a magnetic strip on back.

He wonders what all he's done in the Army. How long has he been in?

Was the man he experienced yesterday his *future* self, then? he wonders. Is that what's going to happen to him if he leaves the Army? He shudders at the thought.

Perhaps he's involved in some kind of top-secret military operation, where his memory has been erased . . . Or maybe something's gone wrong . . .

No, he really will be crazy if he starts thinking along those lines.

Maybe he should call somebody, at least; find out what's happened.

He picks up the phone. It's flat, with a blue screen with lots of colorful icons, like a mini computer. And, unlike yesterday, it appears that he doesn't need a password to use it. But where are the buttons? He pokes at the "phone" icon and the screen changes. There are the numbers.

Whoa . . . Pretty cool.

About a dozen names and numbers are listed. But who should he call? And what would he say? "Hey, man, I'm in New York City and I can't remember a freakin' thing, not even who you are. Send help immediately, please. Thanks, buddy." Yeah, right. He'll leave that as the last option.

Amazingly, it looks like he can even surf the Web on this thing too. But first things first.

He's just picking up the colorful booklet/brochure when the waitress arrives with his breakfast. She raises an eyebrow at all the things scattered about the table, and Clay makes room for the plate.

"So, you on vacation?" she asks, smacking her gum as she pours his coffee.

"Uh, yeah," he says. "Three days, I think."

"Where from?"

"Uh . . . Virginia."

She nods at the backpack beside him, in the booth. "You have any other clothes to wear, besides your uniform?"

"Uh . . ." He looks to it too. "Yeah, I guess I should."

She smiles and leans in. "Well, you might want to change into something a little less conspicuous, you know what I mean?

Something more casual. People around here are pretty opinion-ated. Especially with what's going on." She jots on her pad and tears off the top sheet. "Just my advice, hon. Enjoy. Let me know if you need anything else."

She lays the bill facedown before she goes.

Clay quickly shovels in half his plate before finally succumb-ing to curiosity. He slides the bag over and opens the main com-partment.

It's exactly what the waitress predicted. Only it isn't casual. It's a checkered brown business suit, rolled into a tight bun-dle—jacket, pants, shirt, socks, tie—a leather belt keeping it all together. But now the clothes are laid out on the red vinyl seat beside him. Along with a pair of shiny brown wingtips.

Oookay . . . It's obvious he was preparing to wear this. But why? Where? When?

Shit! He looks to his watch, a bulky black digital. Is he late for an appointment? A meeting with somebody? It's 8:13. He has no way of knowing.

Clay picks up the mini computer/phone again, touches the "calendar" icon. Tuesday, March 2nd. Nothing scheduled. He uses the arrow buttons on the screen to go backward and forward through the days, weeks, and months, until it becomes clear that he doesn't use this feature at all.

Great. He hopes this temporary bout of amnesia, or whatever it is, doesn't cost him a job, or a missed opportunity of some kind. Maybe he *should* call somebody now, he worries.

For the second time, he picks up the fancy orange-and-yellow booklet and opens it to the first page, a table of contents: "A History of the Company," "Why a Managed Account," "Investor Requirements," et cetera. *Aaah,* he thinks. Hence the suit. (Wow, does he have money?) He'll have to call them in a second; maybe they can tell him what he's doing here.

He flips through the booklet's pages. And immediately stops at a photo, a dog-eared page. His heart nearly stops as well, then begins to race.

Once again: it's the asshole. The guy who drove off with Charlene.

Clay has no doubt now why he's come.

It's business, all right. Unfinished business.

His mind is on last night's dream (Was it real? It had to be . . .) as Clay cleans his plate. Then he begins replacing the various items on the table to where they belong.

He signals the waitress; and when she comes over, points to the clothes and shoes still laid out on the seat. Gives her his sweetest smile. "Mind if I use your restroom?"

THE TREE IN the center is a bit shorter, he can tell, less filled out up top. But the building is the same: a towering silver-blue spaceship.

Even the people look the same, dressed so smartly, with their briefcases, strutting purposefully to and fro. If Clay didn't know better, he'd think it really was the next day and not six years earlier.

Let's see if the asshole still has that gorilla with him.

As he crosses the plaza, Clay fingers the hilt of the army knife at his waist, hidden beneath his shirt and suit coat in front. He'd found it in the backpack, in a separate compartment, while getting dressed, along with a fake beard and moustache and a wig, a pair of non-prescription eyeglasses. He'd donned all of this back at the train station, where he'd left the backpack and other clothes in a locker. There's a reason he has the disguise, he figures, so he'd better not deviate from the plan, whatever that plan might be. He'll make it up as he goes along.

09:55, says his watch (the only thing incongruous with the suit). Plenty of time. He has the whole day to figure out what to do. And get it done.

He checks his disguise one last time in the reflection in the revolving door. Smooths the glued-on beard. Pats his fluffy new head of hair. He looks pretty damn respectable, he has to admit. Even without the tie, which he'd given up on and is in his pocket.

Clay takes in the already familiar lobby, checks the posted roster of company names. Prospect Group is on the twelfth floor. The *whole* twelfth floor, apparently. He pauses before the walk-through metal detector and the security guard sitting behind the podium beside it. But he's got to trust himself, he thinks, the part of him he doesn't remember; he had to have known what he was doing. Besides, the knife had looked like glass, or ceramic, not metal.

However, there's a sharp *Beep!* as he passes through the archway. Clay quickly steps back, with his hands up, and prepares to bolt, but then notices the guard simply pointing to a small plastic tray on the adjacent table. It takes a moment before understanding hits, then Clay is patting himself down, putting the phone, keys, wallet, pen, brochure, tie, eyeglasses, even the breath mints on the tray. He can hear the guard chuckle.

But the alarm goes off a second time—*Shit!*—and the guard steps forward this time, with a handheld wand device. Clay freezes—as the man also has a gun on his belt. He may have to run; he can't let himself be searched. But two women are now blocking the way behind.

The wand beeps and stops over his waist. But not the knife, thank God. "The buckle," the guard says with a smile. "Happens every time."

Clay's hands are shaking as he collects his things from the tray; he hopes it isn't too obvious. He can't think of anything witty to say, anything to relieve the guard's suspicion. *Relax, relax. Be cool, be cool.*

Waiting for the elevators, he spies the signs for the restrooms, and for the stairwell farther down. An emergency exit.

Four people leave the next elevator to arrive, and Clay and the two women enter together. The women get off at seven, soft classical music drifting in before the doors close. But Clay barely notices; he's still trying to think of what he's going to do when he lands on twelve.

On impulse, he pushes the button for the tenth floor, and within seconds the doors open. As on seven, there's a large reception area, a secretary sitting behind a long, curved desk. She looks up as Clay walks forward, and waves when he waves and hangs a left toward the stairs, opening her mouth to say something he doesn't catch. As Clay had thought—as he'd hoped—the restrooms are in this direction as well. The stairwell is the next door down. He gives the men's room a quick once over—empty—then tries the stairs. The door handle doesn't seem to lock on either side, but, just in case, he tears a page from the brochure and folds it, places it in the jamb. Then travels two floors up to twelve. The stairwell door opens easily.

In the bathroom there, one man is at the sinks and another at a urinal, holding a conversation. Clay walks in with his head down and quickly enters the first stall, sits, and locks the door.

"Shit, I could have told you that years ago. It was just a house of cards, waiting to come crashing down."

"Yeah. I've seen the prospectuses for those and I still don't understand a word of it. These *new* derivatives, though, are a whole new b—"

"Shit, they're illegal as hell too, if you ask me—if you ask anyone. But—"

"You're still going to sell them."

A laugh. "Damn straight. And so are you. Have to get rid of 'em somehow."

Clay can see both men, now, at the sink, through a gap in the stall's metal door. Neither one is his target.

"I'll bet you no one sells more of this junk than Goldman."

"Shit, who do you think invented it?"

There's the ten-second roar of the hand dryer. Words he can't make out.

"Well, I'm sure we've got a couple of years left on this one."

A chuckle. "Yeah. Thank God for bailouts."

Laughter follows the men out the door, the silence complete when they leave. The only sound Clay's own breathing and the rustle of his clothes.

His watch says it's 10:25. He closes his eyes, trying to recall the page of notes from the day before. On Tuesday, Wednesday, and Thursday the asshole left for lunch around noon. With any luck he still has the same schedule. And with even more luck he'll have to come in and take a leak sometime before he goes.

Clay holds the knife, unsheathed, in his hands. The blade is shiny black, like polished stone, about seven inches long, serrated on both sides. The handle wrapped tightly with cord. He tests an edge with his thumb, and blood wells instantly; it's literally razor sharp. He sucks on his thumb for a while, then makes a compress from a pad of tissue.

He's gone hunting enough times in his life; he knows how to use a knife to skin a deer, a rabbit. But kill a man? . . . He tries to picture it . . . Go for the heart? The lungs? The neck, like they do in the movies? . . . He can't believe that he's actually sitting here contemplating such a thing. That he's actually so willing to do it.

But all it takes is the memory of last night's dream, and the ones before it, to instill in him an adequate level of rage.

He takes out his wallet and the photo of Charlene. "Class of '04." Her face is slightly turned to the right and her lustrous mane of gold hanging down the front on that side. Her lips parted in a sunny smile, her eyes bright and happy. There's that button nose he loved to nibble on, which made her giggle. Those rosy cheeks he would smooth with his thumbs, as he does now to her picture. That softly scented, succulent, swan-like neck. Her glorious pale breasts beneath that fuzzy sweater . . .

He can remember the first time he saw her; their first furtive looks in the hallway, in class, at the games—amazed that such a smart, popular girl might like him back. Their first talk at Judy Paxton's party, outside, by the rabbit hutch. Their first kiss, and more, in his truck. Watching the stars, and sometimes the sunrise, at the lake—nobody else but them in the world . . . Their first full night together in bed (she supposedly at a friend's house), waking up to her in his arms . . . Charlene cooking breakfast for the two of them. Just like a married couple, like they vowed to be someday . . .

It doesn't matter if he can't remember, if his dreams are real or imagined. There is only one reason why he'd have this photo and not another, more recent, one.

You're really gone, aren't you? You're really— He can't say the word but of course thinks it anyway. And for the first time—for the first time that he can remember—he lets himself cry. He lets the tears stream down his cheeks, into his scratchy, fake beard. He chokes back a sob, then another, until there's no holding back and he just lets himself go.

He puts his elbows on his knees, his face in his hands.

Why, why, why . . . ?

What could he have done to prevent her death, if anything?

What even happened? How did she end up like that, on the side of the road?

He's weeping softly into his hands when he hears water running in one of the sinks. He looks up. He hadn't heard anybody come in. Through the crack in the door he can see a man rinsing his hands, and for a moment it appears as if they're looking directly at one another in the mirror.

Then the man's shaking his hands dry and he's gone.

It wasn't the asshole, fortunately; this guy had a dark complexion, dark hair.

Clay wonders if he'd heard him crying. How long had he been in here? *Shit.* He needs to pull himself together. He wipes at his eyes. Blows his nose. Puts Charlene's picture away with a tender kiss goodbye. Takes one deep breath after another. He can feel his moustache slipping and presses it back on.

They had their whole lives planned out together, he remembers, their whole future as husband and wife. School first, at OU;

then good jobs (he a construction manager, she a nurse); then a house; kids . . .

But he's in the Army now . . . Clay shakes his head. How in the hell had that happened? Did he ever take that football scholarship? Did he even go to college at all? Maybe on the GI bill, he supposes. He could never have afforded it on his own.

Clay pulls out the investment company's brochure. Stares at the asshole's photo this time. That perfectly coiffed hair. That cocky grin. *Let our Chief Financial Consultant prepare your portfolio.* Clay tears out the page and replaces the booklet in his jacket pocket.

Whatever happened that night, this asshole is at the bottom of it. Clay is certain of that much, at least.

. . . The asshole's smug grin . . . Opening the car door for Charlene . . . His taillights winking out of sight through the trees . . . Her torn and bloody dress . . .

Clay blinks away the images as he hears somebody else enter the bathroom. Voices. He takes one last look at the photo and crumples the paper in his fist. Flushes it down the john.

He gets only one good look at the man who entered first—the one in the dark blue suit and dark orange tie, the one now at the urinal farthest from Clay's stall, who's broad back Clay can clearly see in the large mirror, opposite—but it was enough. It's him. The asshole himself. Live and in person. A little early, maybe, but right on time.

The other one—diminutive, servile, a classic yes man who hasn't shut up once since he came in—doesn't worry him, he may as well not exist, his rambling merely noise in the background.

Clay doesn't waste a moment. He takes up the knife in his lap and unlocks the stall door. Walks out with the knife held low in his right hand, away from the men with their backs to him.

"Well, unless I'm meeting a client," says the asshole, interrupting, "I'm not going to waste my time going out to lu—"

Clay walks up quickly behind him and bumps him hard, pushing him against the urinal and the wall and holding him there as he stabs him once, twice, three times in the side, twisting the blade and pulling, ripping, upward with each stroke; feeling the cloth and flesh part, tear; the asshole's blood flowing wet and hot over Clay's hand. The asshole grunts and pushes back, but weakly, in vain, tries to elbow him away, but otherwise doesn't say a word or cry out. His knees buckle and he sags.

"What—? Oh my God! What the *fuck!?*" The other man has stepped back, shocked, scared, his dick in his hand.

As the asshole slips slowly to the floor, clutching at the wall, then falling against Clay's knees and turning, as if to look at his attacker, Clay hits him twice more, in the chest, plunging the knife deep each time. Then he gives a final, clumsy swipe to the neck that cleaves through the asshole's face, instead.

He hears the other man gasp and start whimpering, jibbering. "Wha, wha, wha, wha, wha . . . ?"

Clay takes a step back and lets the asshole fall heavily to his side. Then he rears back and, with all the anger he can muster —*This is for Charlene!*—lands a solid kick to the back of the asshole's head, which rebounds with a *crack!* off the wall.

The asshole just lies there; doesn't move. Blood splattered in bright abstract patterns over the urinal and beige-and-white tiled wall.

Clay turns now to the other man, who, he can tell, has pissed himself and is frantically considering his options—fight or flight—eyes darting between Clay and the bathroom door.

Clay holds out his left arm wide, to bar the man's escape, then walks carefully backward to the sinks. "Don't move," he says. "Don't say a word."

The man nods vigorously and backs further into the corner by the first stall, palms out. Slides down the wall, into a squat. Gapes at the asshole (maybe his boss) bleeding-out only a few feet away.

In the mirror Clay's beard is hanging half off his face. His heart is beating madly but he feels strangely calm. Ultra calm. He sets the knife on the counter, his hand slick red with blood. He can see a small red dot on his shirt collar, but otherwise his clothes appear spotless; only the right coat sleeve and shirt cuff are stained wet. He looks at the reflection of the asshole lying dead on the floor in a widening pool of blood.

I did it, he thinks. *I killed him. I made him pay.*

Clay's eyes meet the other man's for a second in the mirror, and then he hurriedly begins washing his hands. Surprisingly, the blood rinses easily away. He steals a glimpse at his watch: 11:09. Gives the knife a quick rinse before sheathing it and putting it in his coat pocket. Only then, hands clean, does he adjust the beard and moustache. His tears must have loosened the glue, somehow. He presses it all back into place as best he can, and it seems to hold.

The man against the wall is staring at him, surely trying to remember some identifying details. He's bound to raise the alarm as soon as Clay leaves.

"Take off your tie," Clay orders. But the guy doesn't move, only shivers, scared. "Take off your freakin' tie!"

The door opens and another man steps in. Stands there. Instantly takes in the blood and the body on the floor; Clay; the cowering coworker. And before Clay has a chance to react, the man, wide-eyed, is backing out the door, then running—definitely running. But Clay hasn't heard a shout. Not yet.

"Stay here or I'll kill you," Clay says to the man in the corner, as if that'll work. And then he himself is out the door and making a mad dash for the stairwell. He can hear yelling now—"Call the police!"—and sees a young woman far down the hall looking directly at him as he takes to the stairs.

He flies down the steps, two three at a time, swinging around each landing with his left hand, using his right to rip off the beard and moustache and wig, and stuff them into the coat's pockets.

He stops for a moment between the ninth and eighth floors to use his unworn tie to wipe whatever gluey residue might remain on his face. Then he quickly strips off the jacket and rolls up his shirt sleeves to the elbow, hiding the blood-stained cuff. Gives his shoes a quick buff with an arm of the jacket and then drapes it over his arm. Runs down the last flight of stairs.

On seven, Clay steps straight to the men's room and, after retrieving the phone, deposits the jacket and knife in the toilet bowl in the middle stall. Gives himself a final appraisal in the mirror: Though a bit frazzled, he looks fine.

Then, as calmly as he can, against his every urge to run, he walks slowly to the elevators. All is quiet. Serene. There's that same soft piano music in the background. Nobody screaming or calling out for help here. He pushes the call button to go down. Waits.

And waits some more . . . His watch says 11:14.

They've called the police by now, without a doubt. Security has to be watching the stairs, the elevators. But they're looking for a man in a dark brown suit, with a beard, and more hair. Glasses . . . Wait, where are the glasses? . . . *Shit.* Oh, well. The asshole's buddy must have told somebody by now that it was just a disguise.

After waiting a full minute, Clay decides to find a fire alarm and start a building-wide evacuation. But just as he begins to move, one of the elevators dings and opens, going down. It's nearly full but there's room for a couple more and he squeezes in, smiling apologetically, nervously probably, and the doors close.

"Are you *serious?*" a woman in the back is saying. "What are they doing?"

"I don't know. Called the police, I suppose," says a man's gruff voice. "They'll undoubtedly want to interrogate everyone in the building, which is why I am heading to lunch right now."

There are excited murmurs among the rest.

Clay stares straight ahead. His pulse pounding in his skull. They stop on three to let one more person on, before the doors finally open on the ground floor. Two security guards, now, are standing beside the metal detector, but facing the elevators and stairs. Both have their hands on the guns at their belts. Both look extremely on edge. The younger one has looked at his watch twice before the group from the elevator reaches them, clearly awaiting backup. Clay can see that a sizeable cluster of people has already been herded off to one side.

"Folks," calls out the older guard, the one from earlier; he holds up his free hand, "we need you all to remain here for a minute. We have—"

"No, no, no," says the man with the gruff voice from the elevator—a puffed-up, broad-shouldered guy, Clay can see now, impeccably dressed, moneyed—"I have an urgent meeting to get to immediately, and I will not be late. I know what has happened upstairs, and I can assure you that I, nor anyone else here, had anything to do with it. If you wish to detain me by force, you had best be prepared to go to court and lose your job and whatever savings you have, for doing so." The man doesn't stop but continues on, brushing off the feeble protests of the guard. Clay follows closely behind, as do a few others and some of those waiting.

Outside, he can hear sirens.

THE SWAY OF the fast-moving train is barely noticeable but hypnotic just the same. Comforting after such a hellacious day. The view out the window has turned from dusk to gloomy black, showing only his ghostly reflection back at him. His haunted eyes. So Clay looks beyond them to the lights moving past—sometimes singly, sometimes bunched—judging their distance by their relative speeds, guessing what they are by their color and size.

He's spent enough time thinking about the enormity of what he's done. The justification for it. And in the end, there's the feeling of satisfaction, of completion, at the back of his mind. Purpose fulfilled. Now his thoughts worry over the more pressing concern: his lack of memory—perhaps sanity. Not to mention the life that awaits him at the other end of this train ride.

A wavering, white reflection appears in the glass. Remains. So he turns.

"Thank you for your service," says the woman kindly.

Clay nods and raises a hand.

He's running, maneuvering around tailgates, bumpers, people. Getting to his truck. He has to get to his truck.

But he finds it blocked by another car. And also in back. Shit! He sees a few other options.

He's in the driver's seat of a Mazda 626, keys in the ignition. He reverses out, fast. Then fishtailing as he speeds across the grass, to the road.

He takes the first turn through the trees too fast and almost loses control. His heart in his throat, pulse racing. Slow down, slow down. Just through the trees, he thinks, just till the main road. The next turn isn't as scary. He's getting used to this car.

He can catch 'em. He will *catch him.*

That asshole!

A short straightaway now and he catches a brief moment of air from a dip. Misjudges the next turn and slides sideways into the ditch—Shit!—bounces off some trees. But he doesn't stop, doesn't let his foot off the gas, but plows through the brush and back onto the dirt.

The final series of turns.

He's flying now, on the main road into town. Pedal to the metal. Engine roaring.

The first hill . . . crests it. No sign.

Second hill . . . crests it. Red taillights blinking through the trees to the left, at the bottom. Just a glimpse but it's enough.

The campground.

I'll kill him!

Skidding, now, onto the narrow gravel road. One turn, two, three, and he has to hit the brakes. It's them, all right—the yellow Camaro.

He flicks on the Mazda's high beams. Sees both of them turn their heads, Charlene raising a hand against the glare.

The Camaro had been going slow, just cruisin', but now quickly jumps ahead. The asshole holds up a finger.

Oh, yeah? Ha!

The asshole can drive but he doesn't know the road, his taillights blinking anxiously.

They're bumper to bumper around the first few turns, then side by side, scraping metal—the asshole's face tense, panicked—braking, speeding up again, never letting up, faster, faster around the next turn, gravel spraying, Charlene screaming . . .

Weightless, the rush of trees—

CLAY WAKES to the sweet smell of milk and Fruity Pebbles. He opens his eyes and sees the face of a child—a little girl, no more than four or five—blowing on his own, her lips puckered in an *O.* Only inches away. Cute as a button. Long, blond, wispy bangs. A sparkly purple horse clutched in her hand as she crouches on the bed. She stops blowing but doesn't move, doesn't blink.

Clay smiles. Blows back.

"Mommy says, get up *now.*" And then she's scooting backward and plopping onto the floor, spinning out the door and into the hall. "I did it, Mommy!"

Clay rolls onto his back. *God!* What dreams! So violent. Not like him at all. He sits up and swings his legs out of bed. Looks out the window, at the tree there, at the little brown and gray speckled sparrows hopping between bare branches, some last clinging red leaves. The sky a cloudless cornflower blue.

Well, it's a good day to—to . . .

Clay looks about the room. It's a bedroom, no doubt about that—a big fluffy bed, night stands, dressers, a rocking chair, strewn clothes, laundry hamper; too many pastels for his taste, too girly—but . . .

It's happening again, isn't it? . . . Oh, no . . . Oh, shit! He closes his eyes. When they open he'll remember. He'll remember everything . . .

"You're going to be late, honey." A woman's voice, behind him. Clay spins, but all he catches is a cream-colored blouse and navy pant leg, a flash of waist-length blond hair flowing behind, moving out of sight in the hallway.

He thinks of the little girl with the same blond hair. "Mommy," she'd said.

Charlene! Oh, thank God! Finally! His real life, this is it.

He stands and takes a step and nearly collapses to the floor as stabbing pains shoot through his right leg, from his toes to his hip, then radiate up his spine. He has to catch himself on the arm of the rocker, lower himself to one knee, then roll to his side on the carpet.

Oh my God! . . . Owww! . . . What the hell?!

When the pain—like an electric, cold-burning fire—finally eases, Clay sits up and scoots gingerly back against the bedframe. Laid out straight, his leg has a thick mean scar running along the top of it, starting at the top of his foot and traveling in an outside arc around his knee to his hip. He has to pull up, then down, his boxers to see the whole thing. It's grizzly.

Oh, my God! No . . . This can't be . . . This wasn't here yesterday, or the day before. Then, of course, there'd been nothing wrong with his leg. In addition to the main scar, he notices, his foot and ankle are covered in a spiderweb of thin white lines.

What the hell's happened?! And *when?*

Slowly, cautiously, Clay eases up the side of the bed and stands, a bit shakily. Takes a few tentative steps . . . The pain isn't as bad when he's careful like this, when he keeps his leg straight. There's just a dull ache now.

He puts on a shaggy blue bathrobe hanging from the closet door, ties it as he teeters down the hall. He's grinning; he can't help it. Charlene will know what to do; she'll understand; she can help him figure this out.

The short, bare hallway ends with a kitchen to the left, a small living room to the right. Two kids are eating at a round wooden table off of the kitchen, beside a sliding glass door to outside—one the little girl from earlier, the other a boy of about eight or nine with unruly brown hair like his own.

"Hi, Daddy," says the girl brightly. "You're up!" She has an empty bowl pushed out in front of her, knees up on the chair. A notebook she's earnestly drawing in with crayons. Colorful little cereal pieces litter the table around her.

The boy looks up once before resuming his attack on his own bowl of cereal. "Hey, Dad." His box says Frosted Mini Wheats.

Ah, Clay's favorite. Like father, like son.

Clay, for the life of him, can't put a name to either child. But that's okay, it'll come to him eventually. Now that he's home, everything's going to be fine. Everything's going to be all right now.

"Where's Charlene?" he asks the kids.

"Huh?" says the boy.

"Who's that?" says the girl.

"Your mom."

"Oh. She's out talking to Linda." Little blondie screws up her face. "Why aren't you dressed?"

Clay spies a bowl and spoon in the dish rack by the sink and limps over to get them. Sits down at the table and pours himself a bowl of Mini Wheats. Both kids staring at him with their mouths open. He adds some milk from the carton on the table. The key is to let Mini Wheats sit for a minute before eating them, get just the right sogginess. He sits with his hands in his lap. Smiles innocently.

"What are you doing?" The boy.

"What do you mean?"

"You're eating cereal."

"Yeah?"

The kids exchange glances.

"You don't eat cereal, Daddy," says the girl.

"What? You're kidding me, I love cereal." And to prove it, he takes a bite. "Mmm, good stuff," milk dribbling down his chin. He digs in, already thinking about a second bowl.

A car outside honks twice and the boy is up and out of his chair like a rocket, taking his empty bowl to the sink, then flying past, behind Clay, into the living room, having snagged a backpack from somewhere. "Bye!" he hollers as he's out the front door.

"School?" Clay asks the girl.

She just nods at him, slowly, watching him eat. Then: "Are we going?"

"Huh?"

There's some movement to his right, and the sliding glass door opens.

Charlene! Clay's heart leaps and he almost stands; but . . .

"Did Waylan leave already?" the woman asks.

Clay can only stare. Way beyond confused. Devastated. But the girl says, "Uh-huh."

The woman hurries into the kitchen and opens the fridge. "Did he take—? No, he forgot it again. Damn it." She slams the refrigerator door. "Will you take it? I don't have time this morning. Will you drop it off for him when you take Crystal?"

She looks over at him but it's only for a second before she's moving again, past him, down the hallway. "Linda says she'll watch the kids tonight," her voice carrying easily, even from another room somewhere. "Just so long as we're back by twelve, because she has to take Philo to the vet in the morning. She didn't say, but I think she's thinking about putting him down; he must be, like, twenty years old, or something, by now."

Clay listens to this as he stares at the little blond stranger across the table, who stares back as if seeing him, too, for the first time.

"Don't forget to ask Will for a copy of the early-release form,"—the woman's back, typing with her thumbs, it looks like, before dropping the phone into her purse—"just in case they keep wanting their monthly payment. I've heard that happens sometimes, like to Terri's brother-in-law." She circles around the table to the girl. "Give Mommy a kiss goodbye."

But the girl won't take her eyes off Clay. So the woman kisses her hair and smooths it down, resumes her circle around. Stops and plants a fat kiss on Clay's upturned face.

"I'm happy for you today," she says, wiping away some lipstick from the corner of his mouth. "Say 'hi' to Will for me. And tell him 'thank you' from me too."

Then she's off again, toward the front door.

Clay's relieved to see her go. He has no idea who she is; he's never seen her before. And he seriously doubts she can help him. He can't believe she's his *wife!*

The woman turns in the open door. "See you tonight," she says with a big smile. "I can't wait to go out and celebrate! Bye, sweetie!"

"Bye, Mommy," calls the girl. Then, "Wait!" She hops out of her chair and runs across the room, tugs at her mother's arm until the woman bends down, whispers in her ear . . . They both look over at him. The woman smiles.

"You're going to get dressed now, aren't you, honey?"

Clay looks down at the robe he's wearing, then back. "Uh-huh."

"You see?" she tells the girl. "Don't forget Waylan's lunch," calling over her shoulder as she goes.

The girl watches her mother drive off. Then closes the door and turns. "Are we going to be late today, Daddy?"

* ✳ ✳

AS CLAY DRIVES, he can't help but be drawn to the changes he sees all around him. The town is the same, but different—modernized. Which should be the case, he thinks, seeing how it's ten years into the future since graduation. Ten years he has no recollection of whatsoever.

Ten years. He'd be freaking out if he hadn't already been doing so over the past few days. It's the same thing all over again. Only now it's four years later than yesterday, and two years *before* the day before that. Who knows what year it was in the alley. (By now he's convinced himself that that day wasn't a dream, as he'd first hoped. It was when this all started.)

And for the first time, he isn't in New York but his hometown. What can that mean?

He's driving around his old high school, past the football field where he used to play, when the cell phone rings. The little girl, Crystal, had been playing with it, and she answers it herself. "Hello? . . . Please hold, please." Hands it to him. Very cute. Like a little secretary.

Clay takes the phone warily. "Hello?"

"Clay. Hey, buddy. Where are you?"

"Uh . . . I'm taking, uh, Crystal to school."

"Oh. Okay . . . Uh, I know you didn't forget about our appointment this morning." A light chuckle.

"Oh, uh, nooo . . ." He looks over at Crystal, who, as usual, is looking right back at him. "But, uh, remind me again, would you? What's it about?"

Real laughter this time. "All right, funny guy. But I've got appointments here and in Eagle City and Canton all day. I can't just see you whenever you decide to stroll in. This takes a little more paperwork than the usual visit, you know. Figure at least twenty minutes, a half hour, maybe. Hold on." There's the sound of muffled conversation. "Can you get here in ten minutes?"

"Uh, listen, uh . . . Is there any way we can do this tomorrow?"

There's a protracted silence. "Hello?" Clay says.

"Tomorrow? Are you serious? Most people would be racing in here to get off probation. Especially early."

Probation?

"Why?" the voice asks. "Did something come up?"

"Well, yeah. I've gotta go outta town. See somebody in Tulsa. Uh . . . An old friend I really need to talk to. I can only do it today."

Another long pause. A sigh. "Tulsa . . . Okay, Clay. All right. I guess it must be something pretty important. Technically, you're not supposed to leave the county, you know, but— Can you be here tomorrow, then, around three-thirty? I should be back from court by then."

"Sure, sure, you bet. Tomorrow at three-thirty." He motions to Crystal to write it down, and she grabs for her pink-and-silver backpack as he ends the call.

Crystal asks, "Are you going to see that lady?"

"What lady?"

"The one you googled."

Clay looks over as he drives. Then he figures it out. "You're pretty smart, aren't you?"

"Yep." She doesn't look up. She's writing 3:30 in big red crayon in her notebook. "Is she your girlfriend?"

"She used to be." His throat swells and there's a sudden pressure behind his eyes. "But not anymore."

Crystal looks up with a grin. "Mommy's your girlfriend now, isn't she." It wasn't a question.

He meets her eyes and smiles reassuringly, though he doesn't feel it. "You got it, kiddo."

When they pull up to the school, Crystal doesn't get out but just keeps looking at the building, then back to him.

"Well? Don't you want to go to school?"

She cocks her head and looks at him in that cute-serious way he's come to like. "This isn't my school, Daddy."

"What? Sure it is." It's the only elementary school in town.

But she just shakes her head. "And we forgot Waylan's lunch."

Shit. "Oh. Okay. Then where *is* your school, then?"

She turns in her seat and points behind them. Scrunches up her face and smiles. "You're funny today, Daddy."

IT'S A HUGE PLACE, the largest hospital Clay has ever stepped foot in. It's taken him a full twenty minutes to find the physical therapy department, where Charlene supposedly works. This part of the complex seems newer and brighter, with extra-wide corridors and doorways, big windows looking in to big rooms filled with exercise machines and other equipment.

His search online for "Charlene Summers" this morning had yielded a number of results, the top ten being news headlines from various years. The ones Clay seized upon—"Presbyterian Hires Hero PT"; "Summers to Wed Her Doctor"; and "Accident Leaves Woman in Coma"—had sent him reeling.

She's alive! had been all that mattered. Until: *How can that be? . . .*

Had he really seen her body by the side of the road? Was it her? Or had that just been a bad dream? . . . Like last night's dream of the car chase and . . .

Oh my God! No! The thought had horrified him. He'd had to push it out of his mind.

Then, later, on the long drive from Taloga, an equally distressing thought occurred to him: Had he killed an innocent man yesterday?

Both thoughts have plagued him since.

In the hallway, Clay passes people on crutches and in wheelchairs, knee- and shoulder braces, and with his lopsided gait he fits right in. Through one long window he can see a bunch of patients rolling around on giant inflatable balls, all different colors, some people arched backward, some forward. It looks like fun.

Room number eleven, he was told, is Charlene's office. But when he passes through the open doorway he sees only a muscle-bound guy assisting a teenage boy to walk haltingly between a set of handrails. "Extend at the knee," the guy is saying. "Good. Like that, that's good."

"Hi," says Clay, and the guy looks up. "I'm looking for Charlene Summers." But the guy just looks at him. "Oh! I mean Charlene *Ritchie*. I hear she works here now." It still hasn't registered that she's married; he can't believe it's true. The article he'd read was posted over three years ago.

"Sure"—the guy motions with his head—"she's right in there."

Clay's hands are shaking as he wipes them on his pants. His stomach is doing flips.

In the next room is a small group of people in wheelchairs. Manipulating large rubber bands of various colors, either attached to their chairs or held between their hands. There's a woman with short, spiky, blond hair in a wheelchair facing them, her back to Clay as she instructs the group.

"Hi," he says, "I'm looking for Char—"

The woman with the spiky hair turns, and the shock of recognition on her face must mirror his own. Her mouth hangs open.

"Charlene," Clay finally manages. "Why—?" *Why are you in a wheelchair?* he wants to ask, but is deathly afraid of the answer.

Charlene's look of surprise suddenly turns to one of anger. Using her arms, she pivots on the large wheels of her chair and speedily reverses away from him, her lips set in a thin line, her eyes boring into his the entire time. Then she's pivoting again and propelling herself through another open doorway, into the larger room he just left.

"Charlene! Wait, I—" He has no choice but to follow.

Charlene's clearly a woman with a purpose. Heading directly toward a spacious, glassed-in office in the far corner. "Scott," she calls out as she goes, "don't let this man near me. I'm calling security."

"What?!" Clay can't understand her reaction. This is the girl he was planning on marrying, himself, just four days ago.

"You got it," the muscle man says; he's put out his arms to stabilize the kid. "What's going on?"

"Charlene, please, I—I really need to talk to you. *Please!*" Clay does his best to ignore the pain in his leg as he hobbles after her. Grimacing and suppressing a curse. "Why are you doing this?"

But Charlene doesn't answer. She stops for only an instant as she adjusts her trajectory to wheel herself into the office. From half the larger room away, Clay can see her pick up the phone on the desk and push some buttons.

Then just before he reaches the office, Muscle Man is there, holding up a warning hand to stop him. But to Clay it feels as if he'd played ball only weeks ago, not years, and he has the momentum behind him, so he ducks low and rams his shoulder into the guy's midsection, smashing him into the metal doorframe, shaking the glass walls. It was a solid hit, but Clay's leg isn't able to support his weight and he goes down, in excruciating pain, with the guy on top of him.

But with a shove, the guy rolls off, holding the back of his head. Moaning. Semi-conscious.

Despite the wrenching pain in his leg, Clay tries to stand. He *has* to talk to Charlene. He has to get some answers to what's going on, to what's happened—to both of them. To his embarrassment, he lets out a cry and has to bite down on his lip as his bad leg refuses to respond. He's left to climb up the doorframe with his hands, instead.

Inside the office he can hear Charlene speaking calmly but hurried. Upset. "Immediately. Yes, please. I believe my life is in danger . . . I have no idea. Please hurry. Hurry . . . Yes: PT. Room eleven . . . Thank you."

Clay's standing, finally, balanced on one leg, face hot, sweat beaded upon his brow. "Charlene, what the hell is this? Don't you recognize me? It's *me!*" Seeing her is everything he wanted—just to know she's all right. But not like this. Something tears inside his chest, and a sob escapes him. "God! I've missed you so bad! I don't know what's going on. You've gotta help me. Please!"

Charlene's eyes move between him and the guy on the floor, who's still moaning loudly. If Clay could, he'd kick him to shut him up.

"Charlene, what—" He points to her wheelchair. "What happened? Why are you . . ."

Charlene rolls slowly backward, away, and pivots, putting the desk between them. Her eyes watchful, wary. Almost like she's *afraid*. She still hasn't said a word to him since he arrived.

Clay gets the feeling he doesn't have much time. This hasn't gone at all the way he'd planned. "Baby, I don't understand. Why are you doing this to me? Don't you love me? What— What's happened? . . ."

But he knows . . . he knows, doesn't he? It's his dream . . . the results of it. And the realization makes him hang his head and sigh.

When he looks up, at the fear and anxiety so plain, now, upon her face, it makes him want to cry. "I'm so sorry, Charlene . . . I really am. I'm so sorry, but—I don't know what's happened here. I really don't . . . I just—" He waves his arm feebly, to indicate everything around them. Reality. "I don't remember anything."

"You need to leave," Charlene says, her voice wavering; and as cold as it is, it's the most beautiful sound. "Now," she adds, when it's clear he won't. "Haven't you caused enough trouble in your life?"

Somehow it's not the same person anymore, he knows this; but it's *her*, the girl he loved—still loves!—the girl he knows so well. He has to make her understand!

He tries to walk but has to hop painfully on one leg toward her desk.

"No!" she cries sharply. "Get out!"

"I love you!" he says, falling against the desk. "I love you so much. I just want things to be the way they were, the way they used to be. Before. With you. Forever. Like you said. Remember?"

There's yelling now, behind him. Many voices.

"We were going to get married, go to school . . . You remember?" He's leaning over her desk, at the waist, reaching out to her, his fingers reaching, reaching—just to touch her, just that—hoping she'll finally reach back. But Charlene is pressed back rigidly in her chair, against the bookshelves behind her. Her beautiful green eyes huge. Scared. Her mouth twisted in disgust.

Oh, God! Clay thinks mournfully. *What have I done?*

Then heavy hands are upon him, knocking him to the floor; dragging him backward by his arms, unresisting, heels scraping the carpet. Charlene at her desk, not watching, but with her face in her hands. Shuddering. Crying.

And it breaks his heart.

Completely.

IT'S WELL PAST nine when he finally rolls back into town. He'd spent much of the afternoon in the back of a squad car. Thankfully, the hospital hadn't pressed any charges. Not yet. Not that he really cares about that, right now. However, he was assured, he *will* be hearing from Muscle Man's attorneys at some point soon. He'd been reminded again and again how lucky he was not to have been arrested, his probation revoked immediately, after all this time—all those years wasted—though it's still a definite possibility. He'd had to listen to the voice from this morning's phone call chew him a new asshole for over an hour.

He's taking the old spur road north, heading home—to the home he used to know, ten years ago . . . a different lifetime ago.

A single light is on in the kitchen when he arrives. But no dogs run out to meet him. No neighbor kids from his youth. And he can't imagine his mother welcoming him with open arms.

But, if there's anybody in the world he can go to, it should be her, he thinks, right? . . . Right?

Unless she's been drinking, of course, which is probably the case. Unless she's too busy at the moment, working the next potential husband who never sticks around—too generous by half with her love, to give anything more to her son—too full of herself to care about *his* problems, for a change . . .

The doorway lights up for a moment, before a large shadow fills the space. A man. Tall, thickset. Who raises a hand in familiar greeting.

But to Clay the man is a stranger. He presses the accelerator, churning gravel, heading back into town. It was enough, he supposes, to see that the place still existed, whether his mom lives there or not.

Less than a minute later his phone rings. Clay ignores it. It's been doing this all day. But it rings only a few times before it stops. YOU HAVE 16 UNHEARD MESSAGES, the screen says.

The familiar, comforting lights of the Old Pines convenience store are growing closer, up ahead, and Clay suddenly craves a beer. A lot of them, actually. And he knows the perfect place to drink them, to drown his sorrows—maybe drink himself into remembering, into understanding, somehow. Maybe oblivion is the answer, he thinks.

First, wipe the slate clean . . .

IT WASN'T HARD to find the house—*his* house, he has to remind himself—in an old, beat-up part of town, even more beat-up than he remembers it being ten years ago. From outside, the place looks too small, too plain, like a shoebox with flower beds and curtains. Nothing like the home he and Charlene had imagined for themselves.

He sits parked for a while, just staring, taking it in.

Shit. Married with kids, for Chrissakes. Wife and kids he doesn't even know . . . Though she's not that bad looking, he recalls . . . And the little girl sure is a doll . . . And he could do some pretty cool stuff with the boy, he supposes . . . A son! Wow.

He finally resigns himself and gets out of the truck. Stumbles slowly toward the dimly lit front steps.

There's a cough, a clearing of the throat, off to his right. He turns. Sees the blue-black shape of a man standing stock still. Until the arm moves just enough for Clay to see the unmistakable shape of a baseball bat hanging down by the man's side; hear the hollow *ping, ping* of aluminum on steel-toed boots.

Instinct, a sense of foreboding, makes him turn to the left, as well. And there another man stands; another grim, dark shadow.

Ping, ping, ping.

"You just don't learn, do you?" The voice on the right is closer than it should be.

Then pain is exploding through both his legs, behind the knees, and he's instantly on the ground, on his back. His head ringing. He can see stars, real ones in the sky, that are quickly blacked out by a looming figure.

"We said, 'Stay away.' And what do you do?"

A kick, he thinks, to his ribs, which makes him arch and grunt. He knows there's more to come. But he won't shout, he won't scream, he won't cry out . . . In a way, he's glad he's so drunk: it'll numb the— "Aaargh!"

Oh, God, help me . . .

The bat—he can hear it hitting—keeps landing on his legs, his arms, his back, until there's nothing but a bright hot ball of unrelenting pain that he can only accept and embrace and curl himself into, in the hope that it will eventually stop. Or that he'll eventually die, if that is what it takes . . .

He doesn't even realize, at first, when it's finally over. He's thrown up his evening's dinner of beer and beef jerky and is lying in the mess. Taking deep, ragged breaths. Whimpering softly, despite his earlier resolve.

"You're lucky we don't kill you, you stupid son of a bitch." A different voice; it reminds him of somebody from his youth. "But if you ever—" *PING!* PAIN "—*ever* come near Charlene again, we will. Do you understand me?"

Clay can barely breathe, let alone speak, from the damage to his ribs, his jaw. But he's able to force out one lone word. One that comes out as a rough whisper:

"No."

Incredulous silence. Then: "What did you say?"

Even more than wanting the pain to stop—or to breathe, for Chrissakes—Clay wants to *understand.* More than anything else, he simply wants to know what the hell is going on—what's happened to him. His life. His memory. So:

"No," he croaks again. "I don't understand."

Fortunately, eventually, thank God, the pain turns to sleep.

He's exhausted. *His throat raw and sore from crying. Bawling. His eyes like swollen wet rags stuffed into his skull—so heavy he just wants to keep them closed. Snot has been running down his face and onto his shirt for so long it doesn't matter. Nothing matters anymore. Nothing.*

Charlene is dead.

Dead.

She's never coming back . . . He'll never see her again . . .

It's been hours, and it's still a shock each time he hears it. A blow to the gut, a ripping out of his heart. As if they didn't know what they were doing.

But now he's cried himself out. He's no longer slumped over the table, head buried in his arms, heaving, sobbing, screaming at times; but sitting back, slouched in the hard chair, head bowed, with staggered breath, his mind as numb and blank as he can possibly make it—no past, no future, only this present moment, then the next, and the next. As he answers their questions, their never-ending questions. The same questions, over and over.

The same questions he's been asking himself.

Why did you leave her, at the party?

What was the argument about?

Who did she leave with?

Why?

Why?

Why?

He's walking now, leaving finally, past rows of desks and filing cabinets, other small rooms with people being questioned. One detective in front, the other behind.

He raises his weary eyes and sees him—*the asshole—also being led, but accompanied by a man in a fancy black suit.*

I'll kill you! he cries, lunging past the cop and knocking him down. I'm gonna fucking kill you!

Then he's on him, hands around the asshole's neck, squeezing the life out of him—for the life he's taken. For Charlene.

Shouting, a crushing weight, hands tearing at his own.

No! No!

Nooo!

FRIDAY, FEBRUARY 22, 2013   **DAY 5**

CLAY WAKES to a beeping sound in the dark. Finds that it's his watch, a digital beast glowing neon blue, its numbers flashing 05:15 A.M. He pushes at one of its multitude of buttons, then another, and another, then just leaves it beeping.

He's lying on his side, curled up tight, on a hard surface. Only inches from his face, from what he can see, is a grimy black wall, a horizontal beam with seemingly decades of accumulated dirt along its edges. He reflexively jerks back and feels a low ridge pressing against his spine. His head is resting upon a bulky cloth bag—black nylon. He goes to straighten his legs—*Aaah!*—and instantly tucks them back in, his heart pounding: it was like he'd shot them out into space with nothing below, his ass right on the edge of a cliff. *Whoa!* . . . Yep, he can feel it with the toe of his shoe: a freakin' edge, a drop-off to something. Or nothing.

He goes to sit up and there's a tugging at his waist. With a gloved hand, in the near darkness, he feels a carabiner attached to his belt. Feels up and around . . . A harness of some kind . . . A flat nylon tether connecting him to . . . He runs both hands along it to determine . . . A large shackle—giant, really—attached to a narrow I-beam along the floor; another beam running at a ninety-degree angle. All of it metal, including the floor, which makes a hollow ringing sound when he taps on it. He keeps feeling—"seeing"—with his hands . . . Attached to the top of the shackle is a large loop of cable as thick as his thumb—he can just make it out in the dark—the tail end clamped about three feet up, the remainder disappearing above him into pitch black. Clay thrums it: solid, taut.

Oookay . . .

Here we go again, he thinks. Once more, he has no idea where he is or how he got here. Or why.

The watch alarm finally stops beeping, and it gives him an idea. He pushes a button—*Nope*—then another, until different functions appear . . .

The date: 02.22.13.

So . . . only one year earlier than before. Not too big of a jump this time . . . But, *why* is it happening, for Chrissakes? For the thousandth time he has to ask himself: *What the hell is going on?*

Blue light from the watch glints off pieces of metal on his harness. He begins patting himself down. It's more a vest, he realizes, with several bulging pockets. There's the feel of a knife handle and long sheath strapped to the left of his chest; nothing in the middle; and—*Bingo!*—a small flashlight in a similar position on the right. He twists it to turn it on.

The bright narrow beam reveals, in parts, a small box-like enclosure of cement and steel. Maybe five by fifteen, with three close walls and the fourth about ten feet away. The floor he's sitting on an approximately four-by-six sheet of welded metal with crisscrossing beams. He reaches out and touches the section of wall immediately in front of him, above that which he awoke to—a solid, smooth, metal rectangle placed into a steel frame and the rough cement around it; a vertical seam bisecting it perfectly in half. The rectangle's about seven or eight feet tall and begins at the level of his waist as he kneels. The number "14" is stenciled large in white in its center, one number to either side of the seam.

To his left is the edge, the drop-off he'd feared earlier. Clay leans over it and shines the beam down, illuminating the side of the metal container he's sitting on and the untold depth yawing below. It confirms his suspicion: He's in an elevator shaft.

Great. Of all places . . . He passes the beam around. *Sheesh. What's next?*

A quick inventory of the duffel beside him produces a thick coil of thin, black rope and an assortment of climbing devices and tools—mostly things he doesn't recognize or know how to use.

What was he planning on doing with it? he wonders. Or has he used it already?

The roof of the elevator is divided into quarter sections by the beams, and the quarter adjacent to the one he's on has a not-so-obvious hatch built into it, the hinges on the longer side closest to him, a recessed handle on the other, and—*something* snaking out of it on that side . . . a thin metal cable, taped down in a few places and ending in a small, funnel-shaped piece of black rubber in front of him. He leans over and picks it up, looks inside. And sees the inside of the elevator, the doors especially, a wide-angle view.

Okay, now we're getting somewhere.

"Whoa!" The shout is involuntary as Clay and the elevator are suddenly free-falling, his stomach in his throat; he has to catch his balance with one hand on the hatch and the other on the central cable, its vibrations coursing through his body. The flashlight held against the roof now casting its beam into a rushing black-and-gray waterfall of cement ten feet away.

The elevator suddenly brakes and slows, comes to a stop. Clay regains his equilibrium and bends to look into the eyepiece. The doors have already opened and a portly, conservatively dressed man with graying temples and two bulging briefcases steps inside. As the man enters and pushes a button on the panel, Clay gets a good look but doesn't recognize him. The man moves slightly out of view, to the back of the compartment, and everything becomes distorted; he looks like a miniature giant, his well-groomed hairdo looming large toward the lens.

Then they're plummeting again and Clay braces himself, ready this time.

What is he going to do? What is he *supposed* to be doing? As usual, he has no idea.

Sooner than expected, the elevator comes to a halt. This time there's another elevator—an identical box (identical roof, at least, its cable near invisible)—beside him; he could easily jump across.

"Good morning, Amos. Is the other elevator still not working?"

Clay can't make out the reply.

"Well, that's all right, just so it's fixed by this—" The voice fades and the doors slide shut.

Clay shines the flashlight on the nearest wall, on the doors above him. "P1" is painted there. So the floor below, where the man just got off, must be P2, he figures. Or maybe just P.

The elevator doesn't move again, so Clay takes the opportunity to search himself more thoroughly. He knows he needs to figure something out, quick. There has to be a clue, an indicator of what he's doing here . . . He turns the light on himself, on his entirely black outfit, his many vest pockets . . . on the gun at his hip.

He pulls it from its holster with an audible *click.* It's not like the gun from before; this one's smaller, more compact—but, he's sure, just as deadly.

Once again, it appears that he's a man on a mission. A dangerous one.

What is it this time? he wonders, replacing the gun. Has he become a freakin' hit man, an assassin, for Chrissakes? A CIA operative? The constant violence is starting to wear at him.

With these thoughts the elevator jerks back to life and soars upward, fast, then faster. Clay steadies himself; ready, he hopes, for anything. The elevator slows. Stops. A quick look: the number "26" above.

Through the snake-eye he watches as the elevator doors open . . . then a single hand appear to catch them before they close. Unintelligible conversation, brief snatches of phrases, then a man walks in, carrying a single thin briefcase, talking on his cell phone. "Good. I'll call you when I get in." He pockets the phone and leans forward to press a button. The doors close. The elevator drops.

At first Clay is too shocked to react. *No! It can't be!* had been his initial thought upon seeing the asshole again. Alive. Not dead in a pool of blood on a restroom floor, but very much alive, talking on his phone, with shiny-wet, combed-back hair, dressed like a million bucks. But now Clay leaps into action; he has to move fast, before it's too late, before the asshole leaves the elevator. This *has* to be the reason he's here!

Flashlight in his mouth, Clay unclips himself from the tether, bends, and lifts the hatch with a clattering bang as it falls open. The asshole's neck cranes up, eyes wide in surprise. And Clay jumps inside.

His blows are frenzied but effective, as a rage consumes him, and the asshole is soon on the floor of the small space, cowering and covering up as Clay kicks him mercilessly, remembering all too well the similar beating he took the night before. But the anger and frustration he feels, he realizes, is more at himself, for not understanding what's happening to him, or why, or what the hell he can do about it. He needs answers more than retribution from this asshole. And it's only in the nick of time that he lunges for the control panel.

The elevator immediately stops. The doors slide open. *Ding!* Clay puts a hand to the gun, terrified, almost expecting somebody to be there. Of the row of numbers above the door, "2" is lit up. On the panel of buttons: "P1," "3," and "4"—he'd hit more than one.

Okay okay okay . . . This is what we gotta do . . .

The asshole looks barely conscious, crumpled against the back wall of the elevator. Clay grabs him by the ankles and pulls him, on his back, out the door and into a small waiting area-slash-hallway. Pauses the doors in closing and grabs the asshole's briefcase and tosses it out. Then, watching as the doors close a second time, spots a long blood-red smear on the carpet inside. *Shit!* But it's too late and the elevator descends. He can only hope nobody notices. He pushes the call button and watches the row of numbers above the door.

The asshole moans. "Shut up," Clay mutters nervously and gives him a backwards kick.

He sees "P1" light up. And stay lit . . . *Shit!* Then finally no lights . . . "1" . . . then, *Ding!* The doors open and Clay's ready with the gun. But the elevator's still empty, thank God.

Clay throws in the briefcase, then drags the asshole back in by an arm and a leg. Pushes "25," where the asshole had gotten on. The doors close, and Clay kneels to use the asshole's coattail to wipe at the blood on the carpet as they ascend. *Ding!* The doors begin to open and Clay, still on his knees, draws the gun. But, thankfully, nobody is there. He'd forgotten about the other buttons pushed, too. He stays wary as the fourth floor's doors also open, and breathes a sigh of relief when the coast is clear. Still, he remains poised with the gun in his hand all the way to the twenty-fifth floor, just in case. He'd hate to have to use it, to take anybody hostage. That's the last thing he needs right now.

Ding! Again he kicks out the briefcase and drags the asshole out into the hallway. There's a long display table with a vase of flowers, a painting, and two doors—one on the left, one on the right. Which one is his?

Clay catches a knee and slaps the asshole across the face to wake him up, get his attention. "Hey! Hey!" he says in a harsh whisper.

The asshole's eyes flicker open, and grow large when they see Clay's face so close to his own. "No! Stop. Please don't."

"Shhh. Which apartment is yours? Point."

The asshole's eyes roll, then close tight. He rapidly shakes his head.

Clay's forced to slap him again, harder, but it only makes the asshole cringe and curl up even tighter into a ball. *Shit!* Clay digs through the asshole's jacket pockets and finds the phone; slips it into his own vest. Nothing in the pants pockets at all. No keys. So he tries the briefcase, which doesn't have a lock but a fake buckle. Finds a wallet and a set of keys in a side pocket.

The asshole isn't going anywhere, so Clay first tries the door on the right: two locks above an ornate brass handle. None of the four keys match the top lock, so he crosses to the other door. And this time has luck with both. But he doesn't open it.

Instead, he drags the asshole over, by his armpits. Props him against the wall. Gets down low to his face. The asshole's eyes are open, watching, one cut badly beneath and swollen almost shut. "Hey. Asshole," Clay says softly. "Is there an alarm?" No answer. Scared silence. "Do you have an alarm?" Still nothing, a slight shake of the head. "You mean, 'no' as in 'No, don't hurt me,' or 'No, there's no alarm'?"

The asshole just shuts his eyes again. "Oh, God," he moans.

Even to Clay, who doesn't have much experience in such matters, it's pretty clear that the asshole's nose is broken: it's crooked now, and congealing blood covers his mouth and chin. So Clay flicks it with his finger, while at the same time covering the man's mouth.

"Aaah! Aaargh!" The asshole raises his hands to his face, shocked, as tears instantly well and spill over. He goes to move but Clay keeps him pinned to the wall.

"I'm serious," Clay says. He removes the gun from its holster. Waves it in the asshole's face. "If an alarm goes off, or if the cops come, at any time"—he pokes him in the forehead with the barrel—"I'm gonna shoot you, a whole bunch of times." Raps him once with it on the head. "And I'm gonna enjoy it, believe me." A tear rolls down the asshole's cheek and Clay wipes it away with his thumb. "But if you're cool, if you do what I say, you're gonna be all right. Okay?" A frightened, hopeful nod. "Good. Now: Is—there—an alarm?"

"No." It comes out weakly. The asshole squeezes his eyes shut for a moment, shedding more tears. "We have security. Downstairs." Gives his head a brief shake. "No alarm."

"Awesome." Clay stands and pushes open the door. Returns. "Now, I'm gonna pull you in. Don't get up. Don't do anything stupid, as they say." He sets the briefcase on the asshole's stomach. "Here, hold this." Drags him far enough inside to shut the door. Locks it twice.

The apartment is semi-dark, the entryway lit by a series of dim orange-yellow sconces along one side. Walking backward, dragging the asshole in further, there's an expansive, elegantly furnished living room to the right, a wall of framed artwork and photos on the left, a short hallway with doors to either side. But for what Clay has in mind he keeps going, his back and arms beginning to strain; he's obviously not in the shape he once was. Then they finally reach the end of the hallway, and the asshole slides easily on the tiled kitchen floor.

Clay drops him. "Sit up, over there," he commands, pointing to the large butcher-block island in the center. He has to lean against the counter, by the sink, to catch his breath.

The asshole slowly scootches over, grimacing, to sit with his back to the island. Clay doesn't see the briefcase; they must have lost it along the way. He finds the light switch and turns it on. Steps again to the sink for a long drink from the faucet.

It's a spacious kitchen, and immaculate, all stainless steel and bright white. Miles of countertop covered with curious appliances. Over the stove hang an assortment of copper-colored pots and pans. Open-faced cupboards holding stacks of china and glass. Atop the island a bowl of fruit and an expensive set of carving knives, probably none of them ever used—it doesn't look like much actual cooking gets done in here.

Clay leans against the counter and stares at the pathetic figure sitting there on the floor, legs splayed, head hung low, his shirtfront stained with blood, a hand clutched to his side, where there are probably some cracked and bruised ribs.

So this is the asshole who drove away with Charlene, Clay's thinking. This is the person who's somehow responsible for everything he's been experiencing these past many days; this is the guy who started it all. How else can he explain the man's continued appearance practically each and every day? And in his recurring dreams every night.

Clay really needs to find out what's going on. Either Charlene is dead, or she isn't. The dreams just confuse things.

But he'd seen her in the flesh . . .

As he's seen this guy before . . . who's also supposed to be dead.

"Hey. Asshole."

The man lifts his head and glares defiantly back; but it's not very convincing. He's pissed, that's for sure—not used to getting his ass beat—and now he's trying to regain some of his lost self-esteem. Probably trying to figure a way out of this fucked-up situation, make it go away. But he doesn't say a word, doesn't plead, which is almost impressive.

"You work at 4 Financial Plaza?"

Now the asshole looks away. Slowly shakes his head; but apparently it's to himself: He sighs, "Yes . . . I do."

Now for the big question—the first one, at least: "Did you get stabbed, back in 2010? In the bathroom there?"

The asshole's glare is back—but confused, now, as much as irritated. It takes him a moment to respond. "No." Drawn out.

"You sure?"

A snort. "Yes, I'm sure." He probes his side, carefully. "Stabbed? Do you think I would forget something like that?" He stays quiet as Clay considers this answer. Then: "Why? Is that what this is all about? Was I supposed to be stabbed?" He tries to sit up a little straighter. "Is this a contract or something?"

Clay doesn't respond right away. Still trying to make some sense of all this. He knows for certain it wasn't a dream. He'd killed this asshole; stabbed him; had the man's blood all over his hands. It was as real as anything as this right now . . .

"Who hired you?" the asshole wants to know. His split, puffy lips make him hard to understand. "Is it Global? Iceland? Bear Stearns? . . . We can make our own deal," he says. "How much will it take? I have an account in St. Vincent; it's all yours. We can both—"

Clay holds up a silencing hand. "Were you ever in a car accident? In Oklahoma?"

The asshole stays quiet for so long that Clay's about to repeat himself, when: "How did—? I grew up there."

"No shit. Were you ever in a car accident?"

"Well, yeah. A couple of little fender-benders, here and there, when I was a kid, but . . ."

"Nothing major?"

"No. Why? . . . Listen—"

"What happened to Charlene?"

The asshole's look, as much as Clay can tell, is baffled, blank. "What? I—I don't know any Charlene."

"Sure you do. Or you did. You put her in your car, a yellow Camaro, back in 2004. You remember now? It was at a high school graduation party. At the lake. There was a big bonfire and everything. Kegs . . . You were there. I saw you." The men stare at each other. "I saw her get into your car."

It's difficult to see in the asshole's ruined face, but Clay thinks the man's eyes widen in recollection. He swallows noticeably. "Oh," he finally says.

Clay nods once, slowly, his arms crossed. "Yeah . . . *Oh.*"

The asshole seems to have found a fascinating spot on the floor in front of him.

"So, what happened?" Clay finally brings himself to ask again. "What'd you do to her?"

The asshole quickly looks up now; puts up both his hands. "Whoa! Look, man, I swear I didn't do anything to that girl. I swear it. I told the police everything I know. Nothing happened."

"What do you mean 'nothing happened'? She's dead, isn't she? What happened to her?"

The asshole's mouth just opens and closes, like a landed fish. Then he shrugs, wincing at the pain. "I don't know. They just found her like that. Someone—"

"Like *what?*" Clay shouts. "Like what? How'd they find her?" He has a sudden flash of the dream from the night before, being questioned by the cops: *Did you do that to her, Clay?*

The asshole flutters his hands, looks like he's about to answer . . . then stops. Stares. "Wait a second," he says. "Are you her *boyfriend?* That guy who . . . ?"

Clay puts his hands to his face and bows as he turns, leans over the sink, suddenly nauseous—overcome with a torrent of recalled and current emotions: fear, despair, anger, hatred, frustration—confusion. The memory of trying to strangle this asshole on the police-room floor . . . for what he did . . .

And in the next instant, hardly realizing that he'd moved, Clay is crouching close beside him now, his right hand again around the asshole's throat, pressing the man's head against the island's wooden cabinet, digging in, feeling his fingers grip the larynx . . . crush it . . .

"Aaraagck . . . aaagck!" Both the asshole's hands are gripped tightly around Clay's wrist, before he finally manages to pull away and fall to his side on the floor. He chokes and coughs and throws up a protective arm. Chokes and coughs some more. "Please . . . ," he wheezes.

"You killed her, didn't you?" Clay's own voice is a hoarse whisper.

"No . . . No . . . ," as he uselessly tries to scoot away.

Clay takes the jagged-edged commando knife from its sheath on his vest. Studies its swirling tempered steel. "I'm gonna ask you one more time," he says, moving closer, making sure the asshole gets a good look at the blade. "What. Happened?"

The asshole's raspy voice is barely discernable at first. "She asked— She asked me for a ride home." He has to cough, massage his throat. "She was looking for her boyfriend"—his eyes flicker to Clay, then away—"but she couldn't find him, so—so she came to me . . . She knew I wanted to leave, that I was leaving." He coughs. Looks at Clay straight on, as if to gauge the reaction. "So I took her."

There seems to be nothing more forthcoming, so Clay sinks the knife to its hilt in the asshole's thigh.

"AAAHH!" The asshole jerks and kicks and finally wrenches his leg free. "Aaah! Oh! *Fuck!*" He scoots away, with a lot more speed than before. And when Clay doesn't follow, pushes himself slowly, painfully backward, to rest against the cabinets below the sink. "Ah, ah, ah, ah!" He's been holding a hand to the wound and it comes away bright red. "Oh my God!"

Clay stays crouched on one knee. The knife pointed downward in his fist. "What. *Happened?*" His voice is dull, deadly serious. No emotions, now, to rule his actions. He's gotta be smart, he knows; this is his best, first chance to find out what really happened to Charlene. And he's going to do whatever it takes. He has all day.

The asshole's eyes, despite the swelling, are huge, frantic; his breath coming faster. "I—We—We made out for a while, but . . . I mean . . . I tried to do more, you know, but—she didn't want to, she was upset, so . . . so I let her go . . . She wanted to go . . ."

Clay can't believe this. "You *made out* with her?"

The asshole nods, carefully. "Yeah," he says.

"You *kissed* her? Did she kiss you back?"

"Uh . . . yeah."

No freakin' way. Clay has to force himself to think about what else the asshole said. "So, you just let her go?"

"Yeah, man, I swear."

"Where? Right there?"

"Huh?"

"Where'd you let her go? Where were you?"

"Uh, we were in the woods, by the lake, but south, in that campground, where the Boy Scouts always had their Jamboree, or whatever it's called—the big cookout."

Clay recalls his dream-memory of chasing the asshole's car through the trees . . . the campground . . .

He says, "So you just left her there? You just left her at the campground? Like, ten miles from town?" Then a wicked thought strikes him: "Did she get out, or did you *throw* her out?"

The asshole's wincing as he squeezes the gash in his thigh, trying to put pressure on the wound. His pant leg has a growing stain to match the front of his shirt. He looks up with a guilty expression, like a deer in the headlights. "No! No way! She left on her own. She wanted to! I wouldn't do that. I mean—" But he just shrugs. Makes a face, in pain.

Clay stands up and sheaths the knife. Walks to the far left drawer, beneath the countertop, and opens it: cloth napkins. The next: dish towels. Another, with more of the same.

"What are you doing?" he hears the asshole say.

Clay keeps opening drawers, searching, going down the line: silverware, and more silverware. "I don't believe you," he says. Wooden spoons and spatulas. Ziploc bags.

"Uh . . . okay . . . So . . . what are you doing?" There's a tremor to the asshole's voice that wasn't there before.

After going through all the drawers, Clay still hasn't found anything worth using. But there has to be— *Ah, of course:* the island; there's a set of drawers on either side; this is where he should have started—the knives on top were the clue: this is where the food is prepared . . . And the first drawer proves him right; it's filled with all sorts of crazy gadgets, most completely foreign to him. He comes away with a long, flat cheese grater.

Light glints off its serrated surface as he turns.

The asshole visibly starts and puts up his hands. "Whoa! Whoa! Hold on, man! I've told you everything. I've told you the truth. That's all I know. Really! Really! I swear!" As Clay comes closer, the man scoots away along the cabinets, leaving a bloody smear on the floor. "Stop! Stop!" High-pitched, panicky. "I can prove it! They tested me! They *proved* it wasn't me!"

Clay does stop. "What? Who? . . . *Tested?*"

"The police. It wasn't my DNA, my sperm, my semen in her. It was someone else's."

The kitchen lurches, spins, and Clay has to sit down where he was standing, a controlled collapse to the floor. He knows he's looking at the asshole but doesn't see him. Instead there's nothing but red, pulsing red, black around the edges. A dissonant hum in his ears.

"She was raped." His own voice, finally. From far off. Hollow. Echoing back at him.

"Right," the asshole says. "But it wasn't me." His voice is slightly calmer now, relieved, but still frightened. "Even though whoever it was washed her body out in the stream, they still found something. And on her dress. It was buried. And the dogs found it, I think, the next day."

Clay's mind is reeling. Confused. *The stream? . . .*

"She was . . . by the side of the road," he mutters.

"What? The road? No, man, she was— They found her in the stream." Through the haze, it looks like the asshole raises a hand, then drops it, in a futile gesture. "I'm sorry," he adds.

Clay is finally able to focus. Meet the asshole's eyes.

"You're sorry," he says.

The asshole nods back, warily.

"Take off your tie."

"Huh? What?"

Clay points to the asshole's leg. "We need to make a tourniquet. Stop the bleeding."

The asshole's relief is palpable. "Oh. Yeah. Right. Okay." He begins fumbling with the knot, but his hands are shaking. Useless.

"Hold on," Clay says. "I got it."

He begins to crawl forward, then notices the cheese grater in his gloved fist; tosses it skidding across the floor, which elicits an "Oh, thank *God*." He gets up close, on his knees, and grabs at the asshole's once-orange-and-yellow tie, now dull red. Pushes the fumbling hands out of the way. "Let me do it." But he's never worn a tie before—or has no memory of it—and it's slow coming loose.

Instead, it just wants to get tighter and tighter.

. . . Charlene looking up, laughing, her hand on the asshole's arm . . . Her worried expression; the asshole's smug grin . . . Getting into his car . . . Driving away . . . Driving away . . . A dirty, bare foot in the grass . . .

Their faces are only inches apart. The asshole's eyes bulging, bloodshot, his mouth working, trying to speak. Plead. A flurry of hands and fists, getting weaker.

Clay raises up and presses his knee even further into the asshole's lap, until the man finally stops bucking. But there's still some movement, some twitching, convulsions, so he pulls and pushes even harder than before, pulling until the asshole's face goes purple and the eyes go dull, lifeless, pulling until there can be no doubt—*no doubt* this time!—that this asshole is finally dead . . . For the trouble he caused, regardless of his guilt or innocence. For the events he set into motion, whatever they might have been. For whatever really happened that night . . .

Clay collapses to the side, his energy completely spent. His heart pounding in his chest, his breath coming in gasps. He sits with his back to the cabinets and stares vacantly ahead. Shoulder-to-shoulder with the asshole's corpse.

Mission accomplished.

Or so he hopes.

Oh, please let this be mission accomplished.

He turns his head wearily to the side. He doesn't want to see this asshole again.

A black mourning sea, swaying, crying. The whole town has turned out. More. And he's caught in the middle of it, lost and alone. He can only stand there, head bowed, hands in his pockets; if he takes them out, someone will grab one, hold it firmly as they give their condolences, tell him how sorry they are. As it is, people pat him on the shoulder, touch his elbow. It wasn't your fault, they say. You couldn't have known. No one could have known such evil existed in our midst.

He follows the procession where it leads, always remaining on the outskirts, never meeting anybody's eye. The priest's voice carries over the distance, as if to him personally—accusing, damning, accentuated by so many sniffles and sobs.

It's only when there's space around him, at last—more green than black in his peripheral vision—that he moves forward. Cautiously. Humbly.

Chairs are set up around the grave, but only a few are still occupied. Charlene's parents, her sisters, her little brother sitting closely together, quietly, cloaked in their own pall of grief. Once, he remembers, they were as much his family too.

Once. But not anymore.

Now he's standing at the foot of the grave, looking down at the polished black wood of the casket. He wants so badly to throw himself in, to join her. The grief he's felt for days has numbed him to anything else that matters.

There is only one emotion that keeps him living, that gets him up and out of bed each day. And that is hate.

Revenge.

I will find who did this, Charlene. And I will make him pay . . . I promise you.

Dark shadow has finally hidden the coffin. There's the sound of chairs being stacked and put away, an idling backhoe. He doesn't know how long he's been standing there, but vengeance and resolve have been etched onto his soul forever.

He turns to go, and Cheryl, the oldest sister, is standing in his way. There's the white blur of her hand and the sudden shock of pain. Her tearful, red-rimmed eyes full of a wretchedness he knows all too well. And recrimination.

Where were you? she spits. You left her. You walked away.

You walked away . . .

CLAY WAKES slowly, rising to the surface. There's the sleepy smell of bed; the pillowy warmth of skin beneath his hand, and against his morning erection. He snuggles closer and squeezes, presses himself firmly between her legs, from behind. Eyes still closed, he nuzzles the softness of her hair, her neck. Kisses her shoulder.

Oh, Charlene, he thinks. Thank God it was only a dream. A horrible, horrible dream.

He opens his eyes to a cascade of raven hair covering the pillow.

Not blond . . . Not Charlene . . .

In the dim light of the room it's hard to tell, but the woman's skin appears brown, more than tan. She's larger, too, than Charlene ever was. The breast cupped in his hand is full and round, the hips thick and wide.

Ohhh, shit.

His first thought is that he's in big trouble. *Charlene's gonna kill me!* But then it all comes back to him—the memory of the past five days . . . the alley, the dingy hotel, the plaza, the train, the restroom, his hometown, the hospital, the elevator shaft, the asshole's apartment . . . each in a different place, a different time, years apart. Always him, but a different *version* of him. Though his mind seems to be always the same . . . still eighteen, unable to remember a damn thing from before all this started.

Clay slowly withdraws his hand, his erection already at half-mast. Carefully eases himself out of bed. He finds a pair of boxers at his feet and puts them on.

It's overly hot and stuffy in the small room. There's the *tink, tink* of a radiator under a narrow window; the view of a fire escape and gray-brick wall; snowflakes trickling down in a soft, early-morning light.

Clay finds the bathroom off the hall. In the mirror he doesn't appear any older or younger, really, than in the past two days. Same crew cut hair. In decent shape but not as fit, maybe, as yesterday. He's just grateful there isn't the flabby, pot-bellied loser staring back at him again this time.

It's a small apartment, and the short hallway opens into a single space—half kitchen/dining area, half living room crowded with a tiny couch and overstuffed recliner, a giant flat-screen TV. The front door, its left side riddled with locks, stands between the two halves.

Clay's wallet and keys are on the kitchen counter, near the door. A flat cell phone, little different from the ones recently. Also, a laminated photo ID attached to a long red-and-yellow lanyard: 4 FINANCIAL PLAZA printed in bold across the top; and beneath his name and photo: MAINTENANCE.

4 Financial Plaza. He works there now? *No way . . .* How did that happen? And why?

He can think of only one answer.

But, no . . . He's killed the asshole twice already. Unless . . .

On the tiny, kitchen table is a laptop computer, which he immediately goes to. He opens it and it quickly comes to life with a checkerboard of colorful icons. 6:48 A.M., reads the time in the corner. The date: 1/7/15.

2015 . . . That's, what? Two years later than yesterday. One year later than the day before. Five years later than . . .

Shit!

Clay stands and paces the cramped space. He has a serious problem, that's obvious; he'd known it before. But *something* has to be done to fix it, stop it, return things to normal. Whatever that is. He just knows this isn't it; he knows that much, at least. And he knows he isn't crazy. This is something different. He doesn't think it's strictly time traveling, either, just popping up randomly, here and there. It's as if he's entering his own life—but a different one each time—and experiencing one day of it. Just one particular day, for some reason. There's no way this could all be just one lifetime. *Shit!* There's no way this could be *real*.

Passing the fridge, Clay stops and opens it, looks inside, more out of habit than anything else; he isn't hungry, really. The shelves are stocked with all sorts of stuff—meats, greens, various colorful containers. At the bottom, beside a stack of Tupperware, is a bulky metal lunchbox, like new—his, presumably. He reaches in for the carton of orange juice and sniffs it, takes a careful sip: alcohol-free this time.

He takes the orange juice to the table and sits in front of the computer again. Clicks on the picture of a globe, which should be the Internet icon. A web page for a site called Facebook appears. He types in "google" in the address bar, hoping the search engine still exists, and is relieved when it does. He enters "psychiatrist, New York" as the search parameters; and in less than a second he has 30,821,597 results to choose from, along with a host of prominent ads. It's too much. Besides, what would he say? "Hi. I've completely lost my mind. And I can't remember anything of the past ten years." What could they do, anyway? How could they help him?

He needs an expert, he decides, a specialist. As in immediately, as soon as possible. As in *today*—the only day he has. He types in "memory expert, amnesia, New York." And this time the results aren't so daunting. In the top ten, one name is referred to almost every time—a Dr. Milton Price, a professor at Princeton University. Author of numerous books, it appears, on the workings of memory and the mind.

Excellent! Now he just has to get in to see him, talk to him, somehow.

Clay does some more surfing.

Princeton, it turns out, isn't in New York, after all, but close by, right next door, basically, in New Jersey, which is connected to Manhattan by a long . . . tunnel? . . . *under water?* . . . *Whoa.*

And according to a local transit website, a "Megabus" can get him there in just an hour and a half. He uses a credit card to book a round-trip ticket online.

A BLANKET OF SNOW covers everything passing by. The scenery has changed from the tall buildings of the city to industrial parks to strip malls to small towns. Farms. Tractors. Black-and-white splotchy cows.

It had taken him forever to get to the bus station. And it was a good thing he'd gotten his ticket in advance, as he'd barely caught the bus as it was leaving. But there were plenty of seats to choose from. Most every passenger looks like a student. And most every passenger has their head bent over their ubiquitous computer phones, typing weirdly with their thumbs (as he'd seen his "wife" do the other day). Most every passenger's wearing headphones, too. Some have laptops plugged in to the outlets in their armrests. Everybody busy, lost in their own little digital world.

Clay pulls out his own phone from the pocket of his heavy winter coat. He thinks again about calling somebody for help, but has no idea who. There are only five numbers listed in his phone's memory: three names he doesn't recognize, one HOME, one WORK. Which gives him an idea. He calls WORK.

"Four Financial Plaza. How may I direct your call?"

"Uh, hi. I'm calling in sick today."

A beat. "Do you work for a company here?"

"No, I'm in Maintenance."

"Oh, I see. One moment, please."

Three rings, then, "Wheeler."

"Uh, hi. Is this Maintenance?"

"Yeah, who's this?"

"Clay. Clay Nehman."

"Clay! Where the hell are you? You're late."

"Uh, yeah, uh . . . I'm calling in sick today."

"Sick? God damn it! You know how much shit we gotta do today? Damn! This is a hell of a way to start your second week. What's wrong with you?"

"Uh, I think it's something I ate, I don't know. I'm puking all over the place."

"Damn it! You don't feel feverish, do you?"

"Uh, no . . ."

"Good, all right; well, at least it isn't the flu. Do you think you can make it this afternoon? The heating on ten through twelve is completely fucked for some reason, and Braedon's team's gonna stay as late as it takes. They could probably use your help."

"Uh . . ."

"Oh, never mind. Damn! But try to be here early tomorrow, all right?"

"You got it. Thanks, uh . . ."

"Wheeler! Jesus." The call ends.

Well, that's out of the way, Clay thinks. No point in getting himself in trouble at work tomorrow. Though it probably won't be *him* him showing up, the way things are going.

He looks over at the shiny metal lunchbox on the seat beside him. What kind of a loser takes a thing like this to work with him? There's a large thermos attached to it now, on the side. Filled with a spicy-smelling tomato soup. The hispanic woman— his wife? girlfriend?—had come running down the stairs with it, to give to him as he left. The spicy kiss she'd also given him had almost convinced him to stay home for the day.

He'd had only the orange juice for breakfast, and now he's hungry. He hauls the heavy box to his lap and flips open the lid. It's packed full, and the first thing he notices is a folded-up piece of paper on top. A note, maybe, a list or something, but it's written in Spanish—what he guesses is Spanish—and he can understand none of it, except for the little hearts at the end.

So, he speaks Spanish now, huh? It's hard to believe.

Just another thing he can't remember.

Inside the lunchbox are a couple of thick sandwiches in clear plastic, a few things wrapped in aluminum foil. A thin Tupper-ware container with some kind of sauce. Two green apples, and a banana, which he peels and starts to eat.

The first thick square of aluminum foil, peeled back, reveals a moist piece of coffee cake—*Jackpot!*—which he sets aside to eat next. The second shiny package contains half a dozen fat enchilada-looking things that make his mouth water; the third a slice of pizza. The last, at the bottom, is triangular shaped, and surprisingly heavy; and once he finds a corner, he begins un-wrapping it, and unwrapping, and unwrapping—until he holds a small gun in his lap, a six-inch black cylinder (a silencer, he presumes) beside it.

Clay glances at the two people sitting across the aisle, but, fortunately, each appear absorbed in their phones. He quickly wraps up the gun and puts it back in the bottom of the lunchbox. Replaces the box on the seat beside him.

Takes a deep, calming breath.

Thinks . . .

It's always one particular day, for some reason . . . And in every case but one (two?) it's been to kill the asshole . . . who somehow refuses to die . . .

Maintenance . . . "Your second week," the guy had said.

Clay takes out the phone.

"Four Financial Plaza. How may I direct your call?"

"Uh, Prospect Group, please."

"One moment."

One ring, two. "Prospect Group. Good morning."

"'Morning." He asks for the asshole.

"He's in a meeting at the moment, but I'd be happy to take a message for you, sir."

The snowy landscape rushes by. Rolling hills. Trees. A barn.

"Sir? . . . Sir?"

THE SNOW HAS stopped falling, but a light breeze keeps flurries of flakes from the roofs and trees dancing in the air. Somebody has kept the main sidewalks of the campus clear, and students traipse back and forth between the buildings. Clay has learned that classes have only just resumed, following the Christmas break.

He'd been dropped off nearly an hour ago at Palmer Square, and it had taken him forty-five minutes to find the Psychology building (one of many) where Dr. Price has his office. However, a notice there informed him that the professor was holding forth, at ten o'clock, in lecture hall number eight. So it's only with minutes to spare that Clay arrives to find a seat in one of the upper rows. Although he isn't here for the lecture, he plans to talk with the professor after.

It's a large space but the room is still crowded. It must be a pretty popular class. Everybody but him has a notepad or laptop out in front of them, ready, many typing away. There's the pleasant, musty, winter odor of wet coats and boots drying in the heat. A happy back-to-school vibe. A murmur that quickly fades as the professor takes the stage.

The professor's photo online must have been taken years ago, Clay realizes, because this man is much, much older—a hundred if a day—shrunken and stooped, with only a tuft of white remaining over each ear. He wears a striped yellow bow tie and at least two cardigan sweaters. Baggy corduroys.

Instead of standing at the podium, the professor retrieves a straight-backed wooden chair from behind it. Amiably waves away a student who's jumped up to help. Sits and takes a tiny microphone from a sweater pocket and clips it to his collar.

"Testing, testing," he says, and chuckles. His voice carrying easily over the sound system. "Welcome to your first class of Psychology 202, The Examined Mind. My name is Professor Price. If you are in the wrong classroom, which sometimes happens, I suggest you either make your escape now or choose to stay. This is a very interesting course, however, and I am not above stealing a student or two, from time to time." He chuckles again and crosses his legs. Takes a sip from a water bottle that has miraculously appeared on the floor beside his chair.

Clay thinks he's going to enjoy this. He's never been to a class like this before. And he may just learn something that can help him. Maybe there will be a question-and-answer period at some point.

"Now," says the professor, settling back, "to examine the human mind, we must first understand the brain and its functions. Which is no small task, as there is no organ in the human body as complex as the brain. In fact, it is quite possibly the most complex system known in the *universe*."

Already the students around Clay are busily taking notes. He doesn't get it. The professor doesn't appear to have any notes at all.

"Modern research into the brain finds that it does far more than figure mathematics, create poetry, and control behavior," Price continues. "It is the monitor and governor of every aspect of body function and chemistry." He lifts a hand and, magically, an enormous, colorful image of the brain is displayed on the wall at the back of the stage. Then with another flick of the wrist, the image begins to rotate slowly, in multiple directions, showing every angle.

"But how does the brain work?" he asks the class. "That is the central problem scientists seek to answer. It is, in fact, one of the deepest questions of all modern science." Even from where Clay sits, he can see the professor smile as he raises a finger. "Indeed, it is the brain trying to understand *itself*." A chuckle.

"However, in spite of many years of research and the most recent advances in technology, most parts of the brain are still only dimly understood. There is still a long way for us to go to find the answers to the important questions. Which are, one:"—the professor again waves his hand, and large text appears in white on the dark background above the still-rotating brain—"How are connections established within the brain?" He shrugs. "We still have only a vague idea, despite what some may say. Only theories.

"The second question is,"—wave, more text—"What kinds of information are handled at those connections? Sensory? Emotion? Logic? Memory? Creativity?" Another shrug. "We simply do not know. Again, there are only theories.

"And third," the professor says, with another change to the screen behind him, "How is that information processed? This is one that really stumps us. Is it energy, electrical impulses? Chemistry?" He shrugs yet again and lightly throws up his hands. "We may never know."

Clay can't help himself: he raises a hand high and begins waving his arm.

The professor, in his chair, shields his eyes; then waves back. "Yes?"

"What about memory?" Clay asks, loud enough to be heard, suddenly conscious of all the eyes upon him, the majority of students turned in their seats.

"Ah! Yes." The professor seems happy for the question. "Which brings us to our greatest challenge, perhaps: How does the brain store memories?" He gives his quiet chuckle. "My favorite subject, actually. Thank you, Mr. . . ." He shields his eyes again to look up at Clay, who can't hide any lower in his seat.

"Uh, Nehman," Clay says, face hot.

Up front a student repeats the name, for the professor. "Well, thank you, Mr. Nehman." The professor gives a quiet cough into his fist and uncrosses his legs, sits up a little straighter. "We do not know much about how the three-pound marvel of nerve tissue in our skulls is actually used in memory. Nor do we know much about which parts are the main ones involved." Again an elaborate shrug. "We assume that the information is somehow stored by the process of experiencing and learning, and is remembered by retrieval. So, what we call memory is essentially 'information in storage.'"

The professor looks behind him and raises his hand over his shoulder, and soon the brain and text disappear, to be replaced by a different image: the cross section of a brain, looking from left to right, but only outlined, all of its various parts in their own bright colors. A bunch of different things at the middle bottom, and in back, where it connects to the spine. A big, open area pretty much everyplace else.

Price continues: "Since scientists as yet cannot say what memory really is, they try to suggest what it is *like*. They have compared memory to a kind of muscle that can be strengthened through exercise, or to a kind of writing or recording device, like Plato's notion of a wax tablet." The professor leans over to retrieve his bottle of water as he speaks. "A third comparison pictures memory as a reference book or library. And a fourth views memory as though it were a computer, where bits of information are stored by some kind of coding system." He gives his now-familiar shrug and takes a drink. "However, none of these metaphors have proven satisfactory. We do store a great variety of material as memory, but just *how* we store them and *where*, and how we *retrieve* them—these questions are still unanswered."

With surprising agility, the professor stands and walks closer to the giant image at the back of the stage, his stoop much less pronounced. With the water bottle still in one hand, with the other he shines a red laser pointer at various parts of the brain. "We do know that the hippocampus"—he points—"is responsible for encoding new memories, and that the medial temporal lobe"—pointing again—"is somehow involved in a transfer of this information to the cerebral cortex. However, most kinds of memory are not stored in any single part of the brain," he says, turning back to the students. "Research suggests, rather, that memories are spread widely in the brain, through interconnected sets of 'patterns.' And where one particular memory may be found one day, it might exist somewhere else the next—or not at all." He raises his hands to the sides in a more expansive shrug. "So, however we do remember, it isn't any metaphor imagined up to now, but by a far more complex system that our minds have yet to figure out."

Professor Price begins to slowly pace before the glowing image above and behind him. "Some say (and I must agree, up to a point) that memory isn't localized in the brain but distributed throughout the body, in every cell. For example, your stomach lining, and your heart, believe it or not, have nearly as many neurons as the brain. And we have all heard of 'muscle memory,' where the body seems to have a mind of its own, having performed certain tasks repetitively."

He stops his pacing and, with some excitement to his voice, says, "Actually, some suggest that the brain *isn't even necessary* for memory. And with good reason. How else do you explain people with hydrocephalus, or 'water on the brain,'"—with his pointer, the professor is moving the bright red dot around the large, "empty," upper portion of the image—"where most, if not *all* of the brain's cerebral cortex is *missing,* but who still live normal, even exceptional lives, including having memories, like anyone else? . . . In fact, these can be honor students with high

IQs—and *virtually no brains* . . . How does that happen?"

Again the trademark shrug. A big smile this time. "We don't know."

"HELLO THERE. Are you waiting for me?"

Clay's sitting on the floor with his knees bent and his back to the wall, beside the professor's office door. He's been waiting there for over an hour, feeling sorry for himself, ready to give up hope.

"Oh. Uh, yes, sir." He stands and brushes himself off. "I, uh . . . I think I really need your help."

With an appraising glance, Professor Price shuffles to the door and unlocks it. "Well, I haven't been able to help anyone yet today, so let's see what I can do for you." He turns back before entering. "You were the one with the question about memory, this morning, weren't you? The one who walked out."

Clay drops his eyes. "Yes, sir."

The professor's small office is well lit from the bright glare of a snowy window behind his desk. Books of every shape, size, and color line the walls, everything very tidy and in its place. The room infused with a pleasant citrusy smell. Price motions to a set of chairs. "Have a seat, please. Would you like a cup of hot water with lemon? It's very good for you. Cleans the blood, they say. Gives you pep."

That sounds nice. "Yes, please. Thank you." Clay takes a seat and lays his coat across the other chair, sets the heavy lunchbox on the floor. He'd already eaten an apple and both sandwiches while waiting. He fidgets while the professor pours from a tea kettle on a hot plate, drops in some lemon wedges from a mini fridge.

"Now, how can I help you, young man?" The professor hands him a steaming mug along with a warm smile. Takes a seat behind his desk.

"Well, sir, I, uh . . . I know you're a memory expert and everything . . ." He's encouraged by a nod to continue. "Well . . . I have amnesia," he blurts. "I can't remember anything."

The professor's eyes brighten. "Do you, now? That's very interesting. Tell me, then: how does it manifest?"

"Huh?"

"How do you experience this loss of memory, this amnesia?"

"Well, I, uh . . . My memory's just . . . *gone.*" He shrugs.

The professor merely looks at him from over his glasses. Silent.

Clay takes a sip of his drink. The water's too hot, but the feel of it in his hands is comforting and it calms him a little. He takes a deep breath. "Every time I wake up, I don't know who I am," he begins. "I mean"—motioning to himself—"I know it's *me,* I know my name and everything, but . . . that's all. I don't know how I got here." He tries another sip and glances about the room. "Like today. I wake up in this apartment, in New York City again, and there's this lady there, in bed with me, and—and I don't even know who she is. But *she* knows *me.* It's always like this. She could be my wife or something, I don't know. She speaks Spanish. And then, I have this." He reaches inside his dark-blue work shirt and pulls out the ID hung around his neck. "I have a job, at a fancy building downtown, but I don't know how I got it. I don't even know how long I've lived here. All I remember is graduating high school, in Oklahoma, like, eleven years ago." He shrugs and gives his head a shake. "That's it."

The professor nods, his fingers tented below his chin. "You said, 'again'—that you woke up in the city 'again.' So you do remember *something,* is that correct?"

"Right, uh . . ." Clay squirms. "I've been here, uh . . . before."

"So, when did this begin? You said that you woke up this morning and did not remember who you were, but . . ."

Clay's already done the math. "This is the sixth day."

"Ah, excellent. But you have no memory prior to this, is that correct?"

"Right. But, uh . . . except for growing up—up until graduating high school, the party that night." Clay doesn't like the new expression Price is wearing. "What? What's wrong?"

"Let me ask you some questions," the professor says, leaning back, "pertaining to your memory." His look shrewd, wary. "Who is the current president of the United States?"

Clay shrugs. "I don't know . . . Seriously, I have no idea." Still that look. "Uh, George Bush?"

"And nine-eleven?" The professor is scrutinizing him, clearly determining whether or not Clay is lying. "What happened on nine-eleven?"

"That's easy. The towers, the Twin Towers. That was in 2001. The planes crashed into them. I remember I was a sophomore. We were in Mrs. Handelman's class when it happened. We got the rest of the day off."

"Hmm, okay . . . And Katy Perry? . . . Blake Shelton? . . . Justin Beiber? . . ."

Clay can only stare back dumbly each time. Shake his head. *"The Matrix?"*

"Oh, yeah. *The Matrix* came out in, like, '99 or something. I remember 'cause we had to sneak in, since we were only twelve. Best movie ever," he adds. "But the sequels sucked."

The professor only nods. "Yes, excellent movie . . . Do you like football?"

Clay smiles big. "Oh, yeah, you bet."

"All right. What teams are in the playoffs this weekend?"

Clay doesn't even try—he already knows it's no use. He tries to match the professor's elaborate shrug from before.

Price sits forward again. Apparently satisfied with Clay's answers and non-answers. "Very well, then. Now: your childhood. You say you can remember parts of it?"

Clay nods enthusiastically. "All of it. Everything. Up until graduation, when I was eighteen; I'd just turned eighteen. Then it becomes . . . extremely messed up. And then it's just *gone*." He moves his hand like a magician. *Poof!*

"What do you mean by 'extremely messed up'?" A flicker of interest.

"Well, uh . . . I keep having these dreams . . . where I think it's my memory—things I'm remembering, from before—but I'm not sure . . . They, uh . . . They kind of contradict each other." He motions with the hand not holding the cup. "So it's hard to trust them being real, you know?"

"You don't remember anything after graduation, except for the past six days."

"Right. Well, today's the sixth day it's happened."

"Where did they begin? What was your first memory, five days ago?"

Clay vividly remembers the alley, the feelings of being so sick, the fear, the confusion, the disgust at the other man and himself . . . the capitulation, the giving in . . . "Uh . . . I, uh . . ." He has to be honest, he thinks, if he really wants this man's help. "I think I was a heroin addict," he says. "I woke up in this alley . . . I'm pretty sure it was in New York."

"You *think?*"

"Well, no, I *was,* but—it was like one of those dreams I was telling you about. I didn't know if it was real or not until later, until I figured it out. And then . . . and then I knew it was."

"So you are addicted to heroin. That might be—"

"No, no, I'm not. See, that's the thing. In *that* life I was. But then the next day I was in a hotel, and—" No, he can't mention the gun. Or the asshole. He can't be *that* honest. Not yet. "And then the day after that I was on a train, and I was in the Army, and—"

The professor holds up a hand. "Wait, please. You are in the Army?" He looks perplexed. "Have you spoken with someone there about this? The V.A.? Were you injured, perhaps? A head injury?"

"No." Clay sighs. "I'm not in the Army anymore. Or at least not *here.*" He's realizing how difficult this is going to be to explain. "That was another life. A different one. In, uh, 2010." He takes a drink of his lemon water, waits for the reaction that's sure to come.

Finally: "But you told me you could not remember anything but the past five days. Now you are—"

"Every day's different," Clay interrupts, impatient, setting his mug on the professor's desk. "Totally different. It's always a different year, even; and they're never in order but keep jumping around. Like, first, it was a six-year difference—*backwards*—then, the next day, four years ahead; and now, like, only a-year-or-two differences lately, but—" he waves his hands "—it's all over the place." He gives up and falls back in his chair, exasperated—at himself most of all.

The look on the professor's face says it all.

"You think I'm crazy, don't you?"

Price indulges him with a smile. "No, no, not crazy, I do not think. Memory is a tricky thing. And very important—it is how we know ourselves. Our past shapes who we are. So I can understand how maddening it is, not to remember properly; how frustrating it must be." He stays quiet a moment, just gazing peacefully. "But, then, perhaps you should speak with a psychiatrist about this, if it is really troubling you. They deal with this sort of thing all the time. Amnesia, I mean."

Clay stares at his hands in his lap. All hopes for a solution, gone.

"But, please. Tell me, while you are here," the professor says. "Have you had any traumatic experiences recently?"

Clay shakes his head. Wearily picks up his mug. "I don't know . . . I'm not sure . . ." He recalls the events of the past five days—the violence, the turbulent emotions. He'd call all those pretty traumatic . . . But that was *after* this all started. "No, I don't think so. But, then, I wouldn't know, if I can't remember, right?"

"Right. Exactly." The professor nods as he puts down his own cup. "But sometimes there are ways we can find out. There is no real cure for amnesia, unfortunately, but it helps to understand the cause. Like head trauma, for instance, caused by an accident. Or alcoholism. Or"—he shrugs—"perhaps there is a psychological cause." He spreads his hands wide. "Dissociative amnesia, for instance—repressed memory—which acts as a sort of defense mechanism, where the mind chooses to forget, rather than deal with the stress of a troubling event. A horrific one, usually."

The professor leans forward and clasps his hands in front of him on the desk. "This is what I believe you may be suffering from," he says kindly. "As it seems you have the symptoms for a limited retrograde amnesia, where you are missing only a section of long-term memory but not all of it. Also, you are able to create new memories, which, to me at least, though I am not a medical doctor, rules out recent head trauma." He smiles and leans back, as if he has it all figured out. "Fortunately, it is usually temporary."

Clay chokes on the last of his drink. "Temporary?!" he sputters. "I can't remember anything since *2004!* How is that temporary?"

The professor looks at him quizzically. "But you told me yourself you were in the Army in 2010."

Clay sighs. "That was a jump."

A moment's pause. "Pardon? A jump? I do not understand."

"In years. Lives. Today is, what?—2015?—and I'm a maintenance guy, in this building. Yesterday was 2013, and I was in a freakin' elevator shaft." He waves off the details of the incident and stands, begins pacing to the door and back—he can't remain sitting, or calm, any longer. "And the day before that was 2014 and I was back in Oklahoma, with a wife and two kids I don't even know, and Charlene was in a wheelchair, scared as hell of me for some reason . . . *Shit!* And the day before that was 2010 and I was in the freakin' Army, for Chrissakes! And before that was 2016, and I was—" He throws up his hands. "—I was a pathetic, pot-bellied slob, who got handled by some stupid gorilla in a fancy suit."

The professor has reached into a drawer and taken out a slim, leather-bound book. "I have the name of a very good psychiatrist, who—"

"I don't need a psychiatrist!" Clay almost shouts. "I don't have *time!*"

He sees the look of alarm on the professor's face. Then retakes his seat, palms out. "Look, I'm sorry, I didn't mean to—I'm sorry." He has to bury his face in his hands. "I just don't know what to do. I don't know what's happening to me."

He sits like this for a while, with no comment from the professor. Then is finally able to sit back, get ahold of himself. "Sorry about that." He wipes at his nose. "I just thought . . . I was hoping you might have heard about something like this before, that's all. Or maybe some kind of memory experiment, or something, I don't know . . . Time travel."

The professor has pushed his chair back considerably from his desk. He sits very still, with his hands in his lap. Looking at Clay with genuine concern, it seems.

"Time travel," he says, at last. "Hmmm."

Clay knows he must sound like a whacko, but he's way beyond caring what anybody might think of him. He just wants a solution to his problem. His very *real* problem.

He fumbles with his hands. "I know you think I'm a nut job, but . . ."

"Yes," the professor says solemnly, his voice subdued, "that could very well be the case, I am afraid." He's turned in his chair, sideways, now, looking out of the partially frosted window beside him. "However, I can understand your reluctance to see a psychiatrist, especially if you truly believe that what you are experiencing is . . ." He makes an ambiguous flourish, then remains silent as he gazes at the snowy world outside.

Finally, after a long minute, Clay reaches for his coat, sighing inwardly.

"However, the proper course of action," says the professor heartily, turning to his desk, "is to explore every possibility—is that not right?—no matter how far-fetched it may seem." He slides a small notepad toward himself and produces a pen, begins writing. "This man, I believe, specializes in issues such as yours. Perhaps; I have no idea; I have never heard of such a thing as you describe happening before." He tears free the paper and hands it over, his smile grim this time. "However, if anyone can help you, young man, this is he."

PSYCHOPHYSICAL RESEARCH LABORATORY, the sign reads. *Finally.* It had taken him a thirty-minute trek across campus to find the place.

The first thing he notices, besides all the colorful artwork on the walls, is the sound of light instrumental music with tinkling bells, a slow drumming beat. The sound of rain in the background . . . Instantly relaxing.

"Hi, I'm looking for Professor—" Clay refers to the piece of paper in his hand. "—D-z-hel-ik-hov—"

"You can just call him 'Dr. Z,' hon." The tall, red-haired woman at the back of the reception area smiles as she comes over. "That's what everyone else does." She'd been burning a long bundle of dried gray-green grass tied in yellow string, and she waves its smoke around a few more times before smudging it out in a bowl on the shelf behind her desk. "Sage," she says with a lovely smile. "It neutralizes the energies, purifies the space. Are you a new student of ours?"

"Uh, no, not really." He shows her the note. "Professor Price said that I should talk to, uh, Dr. Z about something."

The woman's smile fades. "Oh, well, I'm afraid he hasn't returned yet from his trip to Peru. But it's his fourth time there; he's familiar with the jungle, of course. He's just missed his flight, for some reason, that's all. Things like that must happen sometimes, I'm sure." She waves it off. Begins to nervously rearrange a collection of sparkling stones and crystals on her desk. "But, no worries. He'll be home soon, with tales to tell, no doubt. And until then, Marshall and Leanne, the T.A.s this year, will be covering his classes for him—but just till he gets back, of course, which should be any day now. Why, he could walk through that door at any minute." Together they look to the door, her hopefully, it seems. Then she gives a little laugh, appears to think of something, and takes a thin folder from a rack of files. Hands it to him. "Do you have our new syllabus? We've added Shamanic Studies this semester."

Clay holds up a hand, already retreating, defeated. "No, no, I'm okay, thanks anyway."

"Oh, that's right, I'm sorry, I forgot." The woman cheers some. "My name's Rebecca. Is there anything *I* might be able to help you with?"

She really does look very sincere and helpful, Clay thinks, but, "No, I doubt it. It's pretty complicated. But thanks." Again he turns to leave.

"Oh." Then: "Wait. Please. Just a second."

She's come out from behind her desk and places her hand on his elbow, gives him that beautiful smile. "Please. Just stand over here for one second." She points to the near wall, where there's a small painting, and leads him to it; turns him, facing out, arms by his sides. Then takes the lunchbox from his hand before he can react, and sets it down a ways away.

She goes back to stand beside her desk. Puts a hand to her chin, elbow supported in the other palm. Squints her eyes as she looks him up and down, wearing a puzzled expression.

"There's something about your aura . . ." She opens her eyes wide, then squints again. Holds out her hand and moves it, as if molding the air. "It's so *dark* . . . I mean, color-wise. Everywhere. Dark browns and reds . . . maroon. A lot of very dark blue, here,"—pointing to her head—"and here"—to her heart—"it's almost black. Like a sadness, but more than that . . . Are you sad? No, I'm sorry, I'm just trying to help, it's none of my business, forgive me." She gives him a quick smile and makes that squinty look again, unfocused. "So much red, though, too . . . anger . . . hate . . . Is this what you came to see Dr. Z about, hon?"

Clay isn't sure what to say. Or think. "You, uh . . . You can *see* this in me?"

"Oh, yes, of course. Everything is energy, and we're all energetic beings. People, especially, vibrate at certain rates, which make certain colors." She holds out a probing hand again, then steps slowly to the side, a bit farther away. "But there's also a brightness to you that's unusual . . . that encompasses the whole . . ." She stops and looks away a moment, then looks back . . . Smiles. "Have you had any unusual experiences lately?" she asks. "Like angelic? Like maybe trying to help you in some way?"

Unusual doesn't even begin to cover it, Clay thinks. But: "Angelic? You mean, like, in *angels?*"

"Yes. Or maybe any other benevolent spirits." She cocks a hip, thinking. "Have you perceived any communications? Perhaps in your dreams? . . . Dreams are very important, you know."

Ohhh, shit. "Communications? Nooo, I don't think so . . ." Clay moves to retrieve his lunchbox.

"Well, there's definitely *something* of that nature going on with you. I can see it for myself."

The woman removes a single sheet of paper from the folder on her desk, folds it twice, and hands it to him. "Here, hon. These are the professor's office hours and class schedule." She gives his arm a squeeze and smiles with her eyes more than her mouth this time. "Don't you worry about a thing. You've come to the right place. If Dr. Z can't help you, no one can."

Well, apparently nobody can, then, Clay thinks despondently. He does his best to conjure a warm smile for her in return, regardless.

But the woman seems to share his sadness now as she moves absently to a large map on the wall beside them—of South America—one area, up top, dotted with colorful pins. She's touching her fingers to it as he leaves.

CLAY'S UPSTAIRS AND almost to the front doors of the building when the red-haired lady catches up with him. "Wait, wait! Oh!" She's nearly out of breath. "I'd thought I'd missed you. Here. I should have thought of this earlier."

She's handed him a small, flat, circular object, about six inches across. It's made from a few bent twigs lashed together to form the rim, with a dense spider web of string inside. Multicolored beads, shells, and tiny feathers decorate its outer edge. He's seen something like it before, growing up near the Indian reservation, when he was a kid.

"What is it?" he asks.

"It's a dream-catcher," the woman replies, her beatific smile back in full force. "It will help you remember your dreams."

OUTSIDE, THE SUN is shining, reflecting brightly off the new layer of this morning's snowfall.

Clay sits on a covered bench in Palmer Square, where he first arrived, waiting for his bus. Debating on what to do.

Students of the school flow around him, laughing, talking, living their lives.

What is *his* life, he wonders. It seems so long ago that he lived just one.

His attempt at finding some answers here was a bust. He definitely has amnesia, but still has no reason why. He may be nuts. Or not. And the only person who can help him, it looks like, is even more lost than he is, right now.

But Clay knows he'll have to keep trying. He knows that much. Maybe tomorrow, if he can, depending on what the day brings. Then every day. Until he figures this shit out. And puts an end to it. Somehow.

But until then . . .

His watch says it's 1:55. The bus should arrive any minute now. He can be back in the city about 3:30 . . . At work by 4:00 . . .

He contemplates the lunchbox in his lap.

Maybe the day won't be a total waste after all.

Beige, cream, and ash swirls, smudges, little white flecks. No two adjacent squares running in the same direction, he notices, but perpendicular, creating a larger pattern, a swirling chessboard on the floor. The cracks almost nonexistent, invisible. A soft yellow flower petal keeps drawing his eye.

Her favorite color.

It's not too late, he says. There's ways to—

Shut up, Charlene says. It's the first thing she's said all day.

The walls are a light blue-green, the sheet covering the bed bright white. Her back is to him as she lies on her side, unmoving, as she's been since he arrived.

Since he heard the news.

There's drugs you can take now. It won't hurt. It's not like—

You have no right, she says, more forcefully now. It's not your decision.

The emotions he feels are as swirled as the tiles: sadness, frustration, guilt, anger . . .

More than anything—anger.

But what about us? he says. His vision blurring. He swipes at his eyes.

Charlene rolls onto her back to face him. Her beautiful green eyes are wet, too, but hard, like he's never seen them before. Ringed in violet, red, the bruising all but gone. The puckered lines of stitches on her cheeks are getting removed today, he heard the nurse say.

I'm keeping it, Charlene says, her hands pressed protectively over her belly.

He can imagine the tiniest life form in there, curled up, like a cancer, a little demon, threatening to destroy both their lives.

That's my decision, she says. A single tear rolls down her cheek. Falls. *What's yours?*

CLAY WAKES to a kick in the ass.

"We got company."

A giant silhouette of a man towers over him, an orange-red early morning sun rendering the man and the filigreed canopy of branches and leaves above them a shadowed black. As the figure turns away, Clay can see a long beard, muscled arms and shoulders, a thick waist.

Other shadowy forms are moving beneath the spreading tree—at least a dozen. More. The flickering flames of a campfire.

Motorcycles circle the group. Parked riderless. Those in the sun gleaming gold and black. Street cruisers, highway bikes, teardrop gas tanks and lots of chrome. All with the look of long journeys, many miles, many roads.

Glints of silver and yellow and a rolling cloud of dust signal a car approaching a ways away. The unmistakable rack of lights on top thankfully dark.

The man who'd woken him earlier, clad in a white T-shirt and cut-off denim vest, stained jeans, joins another man in the dawn light to meet the vehicle. Neither seems too worried.

The police cruiser rolls to a stop on the dirt road about thirty feet away. Its window is down but Clay can see only shapes, the wide brim of a cowboy hat, a hand beckoning.

The two men approach. The big, bearded man places a hand on the roof of the car as he leans down.

"Mornin', sunshine."

The lilting voice behind him belongs to an attractive pixie of a woman in a faded red tank top and jeans. Packing clothes into a black leather saddlebag. Her light brown hair is pulled loosely back, and silver and gold sparkles ring her ears.

"You slept hard last night," she says, smiling. "First time I ever heard you snore."

These unexpected mornings—these sudden changes in his daily reality—aren't nearly as disturbing as they once were, but it still takes Clay some effort to adjust, get his bearings, wrap his mind around the new circumstances and environment he's found himself in. Yet again.

"Uh, hi." He has to clear his throat. "And a good mornin' to you, too."

The best thing he can do, he tells himself, is just go with the flow. And cope the best he can. After all, what other option is there?

He's sitting on the ground amid a pile of lightweight blankets, a thick pad of some kind beneath him.

The woman comes close and places a hand in his hair, a big kiss on his forehead. "I'll get you your coffee. Your clothes are right here."

She has a nice walk, he notices, nice-fitting jeans. A long, thick, swinging braid down her back.

Clay reaches up to where her hand had been, expecting to find long, straggly hair, like he sees on most of the other men; but his is fairly short, a little curly in back. On his face is a full goatee and moustache, something he's never felt there before.

Shit, how old am I now? he wonders.

He lifts the Indian blanket covering him and, *Yep:* buck naked. Colorful tattoos run up and around his arms and chest. Skulls and snakes, a naked woman, a heart with a dagger through it. Dice. The flames of hell.

Whoa! No way! Tattoos are for . . . Shit!

He wants to get dressed before the woman gets back. Beside him, on the grass where she'd pointed, are a stack of neatly folded clothes. Still sitting, he pulls on the boxers and jeans, wool socks and square-toed, black leather boots. The black T-shirt smells freshly washed. On it, the faded outline of a bald eagle and the words "Live Free or Die."

He's folding the blankets when she returns.

"Ranger's famous rocket fuel," she says. "Here. Don't worry about those, I'll get 'em in a minute. You're doing it wrong, anyway, silly."

Clay takes the large speckled-enamel mug and blows on it. "What's going on?" pointing with his chin to the cop car and bikers at the window.

"Hopefully nothing." She picks up one of the thin blankets and begins shaking it out. "He's probably seen a bunch of us come through here lately, already."

Clay sips his coffee and watches the men talking to the police. The skinny one turns and waves over a large-breasted, older woman in pigtails and a bikini top, who makes a show of begging off before finally relenting. The big barrel-chested slob she's with laughs and slaps her ass as she goes.

For a brief instant, Clay thinks of asking the cop for a ride out of here, to help him escape. These look like some pretty rough characters.

He closes his eyes and takes a deep breath, then another, fighting back the sudden onrush of fear.

"You're still sleeping, aren't you?" The pretty woman has some of the blankets folded lengthwise and is rolling them up inside one of the mats. "Oh!" she says brightly. "Connie heard this town actually has a decent library, so we're going to hang out there, instead, today, okay? Maybe they'll have the second *Hunger Games* book in, or I can find something on candle making, finally." She looks up at him with big brown eyes and a grin. "Plus, there's a bakery right next door. So get ready." She laughs.

He laughs too, relieved. Hanging out at the library sounds like a pretty tame way to spend the day. Maybe this won't be so bad after all.

The woman cinches up the bedroll tight with a long cord. "When you and Pun get back, we'll have a couple of Boston cream pies waiting for you guys. And if they don't have any now, we'll make sure they do. Just you wait."

Oh . . . Shit. So much for that idea.

"Are you going to shave?" she asks him. "I told JoLynn to save you some hot water. She should be almost done. I don't know why she has to wash her hair every fucking day; it's not like we carry extra just for her benefit."

Clay can see a tall, full-figured woman at the base of the tree, toweling her long black hair. She sees him looking, and calls out, "All done!"

He waves shyly. What else can he do now but go over?

Just go with the flow, he reminds himself. Act normal. Be cool, be cool.

Hanging suspended from a sturdy branch near the trunk is a heavy canvas bag, a quarter-way filled with water, an identical mug to the one he's holding submerged at the bottom. A small round mirror hangs from a nail in the tree. The woman, JoLynn, smiles as she finishes drying her hair, says, "Good morning, handsome," then tickles him in the ribs as she leaves.

Clay fills his hands with the warm water and splashes his face and hair.

"That slut," says the little pixie, behind him. "If she ever puts her hands on you like that again, I'll beat the living crap out of her, I swear." She hands him a small, nylon kit bag. "Here you go, sleepy-head. Are you okay this morning? You seem a little out of it. Are you sick?" She reaches up and puts a hand to his cheek.

"Oh, no, no. Thanks," Clay replies, accepting the bag. "I, uh . . . I'm just a little tired, you know, that's all. I'll be all right in a minute. Ha, ha. Just gotta wake up." He gives her a smile.

"Okay. Good." She pulls his face down to hers, kisses him fully on the mouth. Puts some tongue with it.

Then she's off, with a coquettish smile. There's that walk again. *Wow . . . Hot damn.* Things could be worse.

But she's not Charlene.

He takes his time shaving, to check out the scene, the other people milling about the makeshift camp. There are slightly more guys than gals, he notices, everybody wearing blue jeans in various states of wear and tear, T-shirts or less, some bandannas. Sturdy boots. Black leather jackets and denim vests—all with colorful patches—are slung over many of the seats and handlebars of the motorcycles, a few of which are being packed and loaded with gear: bedrolls, saddlebags, water jugs, panniers.

The thought occurs to him that one of those bikes is his. Which doesn't scare him as much as it probably should. He's excited, actually. He used to own a little Honda Trail 70 when he was a youngster, and he's ridden his neighbor's 250 plenty of times. So what if these are a lot bigger? So is he. But which one belongs to him? . . .

In the mirror's reflection Clay watches the police cruiser pull away in a spray of dirt. Only the large-breasted bikini chick standing waving it goodbye.

Clay turns to see the big, bearded guy in the denim vest squat on his haunches beside the fire; accept a heaping plate of food. Clay notices the aroma for the first time and realizes how hungry he is. *Shit.* He wants to interact as little as possible with these people, but knows it won't be easy.

Cheeks freshly shaved, goatee trimmed, Clay carries the shaving kit back to the little woman busy packing the last of their belongings.

She glances back with a smile. "Breakfast is ready." But then she stops, and her look changes. "You parted your hair . . . Why? For the visit?"

The visit? "You don't like it?"

She shakes her head. "Not really. It makes you look sort of . . . square."

"Oh." He reaches up and tussles it vigorously. "Better?"

"Much better," she laughs. "Oh!" She bends and picks up a pint-sized black leather jacket. "Rico called, and I told him what you said: that we'd be there late tomorrow night, about eleven. And he said, 'Cool, everything's ready.'" She looks at him expectantly for a moment; then when Clay doesn't respond, takes out a slim, fold-up cell phone from one of the jacket's pockets. "I'm hanging on to it today, right? Since you can't take it in with you?"

Just go with the flow. "Right, right."

She cocks her head and studies him. Places a hand on his arm. "You sure you're okay? You're awfully quiet this morning. Are you nervous?"

"Hell no, he ain't nervous!" says a booming voice coming up beside them. "What would he be nervous for?" A heavy hand lands on his shoulder. It's Clay's human alarm clock. "It's not like we're gonna be stayin' in there, or nothin'. Just a chat between old friends. And a new one," he adds, giving Clay's shoulder a squeeze. "A little 'bidness.'" A friendly slap. "Come on, partner, you better get some grub before it's all gone. I don't think Shrek's in the mood for sharin' today."

The man steers him away. "What'd you tell her?"

Clay's seized by panic. *Shit!* "Ahhh, ouubt, uhhh . . . ," he stammers. "Nothing. I don't know. She just, uh . . ."

"Ah, don't worry about it. She probably just heard us talkin', is all. Bits and pieces. Tryin' to put it together. I ain't trippin.'" He stops before they get to the small group crouched around the fire. Looks at Clay hard. There's a small black tattoo of a teardrop beside his left eye. More gray than brown in his long beard. "Just so no one knows. *No one.* You never know who's gonna snitch you out when the shit hits the fan. And that can happen any time down the road, you know what I'm sayin'?" He gives Clay another slap on the back, smiling now. "Especially the way we roll, eh, partner?"

Most everybody at the campfire calls out a greeting to him, and Clay does his best to seem relaxed and do the same, nodding and smiling in everybody's direction. Only one scary-looking guy, eating oatmeal out of what looks like his upturned helmet, gives Clay a hateful look, which throws him off a little. He squats by the fire. Keeps his eyes on the glowing coals and the grill and pans atop it. Until somebody nudges him.

"So, what's up?" The man's handing Clay a plate of pancakes and oatmeal swimming in syrup. "We gonna meet you guys tonight, or tomorrow morning?"

"Uh . . ." Of course he has no idea what to say, so Clay looks up to his big, bearded friend standing beside him.

"Tonight," Big Beard says. "We'll probably be only about five or six hours behind you. So if you stop early enough, we should be okay."

Another asks, "How long a visit you guys gettin'?"

"Four hours, since we're out-of-state—"

"Yep, that's us," cracks the woman flipping the cakes.

"—but we're gonna cut it short, so maybe two. Maybe just one. Shit, I hate bein' around that place at all anymore."

This gets some murmurs of agreement.

"Hey, Clay." A scrawny guy his own age (or, at least the age he *was,* last week) has walked up and is beckoning him over.

"Excuse me." It's a relief to leave the intimidating group and stand one-on-one with the kid. "Hey. What's up?"

The guy wears a purple bandanna around his neck and an eager-to-please expression. In his hands is a filthy rag he keeps worrying. "Hey. I got all your shit loaded up on mine, and Tommy's gonna be carrying Big Pun's, so we're all set." He laughs nervously. "You sure you don't want me to take Trudi, too? Ha!" His face has gone beet red and he scuffs at the dirt with his boot. "Hey, just kidding, Clay. But, you know, I'm gonna find me a girl just like that up in Sturgis this time, to ride with me. Somebody with—" He makes melons on his chest and laughs again.

Clay tries to laugh with him, assimilating the information. Trudi must be the pretty little woman he's with. And Big Pun the tall, long-bearded guy with the vest—the one he's apparently going somewhere with today.

To do something highly illegal, by the sound of it. Possibly dangerous.

"We all ready to go, J.T.?"

Speak of the devil. Big Pun has an arm slung around the shoulders of a good-looking young woman who's beaming at Clay with genuine affection.

"Hey, Clay," she says. "You take good care of my man, here, today. Don't let them keep him in there any longer than he has to."

"Sure." Clay smiles. "No problem."

Big Pun asks, "Where's Tommy?" and J.T. points. Then to Clay: "You 'bout ready?"

"Uh, yeah." He puts on a brave face, tries to smile. "Whenever you are, partner." He's hardly touched his plate but has little appetite for it now anyway. He tries to wolf some down, for show.

"Hey, J.T.," says Big Pun, still looking at Clay, "go see if Tommy's got Connie's lid someplace, all right?" The kid runs off. "Connie?" They exchange a glance and she goes, too.

It's just the two of them now, and by the look he's being given, Clay feels caught out. He's in trouble. He starts shoveling in more food, to hide his apprehension.

"Hey, Clay," Pun says, at last, his voice a growl. "What's goin' on?" A tense pause. "You're not havin' second thoughts now, are you? 'Cause if you are, that would really put me in a bad spot. I went out on a limb for you, here, you know what I'm sayin'? My reputation's on the line."

"Yeah, yeah—I mean, no, no," Clay says through a mouthful of food. "I'm all right. I, uh . . . I just slept weird last night, you know? Bad dreams. Kinda threw me off, that's all."

Another scrutinizing look, as if trying to see behind the lie.

"About her?" Pun asks.

Clay thinks about last night's dream. The hospital room. *Does he mean Charlene? Does he know Charlene?* He can only nod slowly back, unsure.

Big Pun nods, too, seemingly appeased for the time being. "All right. Just checkin'." He gives Clay a hard slap on the shoulder. Motions to the plate. "Dump that and let's go. We gotta drop off the girls, and then we got a half-hour ride to McAlester."

There's the hiss and a billow of smoke and steam as somebody pours water over the fire's remaining embers. Clay hands his near-empty plate to the woman washing the dishes, who looks up at him and smiles.

"Have a good visit."

He watches Big Pun approach a low-slung ride with a lot of character, a lot of years.

He sees Trudi talking earnestly with Connie. Sees them both turn their heads his way, a worried look on Trudi's face.

Shit. What has he gotten himself into, now? he frets. What kind of life has he—this version—made for himself? What the hell was he thinking? And *how* the hell did it happen?

He gives his head a shake. It's too late for such questions. "All right. Let's do this," he tells himself. No fear. Just go with the flow.

He picks the motorcycle he thinks Trudi has set their jackets on, and hopes it's the right one.

McALESTER STATE PENITENTIARY, reads the big blue metal sign as they make their turn onto less-smooth pavement, their engines rumbling, then roaring as they accelerate again. It had been a fast twenty-minute ride from the nearest town, the prison stuck literally in the middle of nowhere, the land around it flat for miles.

The tall guard towers, spaced about every five-hundred feet, are the first things Clay sees; then the twinkling glint of razor wire and triple chain-link fencing. The prison walls' sprawling, multi-storied gray-yellow stone with narrow slits for windows. An impenetrable, inescapable fortress.

"We'll be lucky if these are here when we get back," says Pun as they park their bikes. "Crooks runnin' the place are worse than the ones inside."

A sign by the front gate lists the weekend visitation hours and rules. Clay and Pun have to stand there alone for nearly five minutes, neither man moving or saying a word, before they're finally buzzed through. Pun flips the bird to the guard in the adjacent tower, who points his rifle in reply.

Once inside the chain-link maze—NO HOSTAGES BEYOND THIS POINT—they're buzzed through twice more, then finally outside the prison complex itself. Rows of flowers line the building's entryway—a half-hearted attempt to make the place look livable. But nothing can mask the air of hopelessness and despair that permeates the space around them once they're through the doors.

"PUNISHER!" THE MAN shouts, fists raised high as he comes. "Big Pun! What the fuck!" They can barely hear him through the thick Plexiglas. He's wearing prison blues; his head shaved bald; Hispanic, which is surprising at first but shouldn't be; with tattoos on his face and neck as well as his arms.

"Chivo!" Pun hollers back as he stands.

Both men hit their fists at the same spot on either side of the glass. Which elicits a scowl from the female guard at the far end of the row of seats on their side.

Seated, all three pick up their handsets (like an old-fashioned telephone's) to speak and listen through. But Clay just sits there and is greatly relieved when the prisoner only glances at him occasionally while talking with Pun. The two had greeted each other enthusiastically and now ask about people they both know, both inside and outside the walls. Like Pun, the man has a small black teardrop beside his left eye.

Finally, though, after several minutes, Pun slaps Clay on the back. "Chivo, this is Clay, the guy I was tellin' you about. The ladies man. The guy's a fucking chick magnet, I tell ya. It's great havin' him around."

Chivo looks at Clay steadily now. Nods. "How's it goin'?"

Clay nods back. "Good, good, thanks." He has to fight the urge to laugh; has to make a conscious effort to keep his leg from nervously jackhammering beneath the wooden ledge his elbow is resting on. He wants so desperately to know what the hell he's doing here but is worried about what he might find out.

Chivo cuts his eyes to Pun, then back again, a few times. Receives some kind of signal, a confirmation, that Clay can't see.

The man places both his arms on his own ledge and leans closer to the glass. His eyes on Clay. Almost imperceptibly, he moves the handset away from his face and points to the mouth-piece. Gives a slight shake of the head.

Clay thinks he understands. He nods once.

"So you're headed to Sturgis, huh?" The prisoner's talking only to him now.

"Uh-huh. Yep." Clay looks to Pun, who's staring straight ahead at his friend.

"Man, I'm jealous," Chivo says. "Been up there, myself, a couple a times, a long time ago. Had me a blast. Lot of stuff goin' on up there, huh?" He smiles crookedly and makes the universal smoking-a-joint gesture, pinched fingers to puckered lips.

Clay can only imagine. "Uh-huh."

"Hear you *hombres* are swinging through Colorado first, on the way up."

Again Big Pun's no help. "Uh, yep." *Just go with the flow.*

"So you'll be makin' a nice piece of change, I guess." The man's eyebrows, and the tattoos above them, dance.

Clay can feel Pun looking at him now and he tries to stay cool. He just nods back, once, through the glass.

"And you got my number, right? In here? My full name, the address, all that, from this *vato?*" He jerks his thumb at Big Pun.

A glance. Pun barely nods. Clay says, "Uh-huh. Got it."

"Good." Chivo makes a fist, then shows them his palm, five fingers spread wide. He does this twice. "Half now, half later. Shit's gotta be a money order. *Comprende?* No checks. They don't do checks."

Nodding's much easier than comprehending. "No checks."

Pun: "How do we know when it's done?"

"Hell, I don't know." Chivo runs a hand over his gleaming scalp. "Give it a couple weeks, then google the motherfucker. It's gotta come up someplace, right? A police report, or somethin'. What do they call them things?" He snaps his fingers. "The fuckin' obituaries." Then laughs, as if proud to remember. "But it'll get done, I promise you that. On my life, bro."

"You gonna do it yourself?" There's an edge, a challenge, to Pun's voice.

Chivo just shakes his head. Sneers. "Shit, you think I'm stupid, *güey?* I got way too much shit goin' on to fuck with this myself." He looks from side to side, as if anybody is there. "I got a mean-ass *güero* who can get to him. Already in his outer circle. Dude's got, like, three life sentences, stacked, so one more ain't gonna hurt him, you know what I mean?" He smiles slyly. "The thing is, *why*—how—how do I get him to do it, right?" He jabs a finger at Clay, who reflexively pulls back. "Your boy's so rich he got a hundred *culeros* on his payroll. For protection. Ha! Like it'll help him. Like he can't be touched." Chivo chuckles and leans forward, eyes going back and forth between the two on the other side. "But, my guy? He's one angry fuckin' redneck, let me tell you. His sister just got raped, a little while ago, and he's stuck in here with nobody to take it out on. You know what I'm sayin'? He's got motivation. So . . ." He leans back and shrugs grandly, one arm thrown out to the side. ". . . once he finds out what the motherfucker's really in here for . . ."

Pun asks, "He doesn't know already?"

"Naw. Tells everybody it's for manslaughter. Like he's some kinda tough guy." He flips his hand with a sour expression. "No reason for these *pendejos* to doubt him. You know how it is."

Pun looks to Clay, who just looks back, not sure what's expected of him. "But you're gonna convince him somehow," Pun says, turning back to the glass.

Chivo stares, half-lidded, leaning back. Opens his hand wide again. Twice.

There's a pregnant pause in the conversation. Until: "What do you say, Clay?" Pun has one eyebrow raised.

Clay doesn't know what to say. He doesn't know what in the hell they're talking about. He looks from one man to the other, searching for a clue. Anything.

Pun lowers his handset to the counter. "You gotta say it," he says somberly.

Say *what?* What the heck is going on?

Both men are waiting.

"It's gotta come from you, Clay. This is your deal. *You* wanted the asshole dead, man, not me."

And in a flash, Clay gets it, he understands, he knows what they've come here to do . . . Or, at least he thinks he does.

"He's here, isn't he?" he asks Pun, who just nods slowly, like answering a child, a mental patient.

Which is suddenly how Clay feels—his mind set loose from its tenuous moorings, reeling, now, with images—whether real or imagined, he has no idea.

. . . Charlene's beautiful, beautiful face . . . beaming, holding his hand . . . Her hand on the asshole's arm, laughing . . . getting into his car . . . The flashing lights of the police cars . . . her pretty yellow dress streaked with blood . . . Charlene in a wheelchair, calling for help . . . Her casket being lowered into the ground . . . A protective hand over her belly . . . that one falling tear . . .

Clay's eyes come into focus with both men still watching. Still waiting.

"Make it happen," he says hoarsely, overcome with rage. Red lights flashing at the corners of his vision. "And make it hurt."

A crowded room. Murmurs.

Everybody stands as the judge enters. And when he sits, they all do. It's quiet now, pins drop, as the jurors file in. Twelve men and women. No hint of their verdicts, but a palpable feeling of relief that it's finally over.

He can see the back of the asshole's head, turning to whisper to his fat-cat lawyer.

Still no sign of Charlene's parents. They haven't returned in days. But they'll know soon enough. As will he.

The judge speaks, and a woman in the jury box rises. Reads from a trembling sheet of paper.

. . . In regard to the charge of aggravated sexual assault . . . the jury finds the defendant . . . not guilty.

Gasps and exclamations, muted curses. An admonishment from the judge. He feels everything he was so certain of begin to come undone, float away, held on to by only the thinnest string of hope.

. . . In regard to the charge of first-degree murder . . . the jury finds the defendant . . . not guilty.

A roar this time, screams, the BANG! BANG! BANG! of the gavel, yelling from the bench, from every side. Pandemonium.

He can't see for all the bodies standing now, pressed against him, jostling. Seemingly rushing forward to see justice served regardless.

Numbly, he climbs over the backs of the benches, pushes people aside. Leaves the stifling room and its cacophonous chaos.

Stumbling down the wide, empty corridor, oblivious. Bursting through the doors to outside.

Clinging to his last shreds of sanity . . .

He walks in a daze, down one tree-lined street after another. Thinking of the injustice in the world—and what it means for his future . . .

It begins raining, which is fitting. But not cold.

The sodden blocks turn to miles beneath his feet.

DAY 8

CLAY WAKES in a sweat, his legs tangled in the sheets. A warm, humid breeze coming in through a set of open French doors across the room. It carries an earthy, salt-and-spice aroma he's never smelled before—like rotting fruit, but pleasant, exotic.

Sheer, white curtains dance and twirl lazily to either side of the doors.

By the dark blue-purple sky, it's somewhere between night and day.

He kicks free of the sheets and pads across the large room to the doors, the carpet a luxuriant weave he can dig his toes into. Classy, expensive-looking furniture—rattan and mahogany, bamboo and teak. Vibrant works of art covering the walls. An impressive seashell collection.

Through the open doors is a wide balcony filled with large green plants, shivering in the moonlight. And beyond it, from high up, a vast ocean. Dark and fringed with foam, where it laps gently against a sandy shore stretching for miles in either direction.

He's never seen the ocean before, at least not in person, not in real life. And it's all he can look at, or think of, for a few minutes.

It's so . . . *much*. So much more than he ever imagined . . . He can't wait to go down there and touch it, put his feet in it. He hopes he can.

To the right, where the beach curves, are several multilayered buildings—homes, *mansions*—a stately parade of peaches and pinks and creams. Far beneath him, a sprawling patio with a number of round tables with umbrellas and chairs; a long, rectangular swimming pool shimmering off to one side; an expansive glass atrium on the other; other assorted outbuildings spread farther out; a curving, stone pathway to the beach. And Clay realizes, finally, from his lofty perch, that that's where he is, too—a freakin' mansion.

Whoa! This is so cool! He's never been in a mansion before, either.

Or has he? . . . He can't remember . . .

Ah, shit! he thinks. Here we go again. Nothing has changed. He still can't remember anything but the past week. And his crazy, messed-up dreams.

At least he didn't wake up under a tree with a bunch of rowdy bikers this time, he sighs, relieved. However, the party they'd thrown last night had been a whole lot of fun. And Trudi . . . *Wow.* He'd never had sex like that before . . . not that he's very experienced or anything. He knows he should feel more guilty than he does. And hungover. And the fact that he isn't, and isn't puking his guts out right now with a raging headache, just confirms that he's, somehow, once again, jumped to another life, another time.

He looks at himself, naked, in the soft light. His entire body looks tanned a chestnut brown, without the usual band of white around the middle. He's definitely older this time, but not by much, he doesn't think. The bulk he had playing football is gone—even more so than before—but he still has his muscles, he's glad to see, well-toned, and a flat stomach. No gnarly scars on his leg, or anywhere else in sight. Only a day's stubble on his face; but his hair is longer than it's been before, all the way to his shoulders in back, and kinda curly. He sure hopes it's not a mullet.

Clay sighs and resolves to face this day as best he can. Hopefully find some answers—a solution—to his problem, somehow. Hopefully not have to deal with the asshole yet again. May the man remain dead and gone, for a change.

Inside, he walks down wood-covered hallways, through plushly carpeted rooms, turning on lights as he goes, amazed at everything he sees. The subdued opulence, the stylish design. Whoever lives here, he thinks (it can't be him!), sure does like to collect stuff—artwork, mostly, and tasteful knick-knacks from around the world.

One large room upstairs, at the opposite end of the main hall, clearly belongs to a woman, with all its feminine decorations and the feminine products in the bathroom. But nobody's there, thankfully. It makes him anxious that he may not be alone, that he may have to dissemble and play the role, once again, of somebody he has no way of knowing how to be.

The upstairs thoroughly searched, dressed in swim trunks and a T-shirt after a pleasant shower in a ridiculously large bathroom with its own Jacuzzi and sauna and walk-in closet, Clay makes his way down to the next level, the wide winding staircase continuing down even further.

On this floor it appears that the entire side facing the ocean is an office, a business of some sort. A long, open space lined with pale-wood desks and high-backed chairs and shelves filled with books and binders. Water coolers. Plants. A copy machine. Multiple computer monitors at every station. And instead of colorful paintings on the walls: blinking screens—black and blue, with continuously changing figures, bars and graphs; gold numbers, green numbers, some highlighted red; BUY, SELL, HOLD; COMEX, NYMEX, FINEX, CBOT; an entire wall of blinking, scrolling, digital data. None of it making any sense to him as he walks down the room's center—at least a hundred feet long—between the desks and wall of glass on his left and the endless array of screens on the right.

Toward the end, Clay's attention is drawn to a gigantic whiteboard in the center of the farthest wall. And though he's too far away to make out everything written on it, even from here it's easy to see the large round area in the middle that had obviously been erased, in a rush, and now has written large in bold red, as if done during a "Eureka!" moment:

JUNE 16
SELL! SELL! SELL!

And below that, written in black:

DIE!
MOTHERFUCKER!
DIE!

Standing close, the countless multicolored squiggles still covering the rest of it are indecipherable. Cryptic in their complexity. Like a work of abstract art in itself. However, the apparent title to the piece, written above it all—*Prospect Group Holdings*—is a definite key to its design.

The last desk there, beside the glass, is the largest and L-shaped, its short end against the same far wall. Here hang photographs of himself with various people he doesn't recognize; paired and in groups; shaking hands; mugging for the camera; looking serious in a suit and tie. This is clearly his desk, that's obvious. This is probably even his company or whatever.

Wow . . .

Clay turns and looks back at the long, empty office with its many blinking screens, still busy, it seems, without anybody actually being present. But he has absolutely no freakin' clue as to what kind of work he does here.

Pathetic.

* * *

HE'S SITTING ON the beach, in a low, cushioned, wood-slat chair, his feet buried in the sand, the remains of a heavy breakfast on a plate beside him. The sun just making its appearance, finally, over the horizon, turning the ocean waves in front of him a brilliant violet, red, then shimmering gold.

He'd found the kitchen an hour ago and prepared himself a feast of scrambled eggs, ham, and toast from the fridge. Some thick, pulpy orange juice. He'd wanted coffee, too, but all he could find were whole beans.

Then he'd taken his meal to the sea. Where, after eating, he waded through the surf—elated, like a child—marveling at the changing sand and shells beneath his feet, the bathtub warmth of the water, the ceaseless in-and-out of the tide. The water still too dark, though, to go in any higher than his knees.

But since then, he's been sitting and moping, thinking of nothing but his dilemma: his reccurring daily memory loss; the impossible time jumps, spanning years; the strange reappearance of the asshole, despite having died numerous times at Clay's hand; and Charlene, being both dead and alive in his dreams—and in "reality." Not to mention all the totally different lives he keeps finding himself in. But there doesn't seem to be anything he can do about it. At least not without some kind of help.

That memory professor had been so sure that that one guy could help him—the parapsychologist (*not* a psychiatrist, Price had stressed). The best in his field, he said. If anybody could figure out what's going on, it would be him, he said. The same thing the guy's secretary had told him too.

Dr. Z.

But Clay is pretty sure it's going to take a lot more than a bus ride to get him there this time.

"Mr. Nehman! Mr. Nehman!"

Clay looks back toward the house—the *mansion* (he still can't get over it)—to see a dark-skinned black man in khaki pants and an untucked, blue-and-white-patterned shirt walking swiftly in his direction, through the sand. Wearing shoes.

"Mr. Nehman," the man says when he arrives, "are you all right?" He's slightly out of breath; his accent a lilting British, like a TV butler, or aristocrat. "Naina said you'd cooked something on the stove. In the kitchen." Like it was a miracle, or something. Or forbidden.

Oh, shit, Clay thinks, maybe this isn't his place after all. "I'm sorry," he says, "I thought it would be okay. I, uh . . . I was just hungry, and, uh . . . Well, I got up early, you see, and—"

"No, no, that's quite all right, sir," the man says, gathering up the plate and glass. "It was only a surprise, is all. At first we thought someone had been in the house! Or that the men had arrived early, for some reason; or that perhaps you had company, although I know Miss—" He seems to catch himself and takes a breath. "Would you like Naina to prepare your breakfast, sir?"

Much relieved, Clay says, "No, I'm okay, I'm pretty full. But thanks, though, I appreciate it."

"Yes, sir."

Then he remembers: "Can I get some coffee?"

"Of course, sir. It should be ready."

As the man's heading back toward the house, Clay has a thought. He calls after him. "Hey! Uh, excuse me, sir." The man stops and looks back. "Uh, is there an airport around here?"

The guy seems unsure at first of what to say. He stares. "Why, yes, sir. In Nassau."

Clay nods. *Good, good. Okay* . . . It's still early enough. He can probably afford a ticket. And some bus fare.

"Great," he says, hoisting himself out of the chair. "I need to get to Princeton."

* * *

THE CAMPUS LOOKS vastly different without all the snow covering it. Green, with thick grass and shrubs, leafed-out trees, ivy climbing up many of the buildings' walls. Stone and brick, red-and-bronze tiled roofs, pointed spires and towers, like castles in a fairy tale. However, there aren't nearly the number of students as before—very few, actually—and none of the hurrying about and sense of manic purpose he'd seen in everybody then.

He's also heading to a completely different set of buildings than the last time he was here two days ago: the Physics Department.

An online search of the university's website, while aboard the plane (Who'd have ever thought he'd have his *own* plane!), had showed a professor Dzhelikhovsky as head of Theoretical Physics, not Parapsychology. Still, Clay had e-mailed the good doctor and called him, leaving a message that he'd be arriving soon today to speak with him; and that it was extremely important he do so. A matter of life and death, he'd added for good measure—which is true, depending how you look at it, who's life you're talking about, and all.

But the professor still hasn't called or e-mailed him back. And seeing such an abandoned campus has Clay worried.

Shit! He's just realized: it's the start of summer, and school's probably out. He's probably wasted the trip, his entire day.

Once he finds the right building, he spends fifteen minutes searching for the professor's office, getting directions from the few people he meets along the way. It seems like everybody's already cleared out, packed up and gone.

The door to the place he was directed to is wide open, a few small cardboard boxes set beside it in the hall. Inside is a large common room with four separate offices surrounding it, each with a different name on the door. Only one of which is open, somebody moving about inside.

Clay knocks twice on the doorframe, and a slightly older man—gray tweed, short salt-and-pepper beard, bespeckled—stops what he's doing and turns.

"Ah! Excellent," the guy says. "A strong back. Just what I need." He lifts a tall stack of papers off of the corner of his desk and places it into a cardboard box on a nearby chair. "This," he says, "goes to typing, finally, after all these years. And that," pointing to a tall pile of boxes by the door, "goes to the library downstairs, though I imagine we could simply set them in the hallway with the rest, for someone to collect later." He brushes his hands together, then seems to really look at Clay for the first time—the expensive suit, sans tie. "Oh. How can I help you, my good man?"

Clay's already read the name painted on the frosted glass of the door. "Hi, uh, Dr. Z?"

The man hesitates a moment. "Are you a former student of mine?" And when Clay shakes his head: "Because no one has called me 'Dr. Z' in many years."

"Oh. I'm sorry. Uh, your secretary—Rebecca—she, uh—"

"My wife, you mean. Rebecca is my wife." The professor takes off his glasses and pockets them. "Have we met before?"

"No"—now Clay's suddenly nervous—"but I, uh . . . I met your wife a couple of days ago, and she said to come back . . . to keep trying to find you . . ." The enormity of his strange problem, and how to explain it to this man, suddenly hits him. He has no idea where, or how, to even begin. "She, uh— She gave me a dream-catcher. But I, uh . . ."

"A dream-catcher."

Clay nods.

"Oh. Well, any friend of Rebecca's . . ." He goes back to what he was doing. "Now, what can I do for you today?"

Clay wrings his hands. "Uh, well . . . Do you still teach parapsychology at all?"

The professor stops shuffling through his papers and looks up. "Parapsychology? Why would you say that?"

The look on the man's face, and the tone of his voice, say it all. Another dead end . . . And Clay had put so much hope in this meeting. He feels light-headed, all of a sudden, dizzy, weak. "May I sit down, please?" He motions to an empty chair, a hand to his temple.

"Yes, yes, go right ahead." A touch of concern to the professor's voice. "I've never taught parapsychology, or any psychology, for that matter. But I must say that metaphysical phenomena *is* a great interest of mine, especially of late," motioning to the box of papers on the chair. "In fact, I'm embarking on a trip to—," he begins but waves it off. "No, no, never mind. We were talking about you. What is it you would like to discuss? And how is it related to parapsychology, of all things?"

Clay takes a deep breath and sits back. Crestfallen. "Well, Professor Price—the memory guy?—he said that you'd be the best person I should talk to. He said—"

Dzhelikhovsky holds up a hand. "When was this?"

"Uh . . ." *Two days ago,* he almost says. "January, uh, 2015."

"No, that can't be right. It must have been quite a long time ago. Were you a student of his?"

"No, I, uh—I went to a lecture. And then I asked him for help, but, uh . . ." He gives a shrug. "He just thought I was crazy. But he thought you might understand."

"Really? Why me? Did he say?"

"Because of your, uh, 'field of expertise,' he said."

The professor's chest swells. "Ah. Well. That could very well be." He looks to his watch. "But why did you take so long to contact me?"

Clay looks to his own wrist, thinking he may have lost time somehow. "I just flew in. This morning."

"No, I mean, back then. Professor Price must have died at least ten years ago." He looks up, searching his memory. "Yes, 2009, I believe it was. Right here, on campus." His look is puzzled. "What year did you say?"

* * *

THERE'S JUST THE quiet tinkling of ice in his glass as Professor Dzhelikhovsky sits contemplating all that Clay has told him. Clay'd left nothing out.

"It's rather amazing you come to me now," Dzhelikhovsky says, at last, "when my current research has taken such a propitious turn." He finishes the remains of his drink and sets the glass on the coffee table between them. The bottle of Polish vodka there is also empty. The professor had brought it out awhile ago, at the point where Clay was describing his escape from 4 Financial Plaza after killing the asshole. They're in the large common room, surrounded by tall book shelves and comfortable furniture and a large chalkboard covered with lengthy equations. Classical music playing softly in the background.

"You mentioned parapsychology, before," the professor continues laconically, "which we are discovering, more and more, relates directly to quantum physics . . . In fact, quantum theory *explains* paranormal events. Such as yours."

He leans forward and rests his elbows on his knees for a moment, thinking. "If I am to believe that everything you say is true." He holds up a hand to stop Clay's protest. "And I do, I do—too much of what you say is incontrovertible; and your amnesia, it seems, is quite genuine. But we must be rational and approach this from the right direction." He gives Clay a searching look. "Are you willing to subject yourself to scientific scrutiny?"

This isn't the answer Clay was hoping for, at all. "What? *How?*" He throws up his hands. "I won't *be here* in the morning! I mean, this body will, this—version of me, or whatever—but I'll be in some other place, some other *life*." He falls back into the deep leather chair. "There won't be anybody *to* study. Get it?" He motions to himself. "Just the regular me, who probably doesn't even know about any of this, and who wouldn't even recognize you in the morning."

But then a thought occurs to him: *Or will I . . . ?* (He means *he*.) Or will that version of himself just wake up missing a day?

Dzhelikhovsky sits back, himself, to give it some thought. "Quite right, quite right, I suppose." He slaps his knees and stands. "Well, we'd better figure out a solution today, then, shan't we?"

He begins to slowly circle the room, hands clasped behind his back. Then finally clears his throat. "I've never heard of what you've described happening to anyone before, so I am certainly no expert on the matter . . ."

Clay's heart sinks.

". . . However, from everything you've told me, I believe that what you are experiencing are termed 'probable' realities—most often referred to as 'parallel' realities, though I don't consider that to be an accurate enough term." He runs a hand along a row of books on a shelf as he walks. "In quantum physics, you see—because of the Uncertainty Principle, which is at the heart of the matter—nothing is truly predictable, as all possibilities exist simultaneously at some level." He lightly waves a hand. "However, some possibilities are, to some degree at least, more possible than others, so we call them 'probable,' although it basically amounts to the same thing, of course. However, the distinction is *very* important."

The professor checks to see that he has Clay's attention before continuing. "Amazingly, what's been discovered is that the possibilities we actually experience, or observe—at the atomic level, certainly, but at any level of physicality—are influenced, if not determined, by our *attention* to the matter." He looks back with a smile, the lenses of his glasses flashing. "You see, our attention—our thoughts—our beliefs and expectations—our *intent*—skews the results, one way or another. Always . . . So, if we *expect* an electron to be in a certain position, it will; and if we *expect* a photon to behave as a wave, rather than a particle, it will."

He's reached the end of the room and turns, his hands spread wide. "So, you see, what we've learned is that we cannot separate our *beliefs* about reality from the reality we observe. Our beliefs about reality, basically, form it." He smiles. "So, in a very real sense, you see, reality is only as valid as its last observation." A pause. "Do you follow?"

Clay nods once, slowly. This is *way* over his head; but maybe some of it will start making some sense.

"Unfortunately, scientists usually perceive only what appears within our system, and that often appears predictable," the professor remarks as he leisurely returns along the other side of the room. "However, science perceives such a small amount of data, in such a limited area, that the great *un*predictability of any molecule or atom or wave is not apparent. So, 'out of sight, out of mind,' unfortunately, for most. Though our minds, ultimately, are what create what we see in the first place."

He gestures fervently. "The trouble is that many in the sciences do not comprehend that there is an *inner* reality, that is not only as valid as the exterior one, but is the *origin* for it." He holds up a finger, high over his head. "It is *this* world that offers us the real answers and solutions, and that will ultimately reveal the secrets—the blueprints, if you will—that exist behind the world that we experience."

Dzhelikhovsky stops, eyebrows raised. "It is my contention, posited only recently these past few years"—motioning across the room to the box of papers he'd carried out earlier—"that *consciousness* is the deciding factor in reality." He looks to Clay with an exuberant, almost childlike, expression. "Adding consciousness to the equation changes everything!"

He begins walking faster now, gesturing enthusiastically as he goes. "According to my own theory, you see, there are *units* of consciousness, as there are matter—many, many millions of them, let's say, in one atom—which cannot be broken down, but that combine with others of its kind, forming greater units of consciousness—organizations of units, if you will." He passes behind Clay, on his second lap of the room, pausing to give the empty bottle there a dispirited shake as he goes. "Each of these units, by their very nature, is aware of the reality of all the others, and *influences* all others. And, as a rule, they move much, much faster than the speed of light—the speed of *thought!*—and can move backward or forward in time, as well as appear in several—or *all!*—places at once, without going through space."

He glances back, a finger raised. "This is the explanation for Einstein's 'spooky action at a distance,' or quantum entanglement—the one conundrum that had him stumped till the end. Because, you see, neither Einstein nor the others, back then, could conceptualize anything beyond space-time. However, space-time is not the fundamental reality—*consciousness* is!"

The professor stops in place, chuckling to himself, and shakes his head. "If he'd only just . . ."

He shrugs and continues walking, talking, gesturing all the while. "These units of consciousness, I believe, are the vitalizing force for everything in the physical universe—and others as well!—and the varieties of their activities are endless. Because, as each basic unit is endowed with unpredictability—again, at the heart of quantum theory—it allows for *infinite* patterns and possibilities." He stops once again at the far end of the room and turns. Points to Clay. "And as a result: infinite probable realities."

Dzhelikhovsky starts up again, head bent forward, hands behind his back; then stops suddenly and lifts his eyes to the ceiling. "Some might go so far as to call certain organizations of such units 'souls,' and unpredictability 'free will'; but that's just . . ." He waves away the thought as ridiculous and keeps going.

"Consciousness, you see, is energy. *Aware* energy. So thoughts can be thought of as conglomerations of highly charged 'particles' of energy." He looks up to meet Clay's eye. "You follow? And because no energy is ever lost or destroyed—a universal law—the energy within your own thoughts does not dissipate." He raises the finger. "So, therefore, every thought is eventually actualized at some level"—looking pointedly at Clay—"and every probability explored."

He stops and, with a casual lift of his hands, says, "There are probable realities in which the endless possibilities of *one given event* are realized."

The professor steps to the coffee table and lifts his glass, beaming, as he raises it in toast. "Space and time are not modes in which we live, you see, but in which we *think!* Ha!"

Finding the glass empty, Dzhelikhovsky frowns, shrugs, then sets it back on the table. Resumes his unhurried lap of the room, his hands as well in motion.

"So, as it goes, each probable system of reality, of course, then creates other such systems. And any one act, realized in one particular system, brings forth an infinite number of 'unrealized' acts that will also find their actualizations, in other systems . . . You follow?"

He pauses to look back, and Clay's confusion must be plain. "Don't think of infinity as one indefinite line," Dzhelikhovsky advises, "but in terms of numberless probabilities and possible combinations, growing out of each and every act of consciousness—every *choice,* especially."

Clay's head is swimming. "Every choice . . ."

"Exactly. New potential realities are constantly being generated from present choices. And as these choices are being made, certain possibilities are actualized in the present." He turns out his palms. "It's our *choices* which cause our probable futures to become our reality."

"So . . ."

"So"—walking again, gesturing dramatically—"probable realities, in essence, are branches upon branches of various routes of objective reality, based upon our *thoughts*—the choices or decisions we make." He holds up the finger again as he goes. "Although, of course, there has to be some level of *significance* attached to each event; for within a literally infinite field of activity, meaningful order can only arise from the propensity for significance." A sweep of his hand. "A perfect example of how 'possible' becomes 'probable.' And why such insignificant events as what color socks you choose have no real weight in affecting reality."

Clay's just trying to keep up. "So . . . If I do something, or don't do something . . ."

The professor turns with his arms flung out to his sides as if to encompass the entire room, the world. "You create an infinite number of probable realities. And, therefore, an infinite number of probable *selves*—each of whom, I must point out, consider themselves to be the *real* you."

Clay signals a time-out. "So, you're saying I'm, like, *visiting* a bunch of these probable lives, or realities, or whatever? . . . Other *me*'s?"

Dzhelikhovsky begins his pacing again, but across the room, now, a hand to his chin. "Hmmm . . . Exactly, I suppose, in your case." He thinks on it further. "Of course, the probable selves who've chosen the actions you didn't, in other systems, must be, in important respects, quite different from the self you know . . ." A few more pensive strides. ". . . and would certainly be very interesting to compare . . ." He finally shrugs. "But *why* you 'visit,' and for only one day, is a mystery."

His walk has brought him to the couch beside the door, and he lays a loving hand upon his box of papers. "All we can know for certain, in my view, at least, is that your consciousness is somehow responsible for it."

Clay considers this a moment. "But *why*? What's the point? There has to be a point, right? . . . Right?"

The professor can only shake his head. Then, with an expression that says *Aha!,* comes over and retakes his seat across from Clay.

"First," he states, settling back, "you must understand that there are quantum waves which carry information from both the *past* to the present and from the *future* to the present. Okay? Operating well outside of time as we generally know it." He motions with both hands apart then coming together. "Now, consciousness is the resonant gathering of these quantum waves, with one coming from the past and one coming from the future . . . and the focal point where they merge defines the present." He opens his hands to say, *See?* "So your mind is at all times tuned in to *both* the past and the future, making existential certainties out of probable realities . . . by *observing*, then choosing—either consciously or subconsciously—in each now-moment, drawing from the vast bank of probable actions, certain ones that are significant to you."

Clay nods, knowing that it's expected of him, but not really understanding the point. It seems so far-fetched. Like something out of a science-fiction movie. If he hadn't already experienced the insanity of it for himself . . .

Dzhelikhovsky leans forward now, his eyes gleaming. "You see, in terms of energy, *intent* is the stabilizing force." He makes a fist. "*Focus* 'freezes' the moment, so to speak, so that the past and future are closed out; because the particular focus required to live in the present moment necessitates the exclusion of other data . . . Follow?"

Uhhh, nope. Clay finally has to shake his head.

"What I'm saying is that it's the same with probable lives. Your consciousness has focused on *this* particular reality, today, for a reason. Out of all the others it could choose from."

Excitedly, the professor scoots out to the edge of his chair. Makes an exaggerated roller-coaster motion with his hand. "You see, consciousness itself fluctuates as a quantum wave function. Where *each point* on the wave is a specific system of reality." With his other hand, he begins indicating different spots on the curve—high, low, middle. "However, the individual points aren't aware of each other, as each reality is only focused upon itself, by necessity." Now running a finger along the imaginary curve. "Your consciousness, you see, continually weaves in and out of these probable realities, taking on the properties of each system in which it appears, and the characteristics of that environment—each one having no sense of absence, and the *memory of only that one particular reality.*"

He lowers his hands, begins opening and closing the fingers of one in rapid succession. "So, to use an analogy, *this* reality is blinking off and on, without your realizing it—like a trillion, trillion, trillion, trillion times per second (ten to the fortieth power). And just like the frames in a film, or the Earth spinning, it's much too fast to notice, so it in no way bothers your own sense of continuity."

Dzhelikhovsky sits back and crosses his legs. "However, in theory, at least, the fluctuations are actually occurring simultaneously, as all past, present, and probable futures exist *now*." He tosses up his hands. "Ultimately, there is no such thing as time or space."

Clay is totally blown away—discombobulated, bewildered, at sea; and it must show on his face.

The professor sighs. Makes a tent with his fingers under his chin. "I realize this must be difficult for you to conceptualize," he says patiently. "So . . . let's try this." He sits forward to make another attempt to explain. "Think of probable realities as like varying 'frequencies' on a radio. Okay? The 'you' that you recognize is but one signal of one station, tuned in to a certain frequency—a certain *focus*. Your overall consciousness has an infinite number of different 'stations,' which exist simultaneously at other levels, but you yourself are concentrating on only one of them at a time, tuning out the others for immediate practical purposes." He pauses. "Does that make more sense to you?"

Surprisingly, it does. "Yeah. But it still doesn't explain why I'm 'tuning in' to all these other realities. I mean . . . which one's my main one?"

Dzhelikhovsky smiles. "Why, they all are."

"But why do I keep jumping around? And why can't I remember anything but just this past week, since it started?" As much as

Clay has learned after speaking with the professor, he's really no better off than he was before. He covers his face with his hands. "I just want to stick to *one*," he moans. "Where I can remember . . ."

And be with Charlene, he thinks but doesn't say.

Dzhelikhovsky reaches over and pats Clay on the shoulder; finally, it seems, at a loss for words.

The two sit in companionable silence for a while, each with their own thoughts. Clay's mind awhirl with infinite possibilities . . . The intersecting and interweaving of other people's probable realities with his own . . . Total strangers, even! . . .

Until: "Uh-oh!" The professor sits up with a start and looks to his watch. "Rebecca is going to kill me!"

"Why?" Clay can't imagine the woman he met getting angry about anything.

"Our flight leaves in only a few hours, and I haven't done half the things on her list. Or mine. Damn!"

"Your flight? Where are you going? On vacation?"

The professor chortles, shaking his head. "Peru, if you can believe it. Rebecca has been trying to convince me to go, now, for years. Says it's my *destiny*. Ha!"

Dzhelikhovsky pushes himself up from the leather chair. Walks to his office. "I almost went once, years ago, when I was merely a grad student," he calls through the open door. "But then thought better of it, at the last minute. Now, where . . . ?" Clay can hear a commotion: drawers opening and shutting, things falling. "We're to live in the jungle," the professor shouts, "with the natives there, for a time. In relative luxury, mind you, or at least so I've been promised." More clattering, a heavy thud. "A 'shamanic adventure' is how she puts it. The 'real deal.'" *Crash!* "Damn! To *experience* the quantum realm, she says, not just study it. That's my Rebecca . . . Ah! At last!"

Dr. Z appears at the door with a fresh bottle of vodka. Another glass. "However, I think meeting you today qualifies as a quantum event in itself." He grins. "What do you say?"

There he is . . .

The asshole in his Yale-blue sweatshirt, surrounded by adoring fans.

The asshole speechifying outside the Economics building, hangers-on hanging on every word.

The asshole buying rounds of drinks for the bar. The party boy, the pretty boy, the center of attention.

The asshole walking to and from his classes, the student Union, the gym—always with a small cluster of satellites in their orbits.

He's never alone . . .

Until one moonless night it's him throwing out the trash, unexpectedly, in the dumpster behind the frat house. Then skulking away, down the alley, down one dark street after another. Shoulders hunched, hands in pockets, furtive looks left and right, stopping occasionally to look back—tense moments . . . Eventually reaching a neighborhood of run-down apartment buildings stacked too close. Streetlights out.

The asshole darts up one set of crumbling steps and slips through the door already ajar.

And in no time he's back, retracing his route, with a jaunty stroll now, head held high, occasionally swiping at his nose.

But, this time, he never once looks behind him.

CLAY WAKES to a rough jostling, a hand on his shoulder.

"Come on, let's go!"

"Let's bring 'em in!"

Bright yellow and dark blurs of motion. Rustling fabric, stomping feet. The pervasive smell of fish.

He's sitting at a small wooden table—a booth—squeezed in tight, his right side pressed to the wall, where he'd been leaning. There's an empty coffee mug and a plate of crumbs on the table before him, which are quickly snatched away by a pair of large black hands and yellow arms.

Clay watches the man, who's wearing a full suit of heavy, yellow rain gear, take a few steps to deposit the dishes in a sink before hurrying out a doorway to what's clearly the outdoors. Clay can hear a howling wind and see rain splattering the large oblong windows surrounding the small room. The sky a roiling slate gray.

Across from the table is an elevated platform with a man in a thick blue sweatshirt and pair of yellow rain pants held up by suspenders half standing, half sitting in a raised metal chair before a bank of electronic equipment—numerous screens and buttons and lights—in his hands a large steering wheel of sorts.

The room tilts, lurches, and Clay has to catch himself on the table and the seat beside him.

He, too, is dressed in thick rubber rain gear, he now notices—jacket and pants and boots—something . . . a wool stocking cap on his head. His cheeks are stubbly whiskers.

The entire room sways, is jolted again.

I'm on a boat! The realization is as frightening as it is exciting.

The man at the controls glances back. "Jake! What the hell are you doing? Get going! This thing's moving in fast!"

Clay reacts without thinking. He scoots off the cushioned bench and goes to follow the other man he'd seen out the door.

Stumbles and catches himself on the little kitchenette as the boat lurches and rolls again.

"Shut the damn door!" the driver—captain?—yells as Clay stands there uncertainly.

Outside, Clay's face is instantly lashed with stinging rain, and he pulls up the hood of his rain slicker, draws it tight, Velcroes it in place. Keeps his feet spread and his knees bent to absorb the sudden movements of the ship.

A freezing blast of wind sends him stumbling to the side.

At the far end of an expansive metal deck he sees three other men in bright yellow against the all-consuming gray. Working to bring a large cage-like container aboard, dripping wet, partially filled with something unrecognizable.

Buffeted by gusts of wind, staggering against the wild pitching of the deck beneath him, Clay makes his way toward the other men, knowing that he has to help them, somehow—do his part—without the slightest idea of how, or what that might be.

He already knows this will be one of the most challenging days he's had to face so far.

As he approaches the two men handling the cage on the left, the single man on the right yells and waves Clay over. The man has just hauled in a large, round, bright-orange buoy; and in the next moment another metal cage—about four-feet square at the base and six feet tall—appears over the rail on that side, as well, hanging from a pulley. A huge, horizontal spool of cable beside the man keeps revolving.

Together they haul the cage in and lower it to the deck, its sides and metal edges repeatedly bumping into Clay, threatening to knock him down. It must weigh a ton. Inside the cage is a mass of scrabbling giant crabs—spiny pink-red and white—pincers waving, snapping at their captivity. But for as much as the container could hold, he notices, it's practically empty.

With the cage on deck, Clay doesn't know what to do next and he looks to the ruddy-faced, bearded man beside him, who briefly glares before reaching up and unhooking a thinner, branching cable attached to the top of the cage. As he does this, Clay looks over to the other pair and sees one of the men quickly returning to the rear of the boat while holding on to the waist-high railing for support; sees that the man has moved their cage a good distance away, in the other direction. So without waiting to be told by his scowling coworker, Clay bends and pushes their own cage far down the slippery deck. The metal ice-cold in his bare hands, which are rough and calloused.

He returns, hugging the wooden rail with one arm, wincing at the salty spray, and a second cage is already hanging there suspended, his partner struggling to hold it steady.

Shit! Clay thinks. He'd been too slow.

This time, once the cage is down (barely missing his toes), Clay watches how its lead is removed. Then really puts his back and legs into maneuvering it the fifty-plus feet away and into position. It reminds him a lot of pushing the sled during football practice.

"Where are your gloves?" the other man hollers above the roaring wind and rain when Clay is back. He's holding another orange buoy.

Huh? But there's no time to answer or think or do anything as the next dripping, metal cage is swung on board but get it down safely and away.

As he returns again, as quickly as possible without falling, Clay looks out over the turbulent waves rising and falling in endless pointy hills of steel gray with spuming white caps disappearing into the haze. He wonders where the hell he is. It could be anywhere.

Then he's back at the rolling drum of cable and the next swinging cage of crabs. And after getting it down, after it crashes painfully, yet again, into his chest and gut and thighs, he disconnects the lead himself this time, before pushing his way down the deck.

His body is well-muscled and rugged, he can tell, and revels in this kind of work. Despite the exertion, he's breathing easily. It's only his nerves that are taking the strain.

As he nears his orderly row of cages and crabs, the boat suddenly reels and Clay loses his footing, goes stumbling into the rail and nearly over its edge—dangling at the waist, kicking precariously in the air—before being tossed in the opposite direction, to go sliding on his back, on a fresh sheet of spray, clear across to the other side of the deck. And as his head and shoulders crumple against the wall below the rail, he sees all four of his heavy cages sliding swiftly in his direction, hears barely-audible shouting above the din, and, just before the cages go crashing into him and those already aligned on this side (neatly secured with rope, he now sees), there's a massive *BOOM!* and accompanying vibration and a cascade of freezing white foamy water comes crashing over him and the entire deck, obliterating his vision, as the boat rapidly heels to the other side.

STEAM RISES OFF of the three men at the table, Clay still the wettest and coldest of them all. The boat cabin's heat is on full blast and there's the musty sea odor of wet wool, perspiration, and brine. The windows show only black, and shimmering silver rivulets of rain and spray, like the veins on a leaf. The soft yellow lights on the cabin's ceiling and the dim red light at the captain's console create a patchwork of russet shadows over every surface. The small space cramped with tension.

"Dreams," the captain says, frowning. He sits turned toward them, in his chair. His brow lined, a look of incredulity, of absolute bewilderment, on his face.

Clay is the only one facing him directly, and not by choice. He shrugs sheepishly. Nods.

"You get a two-hour nap and have such fucked-up dreams that you forget to lash down the pots *and* clip-in during heavy weather?" The captain just stares; truly, it seems, at a loss for words. "H-h-how does that happen?"

"Well . . . they were pretty bad," Clay mumbles as he rubs his neck. His whole body is bruised and sore from tumbling repeatedly across the deck earlier.

"Ha. I'll bet." The captain points a finger. "You should give these guys half your share for saving your ass and doing all your work today."

Both men at the table with Clay smile. The one named Jerome rolls his eyes and laughs good-naturedly.

Their rain gear hangs along the wall, on the other side of the door to outside, their boots bungeed in place on the floor. Everybody but the captain wearing only their thermal tops and bottoms, Jerome a ratty wool cap as well. Their missing crewmate—Clay's earlier work partner, in a foul mood—had recently ducked through a low arch in the forward bulkhead and down some steps, to go to sleep on one of the bunks there.

The sea and storm have both calmed considerably since reaching their peaks six hours ago. All one hundred cages are lashed together in place on the deck, and their previous occupants in seawater in the cavernous tanks below. Now, as the boat, on autopilot, with a storm anchor dragging behind for good measure, faces directly into the oncoming waves, there's a steep roller-coaster motion—slowly up, then speedily down—that would have been highly disconcerting at any other time, Clay thinks, than after being tossed around like a plaything in God's bathtub.

Soon after taking his first fall, Clay had been clipped-in to the safety line that runs the entire length of the back deck. And though he'd gone down at least fifty more times since then, at least he hadn't gone overboard. But he'd been damn near worthless as a crewman, as if it were his very first day—which in a very big way it was.

"Yeah, at least half," Jerome jokes, sitting sideways on the seat, at the opposite corner of the table. "If I had to pull you outta the hold one more time, I was gonna leave you in there with the crabs."

The other man at the table—Todd, a soft-spoken giant with a balding pate and pale beard—just shakes his head and smiles as he sips his cocoa.

The captain remarks, "You'd better hope none of them were damaged," then slaps the side of his chair. "God damn it, Jake! Our fifth season and I've never seen you so out of it, so fucking clueless. Like a greenhorn! If I didn't know better, I'd of said you were on drugs." He leans forward, peering hard. "You're not, are you?"

"Oh, no no no. It's just—" Clay's much too weary to dissemble or make excuses, and he figures a little truth may help his situation (it sure can't make things any worse). "It's just these dreams I've been having—for, like, a week now. They've been really getting to me. Messing up my mind . . . And it's like, today, I just lost my whole memory, or something. I couldn't think straight. It's weird." He gives his head a shake, then the captain the full force of his gaze. "But I promise I'll be better tomorrow. Just like new, like this never happened. I swear. You'll see . . . Tomorrow . . . I just gotta get some decent sleep, I think, without any more of these crazy dreams."

"What kinda dreams are they?" Jerome asks him. "Nightmares?"

Clay lets out a heavy sigh and looks about the cabin before responding, determining how much he wants to say. "It's my girlfriend. My old girlfriend, from high school. She . . . We had our whole lives planned out together, you know? We were gonna get married soon. Go to school. Have kids . . ." He shrugs disconsolately. "Just have the perfect life, you know?"

"Ah, hell," Jerome says, throwing up his hands, "I know where this is goin'. You fucked up, didn't you?"

Clay's taken aback for a second. "Well, yeah . . . ," he starts, but, "No, no, it wasn't me, it was this asshole. It was his fault."

"Oh, yeah? What he do? Take her away from you, or some-thin'?"

"What's this have to do with your dreams?" the captain wants to know. "And your acting like a fucking moron, all of a sudden?" He gives a quick glance over his shoulder to check the screens behind him, as he's been doing from time to time.

"No— Well . . ." Clay studies his hands on the table. They're red and chapped, and even after finally finding his gloves in his rain coat's pockets, they're still ice cold. "I think she might be dead."

There's an uneasy silence. The stomach-raising acceleration down a wave.

Then: "*What?*" Jerome's toothy grin is gone.

"I mean, I think this asshole might have killed her. Or gotten her killed. Or . . . maybe raped her, even. I don't know."

"Holy shit, bro. What? You don't *know?*"

"It's these damn dreams," Clay says, letting his exasperation show. "I know they've got something to do with it. But they're all so different; they don't make any sense . . . It's, like, sometimes I'll think she's dead—I mean, I *saw* her! I went to her funeral!—but then she's alive . . . but she got raped . . ." He shakes his head, staring at the table. "I never know what really happened. If anything . . . Sometimes—well, once, I think—she was alive, but . . ." He has to close his eyes against the unexpected tears that well and threaten to spill over. That one particular memory, or dream, and the horrible day that followed, may have been the worst for him, by far . . . To think that it could have been his fault . . .

"They're visions."

It's Todd, looking up now, speaking for the first time that Clay can recall. His eyes are a surprising glacier blue. "They mean something," he continues. "Something's going on with her. She's in danger." He drops his gaze back to his mug and takes a drink. "Or else she's dead, and it's her ghost trying to communicate with you."

The group remains silent for a while as they take this in; the other three men looking from one to the other, not sure what to say.

Then Jerome, finally: "Why don't we find out?" He's talking to the captain.

Clay humphs. "Huh? . . . How?" He spreads his hands and looks around, to indicate that they're in the middle of nowhere; in the middle of the ocean, for Chrissakes.

"Google her. What's her name?" Jerome looks back to the captain. "Are we pickin' up?"

The captain gives a shake of his head. "No, not in these seas. Satellite's useless."

"What's her name?" Jerome asks Clay again.

"Uh . . . Charlene. Charlene Summers."

"Summers? Like the season?"

Clay nods. Gives a sad smile. "Yeah . . . She was like that, too—like summer. Real bright and cheerful." He can see her beautiful, beautiful face before him now, in his mind, beaming. "She was the light of my life."

There comes a groan from the forward bunks, below. A plaintive, "Oh, my *God.*"

Jerome asks the captain, "What about the SSB?"

"What about it?" But Clay can tell by the captain's tone of voice that he already knows.

"We can radio Anchor Point and have somebody there look it up. They can call us back, or fax the info. Either way."

The captain's look isn't promising. He glances at his watch. "It's three A.M. It's Sunday now. No one will be there."

"Shit, cap'n. Somebody's *always* there." Jerome waits a beat, then apparently judging the captain's expression, changes tack. Smiles big. "You don't want Jake still dreamin' this shit, do you?"

Five long seconds go by. Then from the bunks below, loud: "Look her up! Find the fuck out, for fuck's sake!"

So as the large boat and small crew ride over one mountain of water after another, the captain picks up the handset beside him and places the call. Then again, half a minute later. And after seven tries it's finally answered. A sleepy hello from a guy named Jim.

There's the anticipated bitching and moaning, which the captain patiently endures, then he's laying out his request. "Charlene Summers. S-U-M-M-E-R-S." He looks to Clay, who nods and adds, "From Taloga, Oklahoma." "From Taloga, Oklahoma. Whatever you can get. We need her current status. Fax me back as soon as you can. Please. It's important to one of my crew. And to me," he says.

Just before the captain ends the call, Clay speaks up again. "Wait!" He reaches out a hand. "Uh . . . There's somebody else. In the dreams . . . Can we find out about him, too?"

"Yes!" is the immediate reply from below.

But the captain's eyes remain locked with Clay's for a few moments before giving in. He sighs. "What's the name?"

ALL FOUR MEN are at the wooden table—Clay absorbed in a nautical magazine, Jerome and Todd playing a high-stakes game of cribbage, and the captain poring over his record books—when the fax comes through an hour later, the machine emitting a short series of rings and tones before the thin white sheet of paper.

The captain gets up and mounts his platform to retrieve it when the machine stops. With a practiced motion, tears the paper free.

"Charlene Summers," he reads, knowing the others are listening intently. "Born 2/14/86. Raised in Taloga, O.K. Went to . . . Jesus, Jim, give me a break." He scans the material for a few seconds. Glances up at Clay. Then clears his throat and stands a little straighter. "Died 5/27/04. Raped and murdered by unknown assailant. Police have no suspects. She is survived by her—" He stops there.

Clay sits still, his eyes on the paper in the captain's hand. His feelings surprisingly non-existent. Calm . . . He'd known already, of course. It was just a matter of having it verified. Just one more piece of the puzzle he keeps having to figure out.

There's a respectful silence as the boat climbs inexorably up the next facing wave, then surfs edgily down.

The captain reads the asshole's name just as the fax machine rings and beeps again. More paper begins spooling out.

". . . Born 7/30/81. Raised—yada, yada . . . Oh. Attended Yale. Finance major. Huh. Uh . . ." He scans. Looks up, then back. "Died 10/12/04. Murdered, apparent drug deal-slash-robbery. Police seek the following suspect for questioning: Clayton Jacob Nehman. Born—yeah, yeah . . . Photo to follow . . . Jim."

Clay's blood runs cold. At the mention of his name, he'd flashed on the memory of last night's dream . . . The felling blow . . . and the many blows that followed . . .

Now he watches as the captain's hand rips the next fax sheet loose . . .

Watches as the captain stares, frowning, perplexed, at the picture in his hands . . .

. . . as he looks up, slowly, eyes wide . . .

. . . turns it to face the table . . .

The blue-white of his headlights illuminates a patch of winding dirt road ahead and a small section of trees to either side.

He has the phone to his ear. *Hi, this is Charlene. I'm not—* He tosses it onto the seat beside him—beside the Wingmaster, loaded and ready.

He wonders again what he'll do with it if he finds the asshole's car. Probably nothing. Probably shoot out a tire. Scare the shit out of him. Warn him off.

The trees glide by like ghosts. Open areas for campsites staggered far apart. On the right: nothing there . . . Left: nothing—

A flash of white, at the limit of his beams. Then again, to the left, through the trees.

He stops the truck and leaps out. Runs. *Charlene!* Dodging trees and branches. *Charlene!*

She's on the ground where she'd fallen, trying to get up. Screams and fights him when he reaches to help. Terror in her eyes.

Oh my God! Charlene, it's me! It's me! Oh my God! What happened?

Her pretty yellow dress has been torn down the middle and hangs low on her arms. Her feet are bare, her knees torn, her hair infused with leaves and twigs. Her face a swollen bloody mess streaked with tears. Blood stains her chest. Her arms. Her thighs.

She's scrambling backward, a cry in her throat, when something registers in her eyes. She stops, stares—collapses as if dead.

He's carrying her cradled in his arms. *Oh my God oh my God oh my God.* Trips and almost falls. *Charlene! Oh my God! Charlene!*

* * * * *

CLAY WAKES with a start.

Rap rap rap! It's a policewoman knocking on the glass, only inches from his head. A car window. A truck or van, by the looks of it—the cop's face even with his own.

"Move it. No blocking the alley."

Clay nods and quickly sits up, signaling his assent. *Jeez! What the hell?* He fumbles with the ignition on the steering column. Watches the uniform with her pad of tickets turn the corner out of sight in the rearview mirror. Starts the engine.

It's a van, all right. A work van with a large open area in back and shelving on both sides. Shelves full of flowers in various arrangements. Gift boxes. Fast-food containers and water bottles litter the footwell and seat beside him.

He's parked back-end to the street, between two dumpsters. A steady flow of people moving past on the sidewalk behind the van. Slow-moving traffic. But the alleyway ahead is clear, so he puts the van in gear and rolls forward. Then stops suddenly. Something in the mirror had caught his attention and triggered a memory . . .

A memory!

He turns and looks through the rear windows of the van. At the large blue-and-green letters on the building across the street: MONA'S. He thrilled at the prospect of a memory—any memory—until he realizes that it's only from a week ago, when all this trouble first started: The notebook; the mysterious list of days and times—places.

Mona's. He tries to picture the piece of paper, in his own neat writing, that had been such a surprise to him then . . . But he can't for the life of him remember which day it was, only the approximate time . . .

He pushes back his jacket sleeve and finds an expensive-looking watch. *Wow, nice.* It's 10:15 A.M.

What's he doing here so early?

What's he doing here at all?

But it's a stupid question. He has a pretty damn good idea.

He pulls forward and stops at the other end of the alley, again between two dumpsters, people and vehicles moving past. He drums his fingers on the steering wheel. Turns in his seat. Even from here he can see the restaurant's entrance clearly, directly across from the alley.

Directly across . . .

As if drawn by instinct, an inner knowing, Clay's eyes go to the long gray bundle on the floor of the van, in the corner, by the rear doors. He'd thought nothing of it earlier.

Ah, shit . . .

He hesitates only a moment; then is putting the van in park, climbing into the back.

The cloth is a thick square pad, like movers use. Wrapped around the baddest rifle Clay has ever seen, except for in the movies. A machine gun, really, with a shoulder stock and pistol grip and long, curving clip of ammo hanging down, a long barrel with at least sixteen inches of it a three-inch-round cylinder at the end. Smith & Wesson stamped into its side. M&P-15.

A loud blast of a horn from the street makes him flinch and raise up, look out the windows, his heart beating fast. He quickly wraps up the gun, removes some of the bouquets of flowers, and shoves it into the bottom shelf. Does his best to cover it up.

He retakes the driver's seat and wipes his sweating palms on his pant legs. Takes a deep but shaky breath and lets it out slowly. Another. *Okay, okay. What now?*

Aha! He's in New York. He can drive himself to Princeton this time. Spend the whole day with the professor if he can. If he's there. Together they're bound to find a way out of this insanity.

Oh, please, please, please . . . Clay pats himself down and—*Yes!*—finds a phone in his coat pocket, almost identical to one he had a few days ago—years, whatever.

He's not surprised at all when the date reads 10/13/16.

However, a quick search of the university's website shows only a few results for Dzhelikhovsky—references to papers he wrote over a decade ago: "Quantum Gravity's Effect on Fifth-Dimensional Spacetime"; "Using Transcendental Quantities to Solve for Infinite Spacial Dimensions"; "Measuring Once-Visible Light Travel with Time Dilation"; "Why M-Theory's Eleven Dimensions Too Limited" . . .

Nowhere is he listed as a professor.

No! This can't be right. *Shit!* Who else can he go to? Who else would believe his crazy story?

But wait! Dzhelikhovsky must be a professor somewhere, right? He has to be. And hopefully someplace close by.

Clay tries Google . . . with success. But . . .

You have got to be kidding me.

THERE ARE SIGNS for wineries every other mile, fruit and vegetable stands in between. The Finger Lakes region, his map says. Beautiful country. Still green amid the profusion of fiery autumn leaves. Rolling hills. Barns. Horses grazing.

The small town of Ithaca is equally picturesque, its bustling main street lined with enticing shops and cafés. At the end of the street, according to his directions, he takes a right, passing a restaurant, a long row of art galleries, a martial arts studio, a large park, before finally arriving at his destination: Universal Fellowship Church.

Along the back edge of a sprawling parking lot surrounded by tall trees are three buildings, a tall A-framed chapel in the center.

Clay parks. Climbs the steps and goes inside. And is immediately dazzled by a kaleidoscope of colors covering every surface, as the late-afternoon sun shines through a beautiful mandala of stained glass, high in the south wall. At the far end of the church a group of women stand in an elevated semicircle by the altar, singing without accompaniment, their harmonious voices carrying easily across the large space.

"Goin' up to the Spirit in the sky . . .
That's where I'm gonna go, when I die . . .
When I die and they lay me to rest,
gonna go to the place that's the best . . ."

Clay takes a seat in one of the pews, midway, to wait till they finish. He knows he shouldn't be surprised but still is when he recognizes the woman with the shiny copper hair among them, swaying to the rhythm: Dzhelikhovsky's secretary—wife—Rebecca. He almost waves.

When the song ends he stands, and a gorgeous smiling woman in faded blue jeans and a bright plaid, flannel shirt meets him in the center aisle.

"Hi," she says, extending a hand, "I'm Pastor Shannon."

Clay's too shocked to speak, for a moment; he's never met a woman preacher before. Especially one so hot. "Hi. Uh, I'm looking for Professor—I mean, Reverend Dzhelikhovsky." He hopes he pronounced it right. And he hopes that nothing has changed from what he read online, that Dr. Z's still here.

The woman turns back to the group flipping through their sheet music. "Becks!" she calls. "Is Doc teaching today?"

Rebecca looks up. "Yep. Till five."

Clay can't help it: he raises a hand. Rebecca smiles and waves back.

"Are you new here?" the pastor lady asks.

"No, uh, just visiting for the day."

"Well, you're welcome to wait here, in the chapel, or next door." She points. "They're getting dinner ready over there and we're expecting a pretty big turn-out tonight. Spaghetti and garlic bread, nothing fancy." She points in the other direction. "Or I'm sure Reverend Z wouldn't mind if you sat in on his class. I think it just got started." She glances at her watch. "Did you come from downtown? Did you see the martial arts center, on the other side of the park?"

It takes a moment for Clay to understand. "He teaches . . . karate?"

"Aikido." The woman grins. "And he kicks ass."

"THE SECRET OF aikido is to harmonize ourselves with the movement of the universe, and bring ourselves into accord with the universe itself," says Dzhelikhovsky as he parries his student's punches and kicks. "He who has gained the secret of aikido has the universe in himself, and can say, 'I *am* the universe.'"

One student after another—kids anywhere from seven to seventeen—each take their turn trying to strike, or even lay a hand on, their teacher, who somehow remains untouched as he delivers his discourse. Earlier Clay had watched them all go through their drills repetitively. This is more fun.

"When an enemy tries to fight with me, the universe itself," Dzhelikhovsky continues as he dodges a blow and pushes the boy away, "he has to break the harmony of the universe . . ." Another student steps onto the mat. ". . . Hence, at the moment he has the mind to fight with me, he is already defeated."

The professor—*reverend,* Clay has to remind himself—no longer sports the thick salt-and-pepper beard. Nor is he portly. And although it's only four years earlier than the last time they met (according to *this* reality's calendar), the man looks half the age. The way he moves so fluidly, and so quickly, on the mat is astounding. It's hard to believe it's the same person.

Or is it, really?

The latest victim is suddenly flying through the air and lands with an *"Oompf!"*

"Truly winning means winning over the mind of discord in *yourself,*" Reverend Z intones as the next student, a small girl this time, attacks with an impressive flurry of kicks. "But, then, how do you do this? How can you calm a troubled mind, and purify your heart, and become harmonized with all things in nature?" The girl continues to twirl around her instructor, who watches her with a smile. "The secret is to make God's heart yours," he says with open arms. "It is the greatest love, and it is everywhere, at all times."

With a leap, the girl lands a solid kick to the reverend's behind. *Thwack!* Her eyes go round with surprise and she stops, looking stunned. There's a silence from the rest of the class, a soft "Whooa."

"Remember, everyone," the man says, smiling, as he bows to the girl. "There is no discord in love." A bow to the class. "There is no enemy of love."

CLAY'S WATCH SAYS it's 7:40 as Dzhelikhovsky says his goodbyes to the last of the volunteers, shaking hands and giving hugs at the door. Pastor Shannon is the last person remaining, laying out the colorful placemats, inscribed with drawings and quotes, along the rows of long tables.

"Go ahead, Doc," she calls, "I'll lock up."

"Thanks, Shannon." Then to Clay: "One moment, I'll be right back." He disappears into his office.

Clay's surprised by how much he enjoyed the evening's dinner-and-a-sermon. He hadn't even realized it was vegetarian spaghetti until somebody told him. And Reverend Z's twenty-minute spiel on forgiveness had touched some chords deep within him—made him think on his problem in a whole different light.

Clay hadn't had a chance to talk to Dzhelikhovsky at all during the meal, or much prior, but he'd been able to explain everything to him afterward as they stood together at the oversized steel sink in the kitchen, washing a copious assortment of dishes for at least a hundred people. This time, however, he'd avoided any mention of killing the asshole, saying only "confronted," instead (the man *is* a preacher, after all).

Dzhelikhovsky himself hadn't said much at all, only listened and nodded, with the occasional interjection and look of concern.

As he had before, Clay worried the guy would think he was crazy. And though it quickly became clear this wasn't the same person Clay had spoken to two days ago at Princeton, it rankled him just a little that he had to start his story all over, from the beginning. This time, however, Clay was able to incorporate the professor's own explanation and ideas on probable realities into his account, which clearly piqued the reverend's interest.

Dzhelikhovsky returns now, carrying his coat. "Come on," he says, leading the way. "Let's go for a walk."

It's already on the dark side of dusk. Dim yellow lights inside the chapel as they pass by beautifully illuminate its many stained-glass windows. The large, one-story building on the right is similar to the community center they just left; and like on the other side, Clay can see a small cottage-like building behind it, lit up and unseen from the road. The men, still silent, walk through a thick stand of tall evergreens and into the wide open park, next door. A low, gibbous moon shines brightly enough to see the still-green grass and scattered leaves at their feet.

"So," Dzhelikhovsky begins, after a few strides, "you say that I was a physics professor, and that I was on my way to Peru for the first time."

Clay knows only too well how difficult this must be to believe. "Right. It was Rebecca's idea. She said it was your 'destiny,' or something. She'd been trying to get you go for years, you said."

"And she gave you a dream-catcher."

"Right. But that was before—the first time. But you weren't there."

"I was in Peru again."

"Right. But you were lost. Or you'd missed your flight, or something. She was pretty worried about you."

"And I was a . . . psychologist?"

"Para—*para*psychologist. I'm still not sure what that is, but that's what Professor Price told me. He said you'd be the best person to help me. That if you couldn't, nobody can."

"Ah, I remember Price. He'd become quite famous for his studies of the mind's effects on the nervous system. Psychoneurology, I believe."

"Uh, it was memory. The brain and stuff. Or, at least it was in that, uh . . ."

"Probable reality."

"Right."

Dzhelikhovsky shakes his head as they continue on. Points. "Let's go down to the water. It's a stream, with a little pond someone dug a long time ago. Just watch your step."

In this direction the bushes are more plentiful and the grass much taller. Dzhelikhovsky has slowed his pace considerably, obviously giving thought to what he's heard, and Clay matches his step.

"I find this so . . . incredible," Dzhelikhovsky says, at last. "But . . ." He stops midstride and gazes up at the moon. "You know I attended Princeton. But I never did teach there."

"Right. Uh, this time."

"However, I have been to Peru . . . And it makes what you say almost believable. Or, I'm sorry—conceivable. By me, that is, because of my experiences there. In Peru . . . And I did finish my doctorate in physics, when I returned, so I can definitely grasp what your professor had to say about—"

"You. What *you* had to say. It was definitely you, I swear, but . . ."

"Yes, yes, right. Me." The reverend has lowered his eyes to meet Clay's. "And because we discussed this before, you're coming to me again for help, is that right? To make some sense of this . . . phenomenon that's occurring?"

Clay doesn't really know how Dzhelikhovsky can help him this time, in his capacity as a reverend, but the man's still the best hope he's got right now. "Yes. Exactly," he replies. "Especially how to stop it. I really don't want to do this anymore. I mean, I just want to go home. Back to the life I can remember, before all this started happening . . . Just one."

With Charlene . . . He has the vision of her running across the field, from the sidelines, dodging his teammates and other fans, to jump into his arms, laughing tearfully, the first year they made it to the finals . . . the year she wore his ring . . . He has to blink away the sudden tears.

The reverend puts a comforting hand on Clay's arm. "I can only imagine how troubling this must be for you."

They begin walking again, the path veering through some trees, the older man leading the way until they can walk side-by-side once more. Not too far ahead the way looks overgrown, impassable.

"Well, I suppose I can give you my take on it, from my perspective," Dzhelikhovsky offers, finally. "However, I can't promise you any solutions, except . . . Well, you'll see that I tend to have one answer for everything." He gives a self-deprecating chuckle. Lifts a hand to point. "There. Let's sit over there. This may take a while to explain. See the pond?"

Clay would call it more a swimming hole, really, complete with the requisite overhanging limbs and knotted swing rope. He can't see but can hear the burbling of a stream nearby.

Dzhelikhovsky takes a seat on a comfortable wooden bench beside the pond, and Clay joins him. The slightest breeze, barely noticeable, rustles the trees around them and creates a shimmering diamond pattern on the water's surface. Just a hint of the moon's reflection.

Dzhelikhovsky takes a deep breath and exhales slowly, like a sigh.

"I traveled to Peru in 1999, as a graduate student in astrophysics," he begins, looking out into the starry night. "I went with a small group of scientists and anthropologists whose purpose was to study the indigenous people there—the Urarinas and Tacunas, specifically, on the Rio Tigre." His hands animated now. "Somehow, these people, with no concept of a radio telescope or other advanced technology, were able to describe, in perfect detail, the rings of Saturn, the four moons of Jupiter, the Sirius system, and other planetary bodies, as well as aspects of the universe that we were only then recently discovering, such as quasars and white dwarves, dark matter, black holes. Not to mention worm holes into other galaxies . . . interdimensional travel . . ." He makes an emphatic gesture. "There was no possible way, we thought, for these 'backward natives' to be so far ahead in their understanding of such things."

Dzhelikhovsky glances over with a shrug. "Our mission, our goal, was simply to talk with these people, their leaders, their teachers, study how they learned what they did; nothing more than that." He sighs. "However . . . when in the Amazon . . ." His hands settle in his lap.

"We drank a ceremonial brew—a religious sacrament, actually—called *ayahuasca,*" he continues. "Highly psychedelic." He slowly shakes his head. "There are no words to describe what we experienced, except to say that it was 'shamanic'; that's the best that I can do . . ." His hands rise and fall, his gaze seemingly in the distance. "I saw and experienced things in that state . . . everything I had hoped for, and more . . . The smallest atomic structure . . . the vastness of the universe . . ." One hand begins to reach out, as if by its own volition. ". . . Other dimensions . . . other worlds . . ." He blinks, gives his head a quick shake. Looks over. "It was a slightly different experience for all of us, but for me, especially. Because, you see . . . I died."

Clay stares, unbelieving, pretty sure he heard correctly. "You died."

Dzhelikhovsky nods. "For quite a while, apparently, before I could be revived." He smiles, mostly to himself, it seems, and gazes out again over the water. "And what I experienced in *that* state, while I was gone, changed the course of my life forever."

The silence goes on and on, so Clay finally has to ask: "So . . . what happened?"

Dzhelikhovsky shrugs. "I went to Heaven. Although, at the time, I didn't remotely believe in such a place. And I met angels, and other beings of light, like myself. Because that's what I was then, a being of light—of intelligent light energy . . . *divine* energy." He clears his throat and sits up straighter. Spreads his hands wide. "And so, you see, when I came back from that experience, I had to learn everything I could about it. I had to understand exactly what it was that happened to me. I had to see if others have had similar experiences, and compare them, find out what they had learned, if anything." He gives a quiet laugh, his eyes twinkling. "Because it was by far the greatest learning experience of my life. More than any school or university could possibly ever teach me."

Clay stays silent, in wonder; and after another few moments of recollection, Dzhelikhovsky turns to him with a smile. "So that's what set me on this path, to be a minister, so long ago. My trip to Peru." He zips up his jacket further, against the chill. "And why I may be in a unique position to offer you some guidance concerning this problem of yours."

Yes! Finally! "Thank you!" Clay grabs onto the reverend's arm, truly hopeful for the first time.

"Well, just wait until you hear what I have to say, before you go thanking me." Dzhelikhovsky pats Clay's hand before it's removed. "Are you a spiritual person, by any chance? Religious in any way?"

"No, not really." Clay's religions, growing up, were Xbox and football, though he'd been to church with Charlene's family and some of his friends plenty of times.

"Well, the first thing you need to understand, whether you know it or not, is that, ultimately, you are a spiritual being." Reverend Z's look is kind but serious. "You are a spiritual being having a physical experience on Earth." He studies Clay's face for a moment more. "Just take my word for it, for now, okay?"

"Okay." But Clay sorta believes him anyway.

Dzhelikhovsky's hands begin moving excitedly again. "Okay. Now, your 'soul' is your spiritual self, the 'you' that never dies. It records your entire life on Earth, primarily through your thoughts and emotions. However, your soul is not all there is. It's a part of your 'Higher Self,' which is your *greater* spiritual self. You got it?" He waits for Clay to nod his understanding before continuing. "And your Higher Self is a part of God—or, the Creator, the Source, Allah, All That Is, whatever you want to call it. But, really, God is completely beyond our comprehension as human beings, so don't worry about that part right now."

Clay nods once. "No problem."

"Now, your Higher Self has been endowed with free will of its own, which means that it is an individual being and can do what it wants. *Anything* it wants. God basically said, 'Make known the unknown! Fulfill your potential! Explore every possibility!,' and then set it loose. Okay?" He waits again for the nod. Gestures enthusiastically. "Now, your Higher Self is doing *a lot*, it's really busy; it's doing all sorts of different things, on all sorts of different levels; and having fun, really enjoying itself. And one of the things your Higher Self wants to do—obviously, because you're here—is experience human form, in order to experience all that can *only* be experienced in the physical world."

He pauses meaningfully to look Clay in the eye. "So your Higher Self is the one who put you here, okay? As a part of itself, called the soul." He waits; gets the nod. "And the main goal, for the both of them, is to *learn and grow through experience,* which usually means experiencing as much as possible—which usually means both the good and the bad . . . You with me, so far?"

Clay nods his head yet again. "Yep." He can think of more bad things he's experienced, lately, than good, however.

"Good. All right. Now, your soul, as a part of your Higher Self, also has free will. And for consciousness to be fully free, it has to be endowed with unpredictability, which basically means infinite possibilities. Because, otherwise, without this freedom, consciousness would forever repeat itself." Reverend Z extends his palms, as in offering. "You see, probability, rather than absolute certainty, gives us the only possibility for free will . . . And what is free will but *choice?*"

Clay lets his gaze settle upon the sparkling ripples of the water. *Choice* . . . Choices . . . It always comes back to that, it seems.

"All right, now, okay. Here comes the tricky part." Dzhelikhovsky turns in his seat, resting a knee on the bench beside him. "Now, to experience the *absolute most it possibly can,*" he emphasizes, "your soul exists in many times and places at once, in many different bodies, different personalities. These are termed 'reincarnational' selves. Plus—now, get ready—there are an *infinite number* of each of these selves, as well, which are termed 'probable' selves, which exist in probable realities—which they *all* are, really."

"Wait." Clay holds up a hand. "'Reincarnational' selves? As in . . . *reincarnation?*"

"Absolutely. Reincarnation simply represents probability in a historical context—projected consciousness fragments in serial existences, rather than parallel." A shrug. "Other lifetimes are like other days to the soul—other aspects—and they tend to build upon one another. So, just like who you are today is a result of all the days you've lived since your birth, who you are in this *life* is a result of all the other lives you've lived, up until this one." Dzhelikhovsky smiles. "From a reincarnational standpoint, you are everything you have ever been, right now."

"Wait, wait, wait." Clay puts his hands to his temples. This is too much. "So . . . how does this relate to what's happening to me? I get the probable lives part. I think."

"Okay, don't worry about the reincarnation stuff, for now. But listen—this is what's most important to understand . . ." Reverend Z's eyes shine in the dark, fired up, intense. "God is not limited. All right?" He waits for this to sink in. *"God—is not—limited* . . . By anything. Including time and space . . . Which means your Higher Self, as a part of God, is not limited . . . Which means your *soul* is not limited . . . Okay? You got it?"

Clay frowns. Finally nods. It's a lot to grasp . . . But he still doesn't see how—

"Think about it." Dzhelikhovsky motions grandly. "Your soul has such vast potential and creativity, that it can never be fully expressed through only one personality." Smiling wide. "So your Higher Self solves this by creating several 'yous' at once. Reincarnational selves, then probable selves, in probable realities—each one experienced as vividly as the next." Pointing excitedly. "You—as you think of yourself, your ego, your unique personality—are but one manifestation of your soul. One of many. An infinite number, actually." He laughs and his smile grows even bigger. "You don't *have* a soul, you are a *part* of your soul."

This takes a minute . . . "A part."

"Right. Like a group of cells form an organ in your body, a group of selves forms a soul."

Clay nods thoughtfully, pretty sure he understands what the man is saying—the gist of it, at least—though it's pretty hard to believe.

"But, how?" he asks, after thinking it through. "How can one soul—right? How can one soul keep track of so many lives? That's, like . . . impossible."

The reverend just smiles. "Remember what I said earlier . . . God is unlimited. And so is your Higher Self; your soul. So they can easily handle it, no problem. Hell, it was their idea in the first place." He laughs.

"And the soul remembers all this stuff?"

"Absolutely. It's what it was designed to do. All of these re-incarnational selves and probable selves, through their own experiences, contribute to the soul's learning and growing. And although the various selves, the different personalities—like you and me, here—come and go, the soul never dies. It's eternal."

Clay waves a hand at their surroundings. "So this life is just a probable one. Just like all the others, too, I guess."

Dzhelikhovsky nods. "Well, not 'just,' but yes. And it, too, can and will be altered, at any number of infinite points. Based on the decisions and choices we make—our thoughts at the deepest level." He turns up his hands. "Again, there's no limit."

Clay's mind has officially been blown. The world—life as he knew it—is a lot more complicated than he ever thought possible. He's learned a lot today. However, none of it has answered his most important question:

"But why can't I stay in just one?" he laments. "Why do I keep jumping around like this, between them?"

Dzhelikhovsky looks out at the trees past the pond. The glittering sky. Finally shakes his head. "That I don't know."

Clay sighs. "So I'm screwed, then."

Silence. Which is probably the most honest answer he could get.

"Come on," Dzhelikhovsky says, after a while, slapping his hands on his thighs. "Let's walk. Get the ol' brain juices flowing."

Together they stand and continue walking in the same direction they started. Clay can see the stream now, to his left, reflected brightly in the moonlight, flowing past lush, overgrown banks. A well-trodden path meanders alongside it, just wide enough for the two of them, their steps measured, in sync.

"Listen to me," Reverend Z says in earnest. Then pauses, as if to find the right words. "Your soul is focused in a human body, in daily life, for a *reason* . . . And there is a reason why you are experiencing *this* probable life, right now . . . It's to learn and grow, as we discussed earlier, but you have also adopted it as a *challenge*."

Clay looks over, intrigued.

"Often, these challenges are predetermined before you get here," the reverend continues. "But regardless of how they originate, within their framework you are meant to learn and grow and develop and *extend* the limits of your consciousness. To become more than you were before. You see? . . . This is what is meant by growing spiritually." A glance. Again the hands, emphatic. "The evolution of man is the evolution of consciousness. And consciousness cannot evolve unconsciously . . . Do you understand what I'm saying? . . . It takes effort. *Thought*. And not by you alone. You are *never* alone. There *is* a higher order of being. There *is* a method to the madness, so to speak. And a reason for everything."

Clay remains silent, waiting for the point, which he hopes is coming.

"So, perhaps you are *meant* to experience a glimpse of these probable lives of yours . . . in order to accomplish something—rise to a challenge of some sort. What do you think?"

This is something Clay hasn't even remotely considered, that his visits are *intentional*. "I don't know," he says, at last. This is something he'll have to think about.

"If this is the case, then," Dzhelikhovsky surmises, "it must have something to do with the man you continue to confront. Or your girlfriend. Are there any clues as to what that might be?"

Clay doesn't have to think about this one, it's obvious. It's the asshole. Clay's mission is to kill him each time, as payback for what he did to Charlene—and to *him,* for ruining his life—for setting into motion so many possibilities—all of them bad.

But he can't explain this to the reverend, as much as he'd like to. He can't just admit that he's a killer, many times over. So:

"No," he says faintly, "no clues."

Dzhelikhovsky says, "You mentioned your memory, that you've lost a large portion of your life. I think this must also have something to do with what you're experiencing." He looks over. "Perhaps it's to help you enter each of these probable realities, with a clean slate, as it were, with no memories of any other lives to confuse things. Does that make sense?"

Clay hadn't thought of that, either. But, "No, not really. Why wouldn't I have just forgotten all of it, then?"

"Hmmm, you have a point. But, then, perhaps what you *can* remember is to provide you with a sense of identity, of who you are. After all, who we are is a result of our past, our memories. And without at least some kind of basis . . ."

The men's footsteps crunch steadily upon the ground, in unison.

Who am I? Really, Clay wonders, not for the first time lately. He's starting to feel much older, and much different, than the eighteen-year-old self he remembers being just ten days ago. Wiser in so many ways.

"Well, regardless of the reason this is occurring," the reverend offers, "remember that your *real* self is your soul. And your soul *always* remembers. It's where your true memory resides—in your consciousness. The brain is merely a temporary receptacle, for this life, a receiver and processor of sorts, and a fallible one at that."

The path has curved to the right and uphill without Clay noticing, and now they're once again entering the large open area of the park itself. Both men keep their thoughts to themselves as they head back toward the church, its buildings barely seen as flickering orange and yellow lights through the trees, far ahead.

Clay can't help but keep coming back to something the reverend had said during his sermon, earlier, at dinner. It was about forgiveness. Something like, "Being unable to forgive is like drinking the poison and expecting the other person to die." In other words, it hurts you more than it does them. Which kind of makes sense . . .

"I wish I could have been of more help to you," Dzhelikhovsky says.

"That's okay. I learned a lot more than I used to, at least. And it's given me plenty to think about, that's for sure." Clay recalls what the reverend had said about a possible reason for what's happening to him: a challenge. "And, well . . . I may have figured out a way to stop it, but . . . I don't know yet. We'll see, huh?"

"I hope so. And please let me know if you do. You're welcome here anytime."

Clay pulls out one of the church's decorated placemats he'd folded and put in his jacket pocket. Shows it to Dzhelikhovsky. "I have your address and phone number, just in case."

Then a thought occurs to him and he stops. Pulls out his phone. "This has a camera built in, right? Do you think it'll work in the dark?"

"I don't see why not. It has a flash function."

"Cool. Could you take a picture of us together, do you think?"

"Of course. I'd be happy to." Dzhelikhovsky takes the phone and presses its screen a couple of times. Holds it at arm's length as he puts an arm around Clay's shoulders. "Smile!" And a second later they're illuminated along with a digital *click*.

Before giving the phone back, Dzhelikhovsky places a call, listens for a moment, then hangs up. "There. That was to my office," he says. "Now if I don't hear from you in a few days, I can call and see how you're doing. Is that all right with you?"

Clay smiles, and his eyes inexplicably cloud over. "Totally. That would be great. Thanks."

Again the men walk in silence across the grass, and then through the trees, to stand in the church's parking lot. Five vehicles are there, still, Clay's white florist's van the farthest away.

Dzhelikhovsky stops at the cobblestones leading to the cozy little cottage tucked into the trees in back. Clay stops with him and holds out his hand.

"Thanks, Reverend Z. I really appreciate it. I really do. It was good seeing you again."

Dzhelikhovsky laughs. "My pleasure. I look forward to seeing you when you have all of this sorted out." He wraps both his hands around Clay's. "Just remember: There *is* a reason for what is happening to you." He smiles warmly. "Often we turn to God for help when our foundations are shaking, only to learn that it is God who is shaking them."

CLAY'S BEEN DRIVING for hours, through and around the town of Ithaca and around its endlessly long, narrow lake. Just thinking. Thinking over everything he's gone through these past ten days. Over everything he's learned recently . . . And how he might possibly put an end to it all. Without having to put a bullet in his brain.

One particular phrase from Reverend Z's sermon keeps coming back to him: *In the end, forgiveness isn't about anyone or anything else—it's about* you . . .

It's well after midnight as he continues to ponder the many meanings of that one simple statement and he pulls into the 24-hour copy shop he'd passed a dozen times already. The place is surprisingly busy at this hour.

Inside he purchases a small, thickly padded manila envelope. A pen. "Can I buy some stamps here too?" he asks.

"Sure, you bet. And we can weigh it for you, if you'd like. Just mail it over there."

At a vacant computer terminal affording some privacy, Clay sits with the envelope and a few pieces of scrap paper. He addresses the envelope to the asshole, at Prospect Group, 4 Financial Plaza, New York, NY. Then takes out the three-inch pointed brass round he'd removed from the rifle's clip. Looks at it one last time, and places it in the envelope.

On a piece of paper, he writes:

You dodged this one, asshole.

Then seals it inside, with the bullet.

On a second piece of paper, Clay writes:

Note to self:

LET—IT—GO!

High fives all around. Back slaps from the guys and hugs from the girls. They didn't just beat Texas, they slaughtered 'em! Sent them home with their tails between their legs!

O-U! O-U! O-U! Gooooo Sooners!

Free beer for the whole team!

He's sitting at a table, toasting their victory, having his shoulders massaged by a pretty coed, when something on the television catches his eye.

He's up and moving, stumbling into tables and chairs, oblivious to anything but the images on the screen.

It's the local evening news. A story that had captivated viewers all across the state two years ago: A young, Taloga, Oklahoma, woman, who had gone missing and was presumed dead.

He's at the bar, hands flat, leaning as far forward as he can. He can't hear the TV, only the din of the pub, raucous laughter, more calls for beer. But there's her face, her beautiful, beautiful face. Her senior photo. Smiling at him from the screen.

Then the forest, the campground, the lake. A dilapidated hunting shack, fenced-in by sagging yellow police tape. A covered body being carried on a stretcher. Mr. and Mrs. Summers, crying in each other's arms.

He can't believe it. They found her . . . They found her . . .

Without thinking, he grips the heavy glass mug beside him and, with a howl dug up from a long-buried pain, hurls it at the television with all his might. The screen shatters and goes black.

★ ✱ ✶ ★ ✷

CLAY WAKES with a full bladder and throws his legs off the side of the bed. Slips his feet into the convenient fuzzy slippers there. Pads across the floor to the hall and to the bathroom lit by a soft blue bulb. Relieves himself and rinses his hands. Happens to catch a glimpse of himself in the large mirror as he leaves.

And is instantly awake.

He flips the light switch and has to blink at the sudden brightness several times before he's left staring in disbelief.

Oh—my—God . . .

It's like he's aged a hundred years overnight. He looks ill.

His hand is shaking as he lifts it to his face, prods his sunken cheeks, the wrinkled sags below his eyes rimmed in red and dark bruise. His pallid skin is dry and flaky, with a sick yellow tint—even on the bony claws of his hands. His nails thick and brown and much too long.

Gone is any muscle he once had, as is any hair worth calling it that on his head. Where are his eyebrows, for Chrissakes? His eyelashes? . . . He looks shorter, too. Frail. A pathetic wretch in light blue pajamas.

Clay just stands there before his reflection, unable to tear his eyes away from the horror staring back. He wants to cry. He can't believe this is him. There's no way—no freakin' way—he would have ever let himself get this far gone.

He lets his gaze drift to the countertop, where beside the sink are arrayed a pharmacy of medications. A long pill dispenser with the days of the week. Crinkled tubes of ointments and creams.

My God . . . He really is sick. No wonder . . .

He lifts one of the bottles and gives it a shake. Allopurinol it says on the label. A prescription in his name. Take three times a day. Another, in a see-through orange container, is marked Chlorpromazine. Take only with food. Do not take with alcohol. There are too many bottles to count.

Clay shakes his head and picks up the pill dispenser. *M* and *T* are both empty, so it must be Wednesday, he figures. He pries open the lid of *W* and pours a colorful mix of drugs into his palm—at least a dozen tablets and capsules—and without thinking or caring, tosses them back, attempting to swallow them dry. But he chokes and has to bend to drink a few handfuls of water from the sink. Then splashes his face. Stares again at his dripping reflection.

He's already given up on this body, this version of himself. He doesn't particularly care what happens to it. Thank God he won't have to stick around, he thinks, and be stuck with it tomorrow.

Let's just get this day over with.

In the hall there's the small musty bedroom directly across and a closed door to the right, at the end, so he turns left, toward an open area suffused with dim light, and walks a few paces to a tiny living room on the right and a grimy kitchen with curling linoleum on the left. Dark curtains are drawn over the one window in the living room beside the front door, but the window in the kitchen has none and reveals a gray, washed-out sky and the upper corner of a red-brick building right next door. It could be any time of day.

Neither room has any decoration whatsoever. In the one half, a brown, patched recliner sits facing a large flat-screen TV; there's a low bookcase full of worn-out paperbacks. A decrepit Formica table with one chair, in the kitchen; nothing but a coffee machine on the counter; the usual stove and refrigerator; cabinets.

Why am I here? he wonders. As Reverend Z said, there has to be a reason. How does the asshole—how does Charlene—fit into all this?

Clay walks to the front door—cheap wood darkened with age—and opens it with a groan from its hinges. A rail-thin, striped gray cat with enormous green eyes looks up at him from the landing and immediately darts down the rickety wooden steps. Across the way, a stout middle-aged woman with her hair covered is hanging the wash out to dry on a clothesline between the two buildings, clothespins in her teeth. When she sees him watching she frowns and quickly picks up her basket and goes inside, slamming the door.

So: he lives on the top floor of an old apartment building in a crowded neighborhood. But where? As things have been going, he's going to guess New York City again.

In the kitchen the fridge is nearly as bare as the rest of the place, its door holding a further assortment of medications. On its shelves, four two-liter bottles of generic cola, jars of mayonnaise, mustard, some relish, two loaves of bread. A bowl of what looks like crusty tuna salad. The freezer is empty of even an ice tray.

However, the first cabinet he opens is packed—with small cans, each one identical. He takes one down to inspect: Tuna. All the cans are tuna. The next cabinet is the same. And the next. *Wow. Jeez.* He can't remember ever liking tuna this much. The final cabinet's stocked with jars of mayo, mustard, and relish.

Clay feels sorry for this guy. He still can't associate the body he's in now with himself.

As he does a final scan of the kitchen he spies a tall blue trash can in the corner, behind the table, the neck of a large brown plastic bottle sticking out of it. He goes over and lifts the bottle out, sees a number of others just like it inside. The name on the label: Old Jed's Kentucky Bourbon.

Without warning, Clay's hand begins to shake, then his whole body shivers and he drops the bottle to the floor as his stomach muscles violently contract, forcing him to bend forward at the waist. He groans in pain but is stopped short as his breath catches and his stomach cramps again. His knees buckle and he staggers against the flimsy table, which barely supports his weight. He lowers himself to the floor. Lies curled on his side, the linoleum cool against his cheek. Takes one ragged breath after another, grimacing at the stabbing, burning pain in his gut—something twisting in there, moving, eating away at his insides—for what feels like forever.

But slowly, eventually, the contractions lessen and Clay can feel the muscles all over his body finally begin to relax. He can breathe easier, and he fills his lungs again and again with much-needed air. Stretches out, at last, easing his legs straight. Gently rolls over onto his back, arms spread out to the sides. Lies there for a long, long while. Grateful the pain is gone. Hoping he never has to go through something like that again. Whatever the hell it was.

Gingerly, carefully, Clay gets to his knees. Stands. Goes to the sink to wet his mouth, splash his face repeatedly. Then leans there, dazed.

He finds a scrap of dish towel in one of the mostly empty drawers. Then, as an afterthought, opens one of the cabinets below. *Aha! There you are:* bottles and bottles of Old Jed's, three cabinets full, the last filled with big bottles of cola.

Shit . . . He's an alcoholic, Clay realizes with as much sadness as disgust. A freakin' drunk. Go figure.

He takes a last look around the two barren rooms. Then with a hand to his still-tender stomach, approaches the closed door at the end of the hall. And with more than a little trepidation, opens it.

The narrow room is the same size as the living room and kitchen put together and extends the entire width of the apartment. There's a cluttered desk and chair against the shorter wall on the left, a filing cabinet and curtained window on the right. But it's the long wall across from him that rivets his attention. The greatest part of which appears to be covered in newspaper clippings and other printed material. Photographs.

Clay steps warily into the room and closer to the wall, fairly certain that *this* is what he's come here to find.

In the middle of it all is a thinly framed piece—about two feet high and one-and-a-half feet wide—decorated with the same type of clippings as the rest of the wall, yellowed with age. Charlene's senior photo smiling at him from its center—the focal point of the entire display.

Framed with her are various articles relating to her disappearance and her body's discovery two years later. All of it incontrovertible proof against everything he's known—or thought he'd known—about what happened to her, up till this point.

As he runs his eyes over the articles, the memory of last night's dream comes back to him in full force . . . The surprise . . . the shock . . . the anger . . .

. . . the hatred . . . That's what he's been left with in this life, isn't it? Unrelenting hate.

It's clear to him because, in a glance, he's already seen the two-foot-high collection of articles and photos concerning the asshole running along the top of the wall. As with Charlene's, the asshole's color photo, from the investment company's brochure, is mounted prominently in the center.

Clay has to step close and crane his neck to read the cut-out newspaper articles immediately surrounding the asshole's face. He can see now that everything is pinned to a layer of cork board attached to the wall beneath.

Many of the articles have sections circled or underlined, which helps, and others are plainly obvious by their headlines. There's one from a local paper somewhere, announcing the asshole's graduation from Yale with a bachelor's degree in finance. Another touting his master's. A small article, printed from the Internet apparently, about the asshole being hired-on by an up-and-coming investment firm.

Clay takes his time perusing the history of his nemesis—the destroyer of his life, the haunter of his dreams—but keeps in mind that this is but one probable history, as he's come to understand it.

Moving to the right along the wall, it looks like the articles primarily concern the asshole's business career—his rise from financial consultant, to Chief Finance Officer, to CEO in 2020. There's the mention of a leave of absence in 2028—for personal reasons, is all it says. Then the herald of his return to the company in 2031. But little else of interest.

2031 . . . Wow . . . What year is this? Clay wonders. But judging by his ancient frame, it must be even many more years than that into the future.

The articles to the left of the asshole's picture run in the opposite direction and deal exclusively with his personal life, it seems. Immediately to the left is a marriage announcement—June 2012; no photo, but it names a Missy Friedlander, of the Boston Friedlanders, as the blushing bride; new money marrying old is the gist of the piece. Then, farther left . . . What's this? The asshole's suddenly one of New York City's most eligible bachelors. Well, that didn't last long, did it? Trouble in paradise, huh? . . . Then it looks like he got married again, in 2016—a photo of the bride this time, a pretty, young thing, Sharon (née Tisdale) her name.

Continuing left: A son is born a year later. Conrad Pierce. Then in 2019, a daughter, Bethany Anne. Here's a photo of them all together—Christmas 2022. How sweet, the perfect family unit . . . Then there's no further mention of his family. Only a large section of candid photos showing the asshole by himself in various places, various situations—all with various looks of distress blazoned across his face. Worry, anxiety, fear. A close-up of him yelling, mouth wide, spittle flying; dirt, sweat, and tears staining his stubbled cheeks; matted hair; a long scratch on his forehead.

It's an infatuation, Clay thinks, appalled. An obsession. It makes him sick that he would ever resort to something like this—ever think it. He's afraid to look at any more of the wall, the majority of which he hasn't seen, and which he has the feeling may be worse. But he has to see, of course; he has to face this, head on.

Directly below the asshole's collage, and to the left of Charlene's, is a section dedicated to a beautiful brunette, a one Missy Friedlander—there's her photo this time, in the center—who'd gone missing from her home in May of 2013, less than a year after her marriage to the asshole.

As in Charlene's case, there are plenty of accompanying articles about her disappearance, the ongoing investigation, and then the discovery of her body two years later, in November—raped and tortured, the medical examiner said, before finally being murdered.

Clay bypasses the next row down and moves to the right of Charlene's section. And in this two-by-three-foot area the focus is on a woman he already recognizes: the slender beauty in the asshole's wedding photo above, his second wife. Who, according to the articles, went missing, like the first, in May of 2023 . . . They'd been on vacation in Hawaii when she disappeared. Abducted for ransom was the initial fear. However, there had been no messages from any kidnappers; no news for two years. Until her body was found in an abandoned fishing boat near Hilo, on the coast of the Big Island. Her body raped and brutalized before she was finally killed, the report says. Her color photo, in the center of it all, shows a smiling woman in a flowing skirt and white blouse, a Hawaiian lei around her neck and hibiscus blossom in her hair, looking off-camera as she walks, holding hands with somebody out of the picture—the asshole, presumably.

I did this, Clay thinks, as the horror of it strikes him. *I mean, not* me . . . Not *him* him of course—he didn't do anything—but the crazy-bastard version of himself, whose body he now occupies. He has to close his eyes and support himself against the wall as a wave of nausea sweeps through him. Rest his hand against the pincushioned wall, ignoring the metal points beneath his skin. *Deep breaths, deep breaths,* Coach Adams would always say; and Clay takes that advice again now.

Eventually, he feels well enough to push himself off the wall. He opens his eyes but keeps them averted, not wanting to see any more of the damning evidence so proudly displayed. Shaken, he stumbles to the chair before the beat-up desk and sits down, hard. Lays his head facedown on his arms, on the littered desktop. And cries.

How could he have ever done such a thing as murder—torture!—an innocent person? How could he have let himself become so consumed with hate that he became the very thing he hated? How could he have ever justified this to himself, no matter how twisted his thinking? No matter how crazy he'd become?

But it worked, says a little voice—the Devil's advocate (perhaps the Devil himself)—inside his head. He can still see the many photos of the asshole's anguished face, and there comes the brief flutter of satisfaction along with the constant ache in his gut. *Now he knows how* I *felt,* Clay thinks, chiding himself for the thought even as he has it. *But I hurt him* twice *as bad.*

Twice . . .

Gathering his courage, Clay slides sideways off the chair and onto the floor. Then, on his hands and knees, begins slowly crawling toward the wall once again, forcing himself to move each arm, each leg—glancing up only once to see that he's on course to yet another section, at eye level now, covered with papers and pins.

He sits kneeling before it all, head bowed. *Deep breaths, deep breaths . . .* Then finally steels himself for what he knows he must do.

The center photo is of a young boy. A school picture, blown up to size. The same square jaw but otherwise angular features of his father; the same wry smile so full of confidence; the same wavy, light brown hair, parted on the left. The spitting image, as they say.

There are several other photos, at various ages, taken informally, outside, almost all showing the boy wearing his school uniform of dark pants, white oxford shirt, and green-and-red-checkered tie.

And the articles surrounding them are exactly what Clay had feared: News of the ten-year-old boy's disappearance in 2028; the search; the questioning; in the end presumed dead. Then the final article, dated November 2030: the boy's body found in the middle of the school's soccer field, dressed as the day he vanished, but horribly mutilated.

Clay has to swallow the bile that's risen in his throat as he finishes reading. He'd cry but his tears have been spent. He can only hang his head, occasionally shaking it in disbelief, as he supports himself with one hand on the wall.

A shudder runs through him, and his hands begin to shake; his whole upper body. His fingers clench and papers crumple in his fist. He drags it down the wall.

I did not do this! he cries out in his mind. *I could never have done this!*

An innocent boy . . .

He becomes filled with a sudden rage—toward himself, toward the vile creature he's become—and reaches up with his other hand to claw at the wall; then with both hands, now, scattering scraps of paper and pins in every direction.

On his knees, still too unsure of himself to stand, shaking like a leaf, he moves to the right, ripping, shredding, determined to destroy as much of the abomination before him as he can.

But then stops as quickly as he began, clutching a torn photograph in his trembling hands. It's of a young girl this time—adorable, maybe eight or nine years old—at the beach, running gleefully from the waves.

Nooo! Clay looks with dread but there are only photos mounted here, no articles.

Not yet . . .

Again the pictures are of various ages. The youngest, it seems, he holds in his hands; the oldest farthest right, where he scoots over; where the image is of a tall, painfully thin young woman carrying a purse over her shoulder, a thoughtful frown, as she walks past a shop somewhere . . . And there *is* an article, but pinned beneath the photo.

Clay rips them both free.

An Internet article. "Sacred Heart Seniors to Visit Museum of Natural History" is the headline. Wednesday, May 20th, is the date underlined. Clay can only assume that day hasn't arrived.

Shakily, he stands, using the wall for support. Rakes a swath through more clippings, in disgust, as he stumbles to the desk. The calendar hanging there shows a tranquil nature scene over the month of May 2037. On various days are written notes in his own cramped hand. On Tuesday, the 19th, it says only "SET UP" in black marker. The 20th is *X*ed and circled over and over in red. But it doesn't tell him what day it is today—how close he's come.

Then he remembers the pill dispenser—*Wednesday*—and relief floods through him.

Still, though, he has to make sure. Do whatever he can to stop it, if it's not too late. He hasn't seen a phone, or computer, anywhere, so far, so he'll check the bedroom, the only place he hasn't looked.

But he has to stop in the open doorway to the hall as the first pangs hit him. *Oh, no . . . No! . . .* He grips the wooden frame with one hand, wipes the sudden sweat from his brow. Waits. Takes a tentative step. Watches as a tremor travels from his foot to his hip. And then he's suddenly doubled over in excruciating pain, once again, just as earlier, but worse this time—much worse—if that can even be possible. Like a seizure but located solely in his gut, his bowels, the very core of his being. He stifles a cry as his muscles cramp and he collapses in a heap to the floor. Curls up around the pain. Takes a shuddering breath. Moans, cries out, screams silently as the next wave hits, so much worse than anything before.

I'm sorry, he thinks. "I'm sorry," he pleads. "So sorry . . . so sorry . . .

"Aaargh!"

AAAHH. HE TAKES a sip and sets the glass down beside him. Feels the soothing fire coat his insides.

He'd finally found the phone, cleverly disguised as a TV remote control, on the seat of the recliner in the living room. The device acts as both, he discovered after many tries. So now he sits comfortably reclined in the decrepit chair well-formed to his decrepit body, while he surfs the Web on the television-slash-computer monitor—the most mind-blowing, bizarre, lightning-fast version of the Internet he's ever seen.

A tall whiskey-and-coke sits close at hand in the drink holder in the arm of the chair. It's his third but he intends to make this one last, to drink as little as necessary. And it is *necessary,* unfortunately. Because although his mind—his current mind—may not crave alcohol, his body most certainly does, and is dependent upon it to function properly—to function at all. Without those first swigs of Old Jed's, earlier, curled up on the kitchen floor, Clay thinks he would have died, eventually, with nobody to take him to the hospital.

The front door to his left is ajar, letting in some of the cool evening air and the foreign smells of his neighbor's cooking. The scrawny gray stray is contentedly eating from one of the cans of tuna Clay had set out for it hours ago, only recently bold enough to come inside.

On the large flat-screen in front of him, at the foot of the recliner, is the website for Fresh Start, a semi-local drug-and-alcohol rehabilitation clinic. Clay has no idea if he can afford it, or not, but the place offers a free four-month stay to those who volunteer to participate in experimental research trials using "all-natural" medications. He clicks SEND, submitting his application.

He's made the first move. Now it's up to this life's usual version to follow through. Hopefully his actions today have helped.

Earlier, he'd sent a copy of a carefully worded e-mail to this and every other alcohol treatment center in a hundred-mile radius, as located for him by Google Maps. Fresh Start has been the first to respond.

All but three of the Old Jed's have been poured down the drain. Their empty bottles already in the recycling bin in the alley out back.

And beside them, in the dumpster, are the remains of his former "wall of hate." He's thrown away everything having anything even remotely to do with his nefarious "project," including the calendar and pretty much every scrap of paper he'd found on the desk and in the filing cabinet. And especially the blue backpack, with its bottle of chloroform, syringes, and duct tape, among the other things he'd found in his car—an ancient station wagon which had dutifully beeped in response to the button on his keychain.

Now, with his many digital cries for help sent, his first official application for rehab completed, Clay, satisfied, pushes himself up from the chair. Takes his drink with him as he heads to the john.

But outside the bathroom door he pauses, then continues past. And in the doorway to his new office, reads again the words written large, now, in black and red marker across the opposite wall:

LET—IT—GO!

He raises his drink in toast before turning out the light.

Ouch! Ooof!

He can almost feel the give in the car door as his head and shoulder slam into it. Almost taste the dust and gravel beneath his cheek. Almost hear his ribs crack as first one boot then another lifts him up off the ground.

Cursing. Laughter. Different voices, which fade.

He tries to get up, but . . . Ow! He'll just wait here awhile before he tries again.

Flash

He's walking past cars and trucks to the club's entrance. His third this night. Blinking pink-and-blue neon, dancing beer bottles and cowboy hats, a twirling lasso.

Inside, it's easy to spot his target: the biggest guy in the place.

It's always the biggest guy.

Flash

The satisfying crunch of cartilage and bone beneath his fists. The snap of a knee bent sideways. The crack of an elbow folded back too far. The sight of blood spraying, flecking his face, drooling from the asshole's mouth as he pleads, No more, no more.

The world is just full of assholes, he's found. They're in every town, every state. Pretty boys with the girls on their arms. Rich kids with Daddy's credit cards and a flashy yellow car. Too-smart college pricks with the world at their feet, their noses held high. All of them with something he'll never have again:

Happiness—the life he was meant to live.

Assholes, all of them.

And himself the biggest one.

★ ✳ ✱ ✳ ★

CLAY WAKES to the sound of cartoon noises. BYOING! PFFL-LIIPPFFT! ZAAP! BWOWOWOW! He tries covering his head with a pillow but it's no use. He rolls over to see a wiry guy with blotchy red skin and a bright blue mohawk sitting shirtless in a pair of surfer trunks at the end of a twin bed separated only a few feet from Clay's own. The guy sits slouched, face glued to the screen, his right leg jackhammering nervously as he watches big-eyed, battling anime figures duke it out amid a riot of flashing lights and swirling colors, zany sounds, on the TV across from him.

Ah, shit. Clay rolls onto his back. Covers his eyes with the heels of his hands. *Not again.*

He lies there for a while, still shaken from the night's violent dreams. It had seemed so real. Not just all the fighting itself but the emotions—the rage and frustration, the self-loathing. He'd felt driven by something he couldn't control. Possessed. He's glad he's woken up, finally.

He sits up and scoots back against the headboard. Takes a look at his new surroundings.

It's a cheap hotel room but many steps above the one he'd first found himself in ten days ago. His bed is the one farthest from the door and, presumably, the bathroom. On the floor, between the bed and the wall, is a dark blue gym bag and, beside it, a pile of clothes. On top of the clothes a bulky black watch and mobile phone.

Clay reaches down and picks up the phone. He can already tell he's much further back in time than yesterday just by the looks of it, the older style.

Another instant giveaway is his body. He's young again (thank God!) and his arms and chest are strong—ripped, even. Chiseled. There's a kind of cool black tribal tattoo flowing across his chest and shoulders. He flexes and moves his arms, reveling in the feel of his muscles rolling beneath his skin, each one defined. Runs a hand over his rock-hard stomach and doubts there's even an ounce of fat there. Stretches his legs beneath the covers and can tell they're as powerful as when he played ball, if not more so.

He smiles happily to himself. This won't be nearly as difficult a life to live as yesterday. *Bring it on,* he thinks.

The phone shares his optimistic view with a cheerful tone as it powers on. No password required.

"Hey. 'Bout time you got up." His roommate has turned sideways to look at him. The guy's mohawk has a shock of purple in front; and his face is a mess. Scarred. His nose looks like a crooked set of steps, and he's clearly missing some teeth. His eyes are wild, bulging in his skull. "Let's get some breakfast," he says in a warbly voice. "I'm starved." Then it's back to the cartoon.

Clay definitely doesn't feel like hanging out with this character all day. He taps the phone's screen and is soon accessing the Net.

He knows that the asshole figures into this life, too, somehow, that he's probably here to kill him again. But he's not going to do it. Something happened to him yesterday that started the day before, after talking to Reverend Z: It felt good to let it go, to get past all the anger and hatred he'd felt, that he'd been harboring for so long, in so many other lives. For the first time, yesterday, he'd felt like he was growing instead of stagnating, moving on with his life. It's just too bad that it was at the *end* of that one.

He's sure now that his visiting all of these different "probable" lives has to do somehow with his being able to forgive the asshole for what he did to Charlene—getting over it—learning how his quest for vengeance has only messed *himself* up, instead. And when he thinks back, he can see now that many times since this started he'd been put in a position where he'd had to make that choice: to forgive or to hate. And he'd hated, for sure. He's here today, he thinks, because, if last night's dreams are any measure, he still needs to purge himself of such violent thoughts. He's obviously still got a lot to learn.

If he can make a difference today, that's great, he will; but more than anything else right now, Clay wants to share his ideas—his theory—with the only other person who understands what he's going through. Or will. Hopefully.

A search for Dzhelikhovsky puts him at Princeton again, not the church in Ithaca, which at first is a bit of a disappointment (the reverend had been Clay's favorite version, so far), until he sees that Dr. Z is listed as the head of the Parapsychology Department, the same place Clay had been on his first visit to the university. So this should be the same guy Professor Price had originally referred him to, he thinks. It feels like he's come full circle.

There's just one thing he needs to know. He crosses his fingers.

"Hey," he says to Mohawk, who merely cocks an ear in his direction. "Uh . . . Where are we?"

The guy looks back, his leg still bouncing, and sees the phone in Clay's hand. "About 10th and West 17th Street," he says. "The Meatpacking District, I think they call it." His expression turns eager. "Why? You looking for somewhere to eat? Let's try that place O'Brien was talking about, with the twelve-egg omelets and all-you-can-eat pancakes. He said they've even got sundaes! And banana splits! For breakfast!" He smiles big, revealing a shiny gold tooth amid the ones that remain.

"Uh, so, New York?"

"Huh?"

"Are we in New York? The city?"

The guy just goggles at him, bug-eyed. "Wow, man, you've been hit in the head one too many times." He laughs. Turns back to the TV, shaking his head. "Are we in New York City. Ha! That's a good one."

Clay tosses back the covers. He'll take that as a yes, for now.

Standing in the narrow gap between the bed and the wall, he picks up the mound of clothes on the floor and sets it on the mattress. The watch says that it's a little after eight o'clock; Clay's going to guess it's morning. There's a light gray T-shirt, a dark green V-neck sweater, and a pair of faded jeans with a brown leather belt and tears at the knees.

"Oh!" Mohawk's looking his way, his leg moving faster, if that's even possible. "Lonnie said to meet him at five instead of three-thirty. He's gonna wait till the last minute to place the bets." He laughs. "The Greek's giving better odds than Vegas. Right now he's got you at five-to-one. Ha!" He goes back to his show.

Clay puts on the jeans, tosses the gym bag on the mattress. Finds a pair of street hikers with thick socks laid over the top, at the foot of the bed.

He's pulling on the sweater when Mohawk says, "Hey, Clay . . . You're not really going to meet Gambarelli today, are you?" He has a sort of guilty look on his face. "I know I'm not supposed to know, or anything, but . . . I heard you talking on the phone last night . . . Sorry."

Clay, of course, has no idea what to say to this. So he just shrugs. "That's okay. Don't worry about it." He sits on the edge of the bed to put on the socks and shoes.

"So . . . are you?" The guy's sitting still for the first time this morning.

"Am I what?"

"Going to meet him?"

"Who?"

"Gambarelli."

"Uh . . . Should I?"

"Hell no!" Mohawk throws up his hands. "O'Brien told me all about that guy. I know what he does. He's no good, man. He'll just get you in trouble, I promise you. I'd stay as far away from that piece of shit as possible. Especially today."

"Allrighty, then." Clay finishes tying his last shoe, and stands. "Gotta go." He grabs the phone and slips it into his back pocket, hefts the gym bag, which he's going to assume is his, too.

"*What?*" Mohawk gets up, himself. He's tall, taller than Clay, all arms and legs and ropey muscle. "What about breakfast? Where are you going?" He holds out a hand to stop Clay as he approaches. "You don't wanna do business with that grease ball, I'm telling you, man."

Clay tries to smile reassuringly. "Don't worry, that's not where I'm headed. I just gotta go talk to a guy, that's all."

Mohawk looks at him skeptically. "What? Who? . . . About the fight?" He goes over to the opposite side of his bed and bends down, comes up with a red T-shirt. "I'll come with you. We can eat after, or on the way."

Clay walks by him and drops his bag in front of an open closet space beside the bathroom door. Sees two jackets hanging there. A bigger, silver-and-blue gym bag on the floor.

"No, I gotta go to Princeton," he says, entering the bathroom. "By myself."

"Princeton? Who the fuck you know in Princeton?" Mohawk's standing in the doorway, a pair of high-top sneakers in his hands. "You mean the university? Where Einstein went?"

But Clay barely registers what the guy has said. He stands stunned before his reflection in the mirror. His once-good-looking face is a wreck. Like his buddy here, his nose has a permanent set of bends to it now, a knobby bump it's never had, on top. There's another, bigger bump on the side of one temple and a slight dent in the other. Pale lines of scars below both his eyes and on his cheekbones, his forehead, cutting through his eyebrows and across his chin, leaving bald stripes wherever there should be hair, including a few curving streaks on his scalp—at least the ones that he can see.

Oh, man . . . This is bad . . . It looks like he's been through a meat grinder. Or been dragged behind a truck for ten miles. Or fallen down one heck of a tall, jagged mountain.

He reaches up and fingers a shadowy crevice along his jaw line. Realizes Mohawk is speaking to him again.

"Huh? What's that?"

"Dude, you're acting weird. What time are you getting back? Princeton's gotta be, like, miles away. What are you doing, taking a taxi, or a bus?"

Clay snaps to as he remembers. "Oh. Uh, yeah . . . a bus." He looks to his watch. Bends to the sink to splash some water on his face. With all the damage to it, he almost expects it to hurt.

"What about your routine?" Mohawk's saying. "A steam. The video. Psyching yourself up. I thought we were gonna do it together; watch it at the Garden; hang out there all day, until it's time."

The cold water is invigorating and helps Clay to wake up. He reaches for a towel on the counter. "Sorry, man. But this is really important."

Mohawk just gawks at him. "Like tonight's not important?" He steps back to let Clay out of the bathroom. Gestures wildly with the shoes in his hands. "Like it's not the most important night of your career? Your *life?*"

Clay stops. "What do you mean?"

"What do you mean, what do I mean? I'd give anything to be where you're at. A thousand guys would. It's the fucking *title*, man. What could be more important than that?"

The title?

Mohawk tosses his shoes onto the floor in front of the television and goes over and plops back down on the bed. Looks over petulantly. "All I'm saying is, I don't see any point in fucking up a good routine, that's all. I don't know why you'd even think about it . . . And I'm pissed, too. Why didn't you tell me you were gonna be taking off?"

Clay thinks fast; he doesn't want to damage whatever relationship this version of himself has with this guy. "Uh . . . It just came up." He takes the phone from his back pocket and holds it up, as if he'd just gotten a message this morning.

"Oh . . ." Mohawk's expression softens. "My bad . . . What is it? Bad news or something?"

Clay slips the phone back into his pocket. "No, not really. Just a personal problem. It's kinda got me screwed up in the head, though." He shrugs. "I'm hoping this guy can help me."

"You gotta do it *today?*"

A thin smile. A nod.

Mohawk looks a little embarrassed. "Oh . . . Well . . . All right. If you need any help, you just let me know, okay?" He busies himself with his sneakers, slipping them on without socks. "You sure you don't wanna get some breakfast first, before you go?"

Clay reaches into the closet and takes out the only jacket that could be his—the one without all the metal loops and studs and zippers—a dark brown suede, and puts it on. "No, I better get going. Try to catch this guy before it gets too late." He picks up his bag and heads to the door, glad to be finally leaving. "See you later."

He's halfway down the hall when Mohawk steps out, calling after him. "Don't forget!" he hollers. "Five o'clock. Don't be late."

Clay holds up a backward hand in a wave as he goes. Then stops and turns. "Where?"

"Huh? What?"

"At five. Where am I supposed to be?"

"What?" Mohawk just stands there. His bug eyes blink. "Are you serious?"

Clay just shrugs. Waits for an answer.

"Oh, fuck. You really are screwed up today, aren't you?" He laughs. "The Garden, man . . . Fucking Madison Square Garden."

IT'S THE SAME bus that dropped him off at Palmer Square, a week ago. And it's the same set of buildings he visited when he first came to the university's campus. The same room. The same sign outside the door—PYCHOPHYSICAL RESEARCH LABORATORY—only partially covered with a taped-up piece of paper with the words "OBE

CENTER" written in marker. Somebody's also added a swirling spiral design with stars all around it, for a background.

The reception area's about the same as before, but there's nobody to meet him. He listens closely and can hear that same soft, trippy music he'd liked so much before.

He takes a quick walk around, glancing at all the artwork, the bookshelves, and the same large map of South America on the wall. Then cautiously enters the dimly lit hallway at the far end of the room.

After a few paces the left wall becomes mostly glass, and Clay can see into a large white space, also dimly lit, on the other side. In it, in a row, side-by-side, are half a dozen large, white, egg-shaped contraptions, maybe seven or eight feet long and four feet wide, four feet tall. "Pods" is the word that comes to mind. Looking closely, he can see a number of hoses and cables attached to each one, at the sides and underneath, running to a wall of white cabinets and machinery at the back of the room. Everything in the room is white.

"Hi there, can I help you?"

Clay turns with a start to see Rebecca standing in the hall. She has on a long white lab coat, like doctors wear, open in front, over a pair of slacks and a brightly colored sweater. Her hair is the same blazing red but piled conservatively on top, a few curling wisps framing her face.

"Oh, hi! Uh . . . Is Dr. Z around?"

Rebecca smiles and nods to the wall opposite the pods, to a long, darkly tinted window there. "He's in the booth. 'Bout halfway through a session," she says, pulling back the sleeve of her coat to check her watch. "He should be done in about an hour or so." She openly studies his face. "Are you a new student here?"

Clay lifts his hands off the gym bag slung across his chest, in a shrug. "No, but he's sorta been helping me with a problem I've been having lately. I'm hoping I can talk to him again, today, if that's okay."

Rebecca's smile grows. "Of course. I'm just surprised I haven't seen you before." She steps forward and holds out her hand. "I'm Rebecca. Dr. Z's research assistant."

"Hi, I'm Clay." He has to stop himself from mentioning they've met before.

"Well, you're welcome to wait in here if you'd like," motioning to the doorway she just exited. "Are you thinking about becoming an explorer?"

Clay follows her into a short entryway. "Huh? Explorer?"

To the right is a glass door leading into a darkened room, where Clay catches a glimpse of glowing computer monitors and blinking lights. To the left Rebecca enters a cozy living room of sorts, with a couch and coffee table, a couple of cushy chairs, an overflowing bookcase, and a round wooden table with chairs beside a long window looking out across the hall, to the pods.

Rebecca motions to the glass. "Are you familiar with what we do here?"

"No, uh, well . . . it's parapsychology, right?"

Rebecca smiles and moves to the far wall in the corner, behind the table. "Yes, in a general sense, that's right. Here, let me show you." She points to a large poster—a schematic with diagrams and pictures—as Clay walks up. "Currently, we're using sensory deprivation chambers to induce out-of-body experiences, in the hope of demonstrating how conscious-ness can act independently from the brain." She points to a cross-sectional drawing of one of the pods. "Participants float in a skin-temperature solution of water and Epsom salts, at a specific gravity that won't let them sink, so it feels as if they're actually floating in space, after a while." She points again, to another drawing. "The tanks are lightproof, soundproof, and even smellproof, so the only stimulus participants experience, so to speak, are their minds."

Clay looks out the window, amazed. "You mean, there's *people* in there?"

Rebecca gives a delightful laugh. "Yep. Those are our current explorers."

"What do you mean."

"Well, that's what we call them. They're *psychic* explorers, essentially, traveling outside their physical bodies. Or, hopefully, I should say; it depends on how successful they are, sometimes, although these six are pretty well-practiced at it by now. They're the best group we've had in a while."

Clay has to process this. He looks from Rebecca to the poster to the pods, then back again, a few times. "So, they're . . ."

"Well, right now they're probably conducting experiments. Or"—pointing to the doorway they just entered—"following Dr. Z's instructions to reach other levels of consciousness. It depends." She laughs and indicates one of the pods, at the end. "However, Bailey tends to go wherever he wants to go. He's fascinated with the Moon, right now. 'Gathering evidence,' he says. Ha!" Her eyes twinkle.

"The moon? Experiments?" As hard as it is to believe what she's saying, Clay wants to understand.

"Yes, well, the experiments are pretty varied, but they're all designed to prove that consciousness can act physically separate from the brain." Rebecca points to the tall bookcase across the room. "One example—one of the easier tests; one of my own—is the color photo I place up there, facing the ceiling, before every session, but *after* the participants enter the chambers, so only I know what the photo's a picture of, right? But afterward, about four out of five times, they can tell me exactly what it is. It's the first place they usually go, as a starting point." She sweeps her arm in an expansive gesture. "But there are other things hidden all over the campus—things that even we don't know about—Dr. Z and I, I mean. Totally random targets for each day, chosen by computer. These are double- and even triple-blind studies, so we won't know the official outcome till the end of the project. But from what they tell me"—motioning to the pods—"they're all describing the same things."

Clay can only scratch his head, incredulous. "Wow."

Rebecca laughs. "Yeah. Wow." She looks again to her watch. "Here, come on, I'll give you a little peek at the booth."

She leads him to the glass door, just outside. Puts a finger to her lips as she enters the darkened room.

Inside, Dr. Z is sitting before a bank of monitors amid a host of other high-tech equipment. He's at a long desk, with a tall skinny microphone directly in front of him. He's gained back his weight plus a little more. "Good," he's saying. "Now, record those images, and let's move on to the next place we need to visit."

There are six monitors—three over three—each showing a person's face bathed in a bright green tint. Both young men and women. All with their eyes closed, as if asleep. Surrounding each of their partially submerged heads is a sparkling, subtly undulating sea of stars.

"The coordinates are 33.581206 degrees north by 69.974825 degrees east . . . The date is August 7th, 2012 . . . The time is oh-four-hundred UTC."

Standing at the back of the small space, looking over Dzhelikhovsky's shoulder, Clay watches the faces on the screens. One guy's eyeballs are moving rapidly behind his lids, while the others' remain completely still.

Rebecca tugs at his arm.

Outside, with the door firmly closed, she says, "Oops. Probably shouldn't have had you in there for that one." She shrugs light-heartedly as they return to the other room. "The military's been showing a lot of interest lately."

She plops down on the couch and waves Clay to any of the chairs beside her. Begins collecting and stacking some of the papers on the coffee table.

But Clay goes to look at the pods again, through the window. "I can't believe they're actually leaving their bodies," he says. "That is so cool." He wonders what it's like.

"Well, so do you," Rebecca says. "Every time you sleep."

Clay turns. "Huh? What do you mean?"

Rebecca laughs. "During sleep your consciousness leaves your body often. Haven't you ever felt yourself flying before, in your dreams?"

"Well, yeah, of course," Clay replies. "But those were just dreams." He picks the big blue chair to sit in, across from her. "Everybody has those flying dreams once in a while."

"'Just' dreams, huh?" Rebecca settles back with her arms laid over the back of the couch. "If you ask me, dreams are just as real as the waking world—they just don't adhere to the same laws."

Clay can't help but think of the sordid dreams he's been having lately, and he has to disagree. They're so screwed up, they can't be real.

Rebecca says, "Have you ever wondered why a third of your life, give or take, is spent asleep, dreaming? It's because it's so important—necessary, even—to our existence." She sits forward intently now and her hands go into motion. "First, while dreaming, your body performs many functions that are impossible for it during waking hours. In fact, the greatest biological activity takes place while you sleep, and certain cellular functions are accelerated. *Healings*," she emphasizes, "can take place in the dream state. Have you ever heard sleep called 'the gentle nurse'?"

Clay shakes his head. If he has, he can't remember.

"Also, think about this," Rebecca continues. "All animals dream. All consciousnesses dream . . . Why is that?"

Clay can only shrug.

"Because it's essential! Not only for our bodies, but for our minds. Our *lives*." She sits back and crosses her legs, obviously enjoying the discussion. "You see, your consciousness doesn't shut itself off or refresh itself during sleep, as most people think. You're just as 'awake' but your awareness is focused in a different direction, toward the dream state—toward other dimensions, other levels of reality."

She flashes that beautiful smile. "You see, in the dream state, or whenever you're out-of-body, your consciousness sort of 'unlocks' itself for a while from its usual coordinates—from the physical plane—and is able to travel faster than light—often *instantaneously*—simply by putting itself in a different relationship with time and space." She holds up two slender fingers, one on each hand. "However, although your consciousness can do this, your brain, of course, can't. Your physical, neurologically structured patterns within it can't capture the perceptions. That's why a lot of people can't remember their dreams, or can't understand much of what they do recall." She gives a slight shrug with her hands. "So, usually, our waking consciousness has to come up with metaphors and symbols and archetypes and such, in order to glean some kind of meaning from them."

Rebecca holds up only one finger this time. "However, that doesn't have to be the case . . ." She smiles slyly. "It's totally possible to remember your dreams and travels outside the body and bring that information back with you: by bringing a portion of your waking consciousness along for the ride, so to speak, in order to comprehend and 'translate' your experience when you get back . . . Plus," she adds, stressing the finger, "with the right intent, it's possible to direct and *control* the entire experience." She gives him a huge grin. "Everyone dreams. Some people are just more active participants. Once you learn how to remain as awake and aware in the dream state as the waking one . . ." She spreads her hands wide. "There's no going back."

Clay says, exasperated, "But why are dreams so weird all the time? They don't make any sense."

Rebecca just smiles. "All dreams are meant for your benefit in some way. They just have to be interpreted correctly. Ask yourself: What is the message?" She holds up another finger. "But, first, you have to change your ideas about dreaming before you can begin to understand them and explore them. Otherwise, your prejudices and preconceptions will simply close the door."

Clay considers this a moment. Says, "My dreams, I think, might be a part of why I need to talk to Dr. Z. But I don't think I've been traveling, or anything like that. I think my dreams are memories. Those are the only kind I've been having lately. But . . . they're all messed up, so they can't be real."

Rebecca looks interested. "What do you mean by 'messed up'?"

"Well, they're all memories of the same night—or a*bout* that night—but totally different, with different things happening each time . . . They don't make any sense."

"Hmmm . . ." Rebecca puts a pondering hand to her chin. "Have you ever considered that they may be other levels of reality, other timelines?"

Now it's Clay's turn to laugh. "You sound just like Dr. Z. He says it's all about probable realities and probable lives and stuff, and that there's, like, an infinite number of them, according to the choices we make."

"Yes, well, there must be some truth to that, because many people have encountered other selves and other realities in their dreams. Past lives, for instance, are very common. Plus, many people are able to see into the future; this happens a lot, too."

Clay experiences a burst of hope. "Really? So I'm not totally crazy, then?"

But does that mean I'm dreaming now? he wonders.

Rebecca shakes her head with a smile. "No, you're not crazy. There's actually a constant communication between other levels of reality and our dream states—a constant interaction, even." She leans forward and places her elbows on her knees, hands clasped. "You see, dreams are as much *psychic* as they are psychological, if not more so. During sleep, you process your daily life, then project it into what you *think of* as the future. Then, in the dream state, you 'sample,' then choose from all of the possibilities, in order to create your own experience." She turns up her palms. "So, basically, everything is first dreamt before it becomes a reality."

Clay just stares, thinking of the implications . . . "My dreams create my reality . . ."

"Well, your *thoughts*, really, but, yep. The world is as we dream it, as they say."

So, if I can somehow change my dreams . . .

"Your present forms your future, of course," Rebecca goes on cheerfully, "just like your today forms your tomorrow. But, in deeper terms, your *precognitive awareness* of your own possibilities *from the future* helps to form the present that will then make that possible future your reality." She laughs, clearly pleased with her explanation. "You see? This way, your *future* creates your *present*. In dreams, you're acquainted with unlimited possible futures, from which you then choose—and for which you're *right now* setting the groundworks." Her face beams as she leans back and lays her arms again over the back of the couch. "So, in a very real sense, you're always living the future *now*."

Crazier and crazier, Clay thinks as he nods automatically. He knows he's just learned something important but can't figure out exactly what that is, just yet, or how to apply it to his situation.

If there was just a way I could relive my past . . .

"So, do you still think they're 'just' dreams?" Rebecca asks him. "Can you see how important the dream state is, now—the out-of-body state—and why it's so important to study both?"

Clay nods his agreement. "Yeah. I had no idea." Though he still barely understands half of what she said. "I can see why you're so into it."

He glances around the small room. Hesitates only a moment. "And I can see why you gave me one of those," he says, pointing to the wall beside the bookcase.

Rebecca follows his finger, then back. "Huh?"

Clay shrugs and smiles sheepishly. "Yeah, well, we've kinda met once, before."

"We have?"

"Yeah." He points again. "And you gave me one of those, but smaller."

She leans forward to get a better look. "I gave you a dream-catcher?"

ACROSS THE WAY, through the window, Rebecca is helping the last of the "explorers" from their pods, removing the various patches with wires connected to their heads and chests, and sitting with them as they come fully awake. The little "wing" attached to the side of each pod, Clay can see now, is actually a seat. Four of the six people have already exited through a door in the back wall, to the locker rooms and shower areas. Only one explorer—the one on the far right—remains in his pod; for "extracurricular" research, according to Dr. Z.

The young man's serene, green-tinted face is displayed on the only monitor still on in the now-lit control room as Dzhelikhovsky makes some adjustments to a control panel beside the screen.

"You don't look too surprised," says Clay.

Dzhelikhovsky spins in his seat to look at him. "The idea of exploring other realities—be they probable or not—doesn't surprise me in the least, as I've experienced them myself." He smiles thinly and stands. Crosses over to the coffee machine for a refill. "What does surprise me, however, is your method of doing so. Usually, people simply teleport their awareness between points—using their minds as a vehicle, rather than a physical body." He turns and leans back against the counter, the mug steaming in his hands. Takes a tentative sip. Gestures languidly. "Which also leads me to wonder: Whatever happened to the 'you' who normally occupies this body?"

Clay turns out his hands with a shrug. "I don't know. I've kinda wondered the same thing, myself. Maybe we switched places, or something."

Dzhelikhovsky scrunches his brow. "Also, your lack of intent—the fact that your visit is unintentional—is what surprises me the most." He blows on his coffee, takes another careful sip. "As long as there is a unique and specific destination held in mind, one can navigate anywhere—to any dimension, reality, place, person, or thing—by simply directing their mental energy, with focused intent. However, that clear and complete *intent* is critical to the process. Always." He blows, sips, scrunches. Pulls at his beard. "Plus, there's the issue of you staying on for a full day at a time . . . and experiencing only that one day . . ."

"And my memory," Clay reminds him. "I can't remember anything about any of the lives I end up in."

Dzhelikhovsky nods absently. Looks up, after a moment. "You say you wake up like this each day. So the transition, obviously, is occurring while you sleep, in the dream state, while out-of-body more than likely." He shakes his head and frowns, pondering. "I've never heard of such a thing happening before, but . . . given the number of multiple realities, and given that similar reality branches could be almost identical in certain areas . . ." He shrugs, raising the cup to his lips. "Perhaps you're lost."

Clay hadn't thought of that. It's as good an idea as any, he supposes.

"All right. Well, uh . . . how do I get *un*-lost, do you think?"

Dzhelikhovsky makes a face to say, *I have no idea*. Then it appears that he's about to speak, when something must occur to him and he stares at Clay for an uncomfortably long moment.

"Come with me," he says, finally.

Dzhelikhovsky leads him from the control room and to the right, to another door—this one with a high-tech security panel beside it. Dr. Z places a card in a slot and enters a lengthy pass code, and when the door clicks open, they enter.

Whoa! Now this *is a laboratory,* Clay thinks.

The large room is crowded with long metal tables covered with exotic, space-age-looking machinery and equipment, complicated spirals of clear and copper tubing and multicolored wires connecting various peculiar apparatuses, just waiting for the bolt of lightning that will set them all into motion. Far to the left stands a gigantic, floor-to-ceiling copper vat, more befitting a distillery than anywhere else. Cabinets and carts and tall stands on wheels vie for space within the criss-crossing maze between the tables.

"You know that I went to Peru as a grad student," Dzhelik-hovsky says over his shoulder as they make their way slowly through the clutter. "But did I ever tell you why?"

Clay recalls his conversation with Reverend Z beside the pond. "Yeah, it was only, like, two days ago. You said you went to study the natives there, in the jungle, by some river, who knew all sorts of stuff about space and things they shouldn't have, without telescopes and all that. Planets and moons and rings. Black holes—no, *worm* holes. Even other dimensions, I think. You said you did some kind of religious ceremony, or something, with the elders, where you drank some kind of brew." Clay tries hard to remember the rest of it. "You didn't really say, but I think that's how they did all that stuff they said they could."

Dzhelikhovsky has stopped and turned and stands looking at him with an inscrutable expression.

"What?" Clay asks, after a few seconds.

"Nothing, nothing." Dr. Z turns back. "I just find this absolutely amazing, is all." Then after a moment walking: "So, did I describe the effects of this brew we drank? Or exactly what it was?"

Clay is eyeing a spiraling, corkscrewing clear tube of bubbling amber liquid within a contraption upon the table beside him, which, after passing through a complex series of other tubes and glass cylinders filled with shiny black marble-looking things, ultimately drips pale yellow into a tiny clear flask.

"Not really," he says without thinking. "Just that you died."

Dzhelikhovsky stops so suddenly Clay almost bumps into him. "What?" His eyes are huge behind the thick lenses of his glasses. "I *died?*"

Clay backs up a step, stammering. "Yeah, well, uh, you did, but, uh—it wasn't permanent, or anything. You said you went to Heaven and, uh . . . It's the reason you became a priest—or, a minister, I mean." He takes in Dr. Z's shocked expression. "In *that* life," he adds.

At last Dzhelikhovsky just shakes his head. "Absolutely amazing," is all he says.

At the end of the long room, two things immediately stand out: to the left, an expansive glassed-in enclosure filled with thick green plants partially obscured within a steamy mist; and on the right, another one of those big white pod contraptions. Between these is a wide desk with a single computer monitor and microphone, four high-backed cushioned chairs, and a set of tall wooden cabinets and a refrigerator against the wall. Around the space a number of lab tables covered with the usual curious paraphernalia.

Dzhelikhovsky motions Clay to a chair as he occupies himself at the desk for a moment, takes a large swig of his coffee and sets it down. Then heads over to the greenhouse, beside him. "I'll be right back."

Instead of sitting, Clay inspects a nearby table. On top of which are at least a dozen identical metal bowls, each filled with a course, dull-colored powder. Not one, he notices, is labeled. He runs a finger through a flaky, reddish-brown substance and takes a pinch and smells it. Sneezes.

On the shelf below are many wooden boxes—crates—labeled as various roots and barks, in English and what looks like Spanish, and covered in intricate shipping stamps and seals. He sees one from Ecuador, from Bolivia. Brazil. He sees one with an unmistakable skull-and-crossbones symbol.

"This," says Dzhelikhovsky grandly as he exits the greenhouse, his shirt slightly damp and clinging, "is *Chacruna,* or *Psychotria viridis*—one part of the reason I first went to Peru and continue to go, now, every few years." He's waving a fat, emerald-green leaf. "It contains extraordinary amounts of DMT—dimethyltryptamine— which is considered the most potent psychedelic on earth." He holds up, in his other hand, a short length of something dark green and finger-thick. "And this is *Banisteriopsis caapi*, which is unique in containing a number of different alkaloids that help DMT diffuse past membranes in the stomach and small intestines and cross the blood-brain barrier, to activate certain receptor sites in the brain." He chuckles, eyes beaming, sans glasses, which are in the man's shirt pocket. "Thousands of years ago, South American Indians discovered the combination and eventually developed various recipes including many other types of plants." He holds out both, for Clay to take. "They call it *ayahuasca*."

The wide leaf has a smooth, oily texture; and the vine is rough but springy, with tiny orange-and-yellow bumps. A sticky sap has coated Clay's fingers.

"You boil them together," says Dr. Z, replacing his specs. "The resulting brew is what the shamans in the Amazon have used for millennia to leave their physical body and explore other dimensions, other realities, as well as our own physical universe. Like many hallucinogens, in sufficient amounts, it completely dissolves the ego, the human personality, and allows one to subjectively experience themself in a much more unlimited context, without the brain's usual filter."

He's gone to the large stainless-steel fridge against the wall. Inside, on racks of shelves, are a number of pint-size bottles of a dark amber liquid, and he takes one out. Gives it a shake. Holds it up to admire its contents through the glass.

"After a great deal of trial and error, I've come up with my own favorite recipe," Dzhelikhovsky states with obvious pride. "One that I believe perfectly balances all of the plants' distinctive properties—both the yin and the yang, so to speak—both power and serenity, strength and wisdom, ecstasy and insight."

"Uh, but is it safe?" Clay asks, glancing at the wooden crate with the skull and crossbones and remembering the reverend's previous fate.

Dzhelikhovsky looks over, as if surprised. "Why, of course. I myself and many of my students have taken this exact mixture, several times. In the Amazon it might be important to have a shaman—a medicine man—present, because you're never quite sure of what you're getting, you know; but here we have the dosage of DMT and other drugs calibrated to a *T*." He shrugs, says offhandedly, "Except for the initial vomiting, there's really nothing to worry about."

Other drugs? Clay swallows and takes a seat. "So, what does it do?"

Dzhelikhovsky moves back to the front of his desk. "Primarily, it affects the pineal gland, in the forward center of the brain, which many ancient traditions around the world refer to as our 'third eye,' or 'sixth chakra,'"—making air quotes—"allowing us to see 'beyond,' into other realms, and connect to 'higher' aspects of ourselves." He swirls the liquid and watches as its sediments rise up and cloud once again. "People taking it generally have spiritual revelations of the highest magnitude regarding their purpose in life, the true nature of the universe, and insight into how to be the best person they possibly can." A shoulder shrugs. "It's also been used quite successfully in treating alcoholism and opiate addiction, as well as anxiety and depression and other psychological disorders." He looks to Clay with an eyebrow raised. "However, for my research, I'm most interested in its function as a catalyst—a gateway, if you will—in providing transcendental out-of-body experiences—gaining access to the so-called Divine realms, and making contact with extra-dimensional beings."

Clay sits waiting for Dr. Z to return his grin, but it never comes. "Uh . . . beings?"

"Absolutely. We're surrounded by them all the time. Beings just like you and me but inhabiting different energy bodies that we can't see." He waves a hand dismissively. "But those I seek are enlightened entities, with special insight into The Game." He sets the still-swirling cloudy bottle on the desk.

Clay's afraid to ask but his curiosity has been piqued. "Uh . . . What's 'The Game'?"

Dzhelikhovsky spreads his arms wide and turns in a circle. "This. Everything. Life. We live in a virtual reality created by a digital simulation—a 'game'—where we're learning to evolve the quality of our consciousness." He smiles fully now. "It's a training machine!"

Ohhh, shit, Clay thinks. Just when he thought he'd found a version of Dr. Z who could really help him.

"What we perceive as our local physical reality," Dzhelik-hovsky goes on, "is actually a nonphysical virtual reality, a subset of a larger, more fundamental one." He gives a casual flip of his hand. "The reality we experience is merely an illusion, albeit a very persistent one." He chuckles. "A sort of optical delusion of consciousness."

He begins to slowly but firmly pace between the sur-rounding tables and his desk, clearly in lecture mode now. "What's important to understand is that we are nonphysical consciousness beings experiencing a virtual physical reality, not physical beings experiencing consciousness. It's our lim-ited physical-matter-reality perspective that makes us believe the tail is wagging the dog, so to speak." He glances Clay's way, motioning ardently with his hands. "Consciousness, you see, is the fundamental reality, where each level of existence is derived from the consciousness above it, with every unique reality dimension having its own rule-sets which constrain the possibilities within that dimension—a kind of self-organizing, self-modifying consciousness-evolution process fractal, where each new layer is built upon the previous one. Consciousness acting upon consciousness." He stops and brandishes a finger. "And you—both the physical and nonphysical you—are but one small individual part that contains the essence, the pattern, of the Whole—an evolving, individually conscious piece of the larger evolving consciousness."

Clay raises his hand. "That's sort of what the professor said— what you told me when I first met you—that there were, like, these *units* of consciousness that pretty much did everything."

"Exactly!" A look of surprised disbelief comes over his face. "*I* said that? As a *scientist?*"

Clay nods. "Yeah. It was your new big theory, I think. You'd just finished writing a paper on it, that you were gonna have published, hopefully." He smiles. "You thought everybody'd think you were nuts."

Dzhelikhovsky scoffs. "Of course. To scientists, consciousness is seen as merely a hallucination of physical biochemical processes in the brain." He gives a snort and waves the notion away. "As if a physical object could create our *minds*."

Dzhelikhovsky begins his pacing again, but faster now, agitated. "'But where is the hard physical evidence?' they say. 'What about the scientific method?' Ha!" Up goes the finger, high over his head. "But I say there is one thing even more vital to science than intelligent methods; and that is the sincere desire to discover the *truth,* whatever it may be." He stops and points the finger at Clay. "And truth is not decided by a show of hands."

Clay looks to his watch as Dr. Z resumes his manic pacing. He figures he needs to catch the three-o'clock bus to get back to the city by five, for whatever's going on that must have something to do with the asshole. But he may just be leaving much sooner, he decides.

"You see, the scientific method has a limited validity to only physical-matter reality," Dzhelikhovsky rants. "But how can we accurately evaluate such paranormal activities as divination, mind reading, telepathy, remote viewing, precognition, psychokinesis, and other psi effects, in physical terms, when such things are *beyond* it? Even though they have been demonstrably *proven* to exist, time and time again, we cannot explain *why,* based on classic Newtonian physics." He throws up his hands. "For physically focused mainstream science, the lack of physical control makes the serious study of psi almost impossible. The traditional scientific requirements for tight *physical* control over something *completely nonphysical,* such as consciousness, in order to prove its *physical* existence, makes absolutely no sense. It just isn't logical.

"Psi and other aspects of nonphysical reality aren't best studied objectively," he concludes, stopping in place, "but subjectively. They must be *experienced* to be understood." He strides to his desk and lifts the previously extolled bottle of *ayahuasca.* "And this is simply one method of doing so."

Clay dutifully nods. This is all fine and well, but he doesn't see how it can help him. He'd learned more today talking to Rebecca.

It's as if Dzhelikhovsky can read his thoughts: "It's just too bad you're not a student here," he says now, indicating the bottle in his hands. "I really believe this may be a solution to your problem."

Huh? Clay's expression must say it all: confusion and worry suddenly eclipsed by a ray of hope.

Dr. Z smiles. "If—*if*—you were enrolled at the university as an official research participant, I would suggest that you access the nonphysical in this way"—shaking the bottle—"and use it as an intermediate hub—or router, if you will—to transport your present awareness to a space-time point on your history thread that conforms to the last memory you possess of it. Simply by focusing your intent." He shrugs nonchalantly. "Just think of it as hopping between different locations within The Big Computer."

The . . . ? *Don't ask, don't ask,* Clay tells himself.

"I could have talked you through it," Dzhelikhovsky adds, motioning to the pod, "but, alas—" he sighs loudly "—you are *not* a student." Deliberately, he places the bottle at the corner of his desk. "And most likely, you will not even be in this reality, come tomorrow—or possibly even today," he remarks, tossing a final glance at Clay before turning away.

Dzhelikhovsky walks over to a cluttered table on the left and opens a bulky laptop computer there, between a tall microscope and tier of stoppered vials. "But perhaps we can think of something else," he calls over his shoulder. "The Internet these days seems to have an answer for everything."

Clay can hear him typing away.

"Then again," Dr. Z offers, his back still turned, "think how fortunate you are to be having this experience! Most people go their entire lives having no concept of the existence of probable realities—probable *selves*—each digital copy evolving independently under different circumstances, different motivations, within The Big Computer. Ha! Parallel processing at its best! Each 'you' exploring the possibilities within a virtual simulation—The Game!—projecting and calculating potential value into all the known options, choosing the best states or outcomes, and then progressing those forward by their actions and choices. Each you making choices, and the choices you make, making you. Each version—each player—evolving to its fullest potential. (Or, of course, dying by the wayside.) Ha! I envy you—I've had only glimpses of other realities, where you have spent *days!* What insights you must be gleaning from each life you visit! How many has it been, now? Ten? Twelve? More? Ha! Who knows? It could go on like this *forever!*" He shakes his head, still typing. "It's too bad we can't empirically study what's happening, in your case. But, even so, who would listen? So many people are fascinated by the concept of the multidimensionality of our beings, but then are scandalized at the hint of any evidence that actually supports it—such as past-life regression, or channeling, or near-death experiences."

Dzhelikhovsky turns with a knowing look. A mischievous grin.

Clay stands nervously beside the desk. He sets the empty bottle down with one hand, while stifling a burp with the other. Grimaces at the bitter taste.

"How long did you say this stuff lasts?"

★ ✳ ✺

HE'S SOARING, SPIRALING upward, then down and around, through various realms, each separated from the next by only the flimsiest veil, each with its own atmosphere and worlds, its own colors, its own life forms—most of whom are oblivious to him, but some appear startled and call out as he passes by. However, he never stops, never tarries, too excited, too full of boundless energy to do anything but race on, like the wind, taking in everything he possibly can, amazed and elated at all he sees.

Who ever knew such places existed?! he marvels. *And so close to home!*

He's entered into an area of utter blackness—a void—when a formless, phosphorescent cloud attracts his attention and draws him near. Its shape and movement like a thousand intertwined scarves of silk, underwater, hypnotically weaving in and out; the whole thing slowly pulsating, as if with breath. And as Clay watches, still moving swiftly, circling 'round, the cloud begins to spin with him—then faster, much faster, until it's become a swirling tornado of sparkling light, growing taller, wider, with every revolution. Then in an instant, it's exploding outward and enveloping him in its turbulent gale, taking him with it in a stormy sea of varicolored pixels, spinning him dizzily and for so long that he wonders if it will ever end . . .

HE'S HURRYING WITH his wooden staff through the desert. A few tall cacti but mostly barren waste, prickly scrub, scattered red rocks in the sandy red soil. A blazing inferno somewhere overhead, making the thin air around him shimmer and shake, the distance fade. Strangely, he isn't sweating, or thirsty—only anxious to reach the other side, where . . . something, he feels, must await him.

A hiss and rattle, and a snake is rearing its head in his path, swaying from side to side, striking at the empty space between.

212 • **ERIC ARTISAN**

Clay doesn't hesitate: he swings his staff like a sword, and the snake's head goes spinning into the dirt. He feels triumphant and goes to move on, but where the snake's living head had been, there are now *two*—hissing, spitting, serrated mouths open wide.

Clay brings his staff to bear once again and now two more heads have been severed. But before they can even touch ground, *four* are in their place.

Clay's worried, suddenly, but he's faced bigger foes on the field. So he swings again. And again, and again . . . Now dodging as the snake's body grows thicker, longer, to accommodate the burgeoning heads and necks sprouting from its base. The serpent—now a dragon—towers above him, countless yawing maws snapping at him from every direction, venom dripping from razor-sharp fangs.

Yet Clay still swings and swings, yelling, now, in his fear, his magical staff having no effect—hindering rather than helping, making the problem worse. He can feel slithering scales twining around his legs and waist—his throat!—as the first teeth find their marks and cavernous jaws descend from above.

✶ ✶ ✶

HE'S HURRYING THROUGH familiar desert—uneasy, impatient—its small red rocks turning to boulders turning to twisting spires as he goes, when canyon walls appear through the haze and rush up to meet him.

He's entering the narrow mouth of the canyon—his destination surely at the other end—when he hears the hiss and rattle, sees the snake rise above its coil directly in his path.

Shit! He wields his trusty staff—then thinks again. For the first time he can feel himself sweat.

Keeping his eyes on the menacing serpent, his staff held upright before him, in defense, Clay eases his way carefully along the rock wall. There's very little room; and it feels as if his fear is drawing the snake even closer. Then, in a blur, the thing strikes, accompanied by a burning pain; then strikes again when Clay lands closer still.

"Aahhh!" Clay brings his staff down, but is able to check himself at the last second, recalling his previous disaster. The snake attacks again and Clay stumbles and falls, scrambles backward. Tiny spots of blood appear on his pant legs, and the pain begins to throb. He hopes the snake isn't poisonous.

As he crouches there, considering what to do, he begins to feel faint and realizes he has to move fast.

So Clay tentatively extends his staff out in front of him and carefully, oh so carefully, uses it to ease the snake out of the way, ready to run, if necessary.

But after striking at the wooden stick a few times in vain, the snake cooperates and, without pause, slithers away, its diamond-back skin disappearing into a crack in the wall.

* * *

HE SITS WAITING patiently before the entrance to the canyon. Hours go by, precious few clouds blocking the sun. But there's no hurry. Wherever he's headed, whatever awaits him, is up to him alone; and it will still be there regardless.

The snake keeps up its incessant hissing and rattling, putting on a show, until it finally seems to tire of itself and Clay's company and lowers its head to the ground. Gliding away in infinite Ss past Clay's knee and into the desert.

* * *

HE'S WALKING RESTLESSLY through dense jungle of colossal trees with clinging vines, broad palms and pointed swords, leafy daggers—impenetrable foliage to either side—its spreading canopy, miles above, admitting but token light. The tangled, detritus-strewn path before him branching, then rebranching itself with his every step—the way behind instantly closing in and choking off any possibility of return. He has no way of knowing where he's going, or how to get there.

The hours and days go by as he continues to struggle, lost. And eventually he becomes so despondent that he simply stops. After all, what's the point?

But after sitting in place for a while, with no thoughts of coming or going—no thoughts at all—he begins to become aware of the sounds of birds in the trees around him, high above. One in particular seems to be calling him, urging him on—pointing him in a certain direction.

So Clay gets up and continues on his way through the labyrinth, following the resonant birdsong. Which slowly begins to fade as he tires.

So he sits again, more optimistic this time, and in time can hear the music once again. It's calling him *upward,* he realizes, up into the trees.

He doesn't understand; but instead of remaining lost in the jungle, Clay decides to climb, as impossible as it seems. He climbs higher and higher, ever so slowly, using the thick, twisted vines and occasional limb to make his way—sometimes sliding down the tree's slick surface, only to continue his slow upward progress—the golden bird guiding him on, visible now as well, flittering through the misty atmosphere of the upper reaches.

Then one day, without warning, Clay has suddenly broken through—brilliant sunlight dazzling him, filling him with an energy, a vitality, a spiritedness he's never known, his worry and fatigue long forgotten. And from his new vantage point, high above the world, he can see forever, in every direction . . . His paths are clear.

In melodious song, the radiant, mystical creature that had led the way now lands beside him. And with his own cry of joy, Clay leaps upon its back, and together they fly away, even higher.

HE'S RUNNING THROUGH the forest, faster than ever before, his heart ready to burst in his chest, his breath coming in rapid bursts that steam in the freezing air, as the predators close in. Glimpses of the shadowy figures racing alongside, keeping their distance.

Finally! He breaks through the trees and into open space, where he knows he has the chance of escape. But the snow is suddenly deeper here, and it takes even more of his energy to plow through the drifts, bounding high, and he nearly falters, stumbling, barreling through snow up to his chest. Excited yips from behind propelling him on.

And then he's free and running full out again, his hooves kicking up a plume of powder. He needs to make it to the ridge, and its safety beyond.

But from the left, and somehow ahead, come the silent pack, and he's forced to turn, two of the beasts lunging in, snapping at his flanks, making him leap in panic. They stay to his left, between him and the ridge, driving him irrevocably down into the bowl—which he realizes too late is a trap.

He feints and tries to double back, but they're there, waiting, leaping at his throat. He's able to spear one, then another, with his antlers, connect with his hind legs as he kicks out blindly; but there are too many—darting in, taking their turns, taking their toll—and when he runs, now, he's too weak, too slow, and soon there is nothing to do but fall.

As he watches from above—his body lying in the reddening snow; wolves tearing at his neck, his stomach—he is completely at peace. He feels no fear, no anger, no remorse. He forgives, knowing that it is the cycle of life, and he is happy to have played his part. Exhilarated! So grateful to have experienced such life at all. It had been a good one.

And someday, he knows, he will live again.

THE GROUND BENEATH him is shaking and he's running through the street, falling painfully, then running again. All around him is chaos, people screaming, buildings collapsing, a torrent of rocks and boulders from the mountain above tearing through the village, destroying everything in their path.

Only minutes ago he had accompanied his two young children to school, where he'd presented their beautiful teacher (widowed, like himself) with a small jar of honey from his own hives; and she had dipped her finger into it, right then, and given him the sweetest smile.

But now as he stumbles and crawls back toward the school, unable to stand atop the rolling earth, he can see that the entire structure is gone—only rubble in its place—and he cries out in despair, his screams just one of many, before he is mercifully crushed by falling stone.

And as he rises up, taking in the whole tragic scene, he feels no fear, no anger, no remorse. Because he knows that it was merely a natural event, a result of the wonderful planet they live on growing and changing and replenishing itself, in conjunction with the pull of the moon directly overhead, exerting its own heavenly force. So he is easily able to forgive the earthquake that took his life and of those he loved.

Besides, he knows that he will be seeing them again soon.

SHE WEEPS INTO her hands, unable to bear witnessing any more violence and cruelty this day, as she's herded into the small wooden grain shed along with the others. All of the sacks have been removed—stolen—by the marauding gang of Hutu rebels who had inexplicably attacked their village at dawn. The shed's door slams shut behind them, and she can hear its padlock being replaced.

For another fitful hour they wait, listening to the frightened screams of young women and girls as they're brutally raped; the sickening *thwacks* of machetes cutting down the remaining men—those not off fighting elsewhere. Pleas and curses. The occasional explosion of a rifle bullet. Excited shouts and bursts of laughter amongst the killers as they haphazardly ransack the surrounding homes.

It's dark and stuffy inside the shed, the only light and air coming through near-invisible cracks between the sturdy planks. Everyone crowded together, crouching or standing in place—most all, she thinks, elderly women, like herself. A few voices praying softly, asking the good Lord for his help, his mercy. She's no longer crying, too shocked and afraid to do more than wait—and worry desperately for her daughter and grandchildren.

It's the sickly smell of fuel that registers first; then the sound—a sudden whoosh and moaning roar, like the wind; before thin sheets of flame and choking smoke coming through gaps confirm that the shed is on fire.

Their clothes catch first amidst the wailing cries, as the women hopelessly pound and kick against the door and walls—then at each other, thoughtlessly fighting for the center as the fire spreads.

She can see the burning shed, the entire village with its dead and dying, from high above. She feels no fear, no anger, no remorse. Because she can also see the murderous looters for what they are—*children!*; if not all in body, then in mind—ignorant, scared, insane on drugs, brainwashed and controlled by threatening figures; unloved; with no other purpose than to take and to kill, out of some wholly manufactured and nonexistent threat to their own worthless lives; not driven by greed and lust, like their masters, but by *fear*.

So she forgives them. Completely. Knowing that it isn't their real selves who performed these heinous acts but their human egos, who often have to go through thousands of lifetimes before living into the truth of who and what they truly are as spiritual beings—as beings of Love.

But they'll learn eventually, she thinks with compassion as she goes. They always do.

SHE STANDS STARING, uncomprehending, at the desolate wasteland that had once been her home, the city she grew up in. But now there is nothing. No living thing. The fires she had seen on the horizon for days are now cold and have left only a smoking ruin. The landscape, as far as she can see from her hilltop view, has been obliterated. Impossibly so. As if crushed beneath the fiery foot of an angry god.

She has a bit of an idea of what's happened—she'd heard her teachers and some of the older kids talking about Hiroshima a few days before—but her mind can't wrap itself around the level of absolute destruction laid out before her. She can't even begin to fathom how something like this could possibly occur. Or why.

Now, seeing that her epic trip has been in vain—that there's no chance of her parents being alive—she lets herself collapse. Lets her restless spirit go.

And, joyfully, she flies.

At peace.

She feels no fear, no anger, no remorse. She can see the battle-ships and bombers surrounding her island home, and she forgives them. She knows she cannot blame an entire country of innocent citizens, nor the fighters charged to protect them—from enemies real or imagined. Nor can she blame their elected rulers, corrupted by the love of power and newly discovered science, who are as ignorant and fearful as anyone else, if not more so, and who cloak their cowardice in rationalization—who somehow think that one person's life is worth ten thousand others.

They have a made a mistake.

A big one.

And someday they will realize this.

HE LEANS PRECARIOUSLY out into space, the slick soles of his shoes barely clinging to the metal rail, his right hand clutching the vertical beam at the center of the bridge. Far below him, the river's surface glints with the reflected lights of the city's towers, hypnotic in their effect—lulling him into a state of acceptance, of the inevitable—seeming much closer than they really are, as if he's simply stepping onto a sparkling, black, magic carpet that will whisk him away to a land without any cares; where he isn't a failure; where his life has some meaning. Where he is loved.

He stands in limbo, in a solipsistic trance, his thoughts swirling madly through his miserable and misunderstood life, until the invisible, unshakable weight that has been bearing down on him for years finally overcomes the emptiness inside, and he lets go, tipping forward into the abyss, into oblivion, with a sudden shock, a silent cry of exultation—he is *doing* something! something *major!*—as the wind rushes around him, billowing his coat, and the river and its stars, growing larger, rush up to meet him.

And for that brief instant, he feels alive. And terrified.

Then, in a blink, he is circling his body, watching it sink open-mouthed, open-eyed, deeper into the inky depths.

He feels no fear, no anger, no remorse. He was an idiot, is all, a self-absorbed fool, who cared more for himself than the concerns of others. However, in his ignorance, he hadn't known any better; and in his worry and fear had been blinded to anything that really mattered.

Unfortunately, it had been a life wasted, with no real lessons learned—until now, of course. Until too late.

He'd been too proud to ask for help; that was to have been his greatest lesson, his primary obstacle to overcome. And he'd failed.

But he can forgive himself. As there are just some things you have to experience to understand.

He raises a mental hand goodbye as he watches the river's current slowly carry his old body away . . .

Better luck next time.

HE'S AGAIN IN a dark void, moving rapidly toward a speck of light in the distance, which soon becomes a vast, white "hole," concentric halos diminishing in brightness around its rim.

He enters gleefully, and the hole quickly funnels to a luminous tunnel, which he flies through with no point of reference as to how fast or how far he's really going.

Then after a time he emerges into a much larger tunnel with countless small openings, like the one he just left, dotting its surface. And from many of these smaller tunnels come glittering gold balls of light—like *himself,* he now notices; like miniature suns—and together they go speeding on, with more and more continually joining the flow and eventually merging into one, larger, brighter star.

Then, finally, this tunnel enters into an even broader one, again with many smaller tunnels covering its sides, and again through which many other brightly shining orbs like himself are exiting and sharing his flight—eventually merging, once again, into an even greater, even more radiant being.

The pattern continues to repeat itself: More consolidating tunnels. Lights joining lights. Becoming greater, becoming more. The experiences of all becoming the experiences of one.

He races on.

Time and distance have lost all meaning, but at last, at some point, he has left the final tunnel—a single spark—and is now floating through space, toward an enormous, breathtaking light of incomparable brilliance . . . as if being pulled by a magnetic force.

He goes willingly, joyfully. And soon he is merging with this extraordinary being.

Home! His true, higher self.

And here he will stay until he's sent out again.

"THANK YOU, SIR." The taxi pulls back into the evening traffic, leaving Clay standing directly across the busy street from Madison Square Garden, his gym bag slung across his chest. He stands staring, transfixed, at the huge, brightly lit marquee above the entrance—rows of gold-yellow lights running opposite each other in a blinking race, then reversing their directions, around the edge—surrounded by red and purple neon strips—a bright white, shimmering center:

* UFC FIGHT NIGHT *
LT-HEAVYWEIGHT CHAMPIONSHIP
CLAY NEHMAN vs DEMARCUS RASHAD

The revolving lights continue to swirl, laser white rays shooting into the dusk, a steady flow of shiny metal and red-and-white streams passing before him, beneath, all vying for his attention; but it's the stark lettering, the words—his name!—which continually command his focus . . . his need to understand . . .

And when he does—when it all finally comes together in his mind, along with what the kid had told him this morning—he stands shocked, incredulous, both terror and adrenaline coursing through his system.

Today's mission—today's *challenge*—be damned.

There is no way in hell he's going in there.

"WHAT THE FUCK were you thinking?" the man continues to rave. "What in God's name could be more important than this fight? Huh?" He slams shut a locker door. Glares, breathing hard. Then bends to peer into Clay's eyes, where Clay's been sitting chastised on the bench. "And what the fuck are you on, anyway? I could park my Chrysler in your pupils." He throws up his hands as he straightens. "Jesus Christ! Are you gonna come up dirty after the fight? For God's sake!" He turns and kicks a locker now, denting it. Puts his hands to his bald head, as if to pull out nonexistent hair. Then he's back in Clay's face, apoplectic, shaking, a stubby finger beside his bulbous nose, each pore a glistening pit. "I tell ya, Nehman, I got everything on this fight. Everything. You fuck this up, it won't just be me who's ruined. You understand me? . . . Do you?"

Clay doesn't, but he gives the compulsory nod anyway.

The man's up and back to hitting and kicking the lockers again, fuming. Then pacing, with his hands to his head.

"Come on, Lonnie, calm down," comes Mohawk's treble voice from the periphery. "He's here, ain't he? And they didn't cancel it after all."

The man stops side-on to the both of them, face livid, and throws back his head to the ceiling. Lets out a long-held breath with a *whoosh*. "All right, all right . . ." He points a finger at Clay. "But, damn it, Nehman, you'd better give it all you got. You think that just because you're favored five-to-one you've got a lock—that you can just waltz in here at the last minute, without getting ready, without a fucking care in the world, and just *take* this championship away from Rashad? Well, let me tell you one thing . . ." His finger quavers. "He who hath pride, the gods destroy."

Clay can hear Mohawk snigger, and Lonnie redirects his scowl. "You! Get him ready. I gotta go talk to the organizers," he says, storming off. "See if they can give us a few extra minutes." The door to the dressing room slams shut behind him.

"Wow. I haven't seen him that mad," Mohawk remarks, "since . . . ever." He comes and stands before Clay. He's been through a beating. His forehead and cheeks have been rubbed raw and his whole face is swollen red, his left eye a violent shade of purple and practically closed shut; criss-crossing bandages cover his nose, and pieces of clear tape cover cuts on both his cheeks and his brow. Yet his gold tooth sparkles in his grin. "Can't say I blame him, though. Come on, get up, let's get you dressed."

But I am dressed, Clay thinks, standing.

Mohawk's going through Clay's bag and setting out some of its contents on the bench: a pair of thin black fighting gloves; a fluorescent yellow mouthpiece; rolls of athletic wrap and white tape; a jock strap with a cup; a pair of black-and-blue trunks with some company's logo in white.

"Come on, come on, hurry up, get out of 'em." Gesturing. He helps Clay off with the sweater, pulling it up over his head. "So, was that guy today able to help you, like you wanted?" he asks. His look is sincere.

Clay simply nods, words being unnecessary. Dzhelikhovsky hadn't presented him with a solution to his problem, but what Clay had experienced today has helped him, he thinks. What he'd understood of it, at least. He's still trying to figure it out.

He manages the T-shirt by himself and gets to work on his shoes and pants as Mohawk unrolls the athletic wrap, which becomes four smaller pieces.

"Well, I hope it was worth it." He tosses Clay the cup, without looking, and begins tearing off strips of tape, which he lines up along the edge of the metal bench. "At least I know you weren't talking to Gambarelli. His goon's been looking all over for you. And he didn't look too happy, neither." He hands over the trunks. "But he's stayed away from Lonnie, I noticed, so that's a good thing."

Clay pulls up the trunks. They're a lot tighter than he expected, not like the kind he's seen boxers wear at all. He looks to the kid, trying not to let his anxiety show. What's next?

But Mohawk just stares back. "Boy, you're really out of it, aren't you? Holy shit, dude! Come on, sit your ass down . . . Give me your hand . . . No, the other one, stupid."

Clay obeys. Glad to have at least one person in his corner—literally. He's already resigned himself to following through with this day, but it's a minute-by-minute struggle not to turn tail and run and just try again tomorrow. In hopefully a better, less dangerous, life than this one.

Mohawk's wrapping a layer of tape around Clay's knuckles when he says, "Oh, hey! Your VIP showed up, just like you wanted. With a buddy, too, it looks like, and a couple a hotties. Used all four of the tickets you sent him." He catches Clay's eye. "You ever gonna tell me who this guy is? . . . No? Other hand. Well, I'm gonna guess Under Armour. Or Red Bull. The big guys." He barks a laugh. "I can see it now: 'Clay "The Fury" Nehman wears Depends undergarments, and so should you.' Ha!"

Clay's mind is racing. *Finally!*

"What's he look like?"

"It speaks!" Mohawk finishes wrapping the palm. "Oh, I don't know. Regular high-class schmuck in a suit. But you should see the girl he's with! Wowza! Tits out to here; all cleavage. Bright yellow dress. Can't miss her."

"What?" He has the sudden flash of Charlene at graduation. "A yellow dress?"

"Yeah. Looks just like Jessica Simpson." He stops. "Wait. Holy shit! It might *be* her!"

Clay's heart slows a fraction. Of course it isn't Charlene. "Hey. Can you do me a big favor?"

Mohawk laughs. "Like I'm not already?"

"Could you give this, uh, VIP a message for me? . . . Tell him to meet me back here after the fight. Okay? It's really important." He feels relieved; back on track; one step closer to making this day a success and doing what he knows he has to do. It doesn't matter what happens to him tonight, so long as he manages to forgive the asshole. Even if it's from a hospital bed. "Uh, we *are* coming back here after, right?"

Mohawk finishes up. "Sure, I can do that." He slaps the hand down. "For a hundred bucks." Then laughs at the look on Clay's face. "Naw, man, just kidding. I'll tell the guy when we head out to the cage. Me and O'Brien are gonna stay close to Lonnie tonight. One more win and he'll be three for three. We wanna be there when you kick some ass."

From the door: "Yes. And everyone loves a winner, don't they?"

Both men turn to the voice—deep and gravelly and dripping with menace—as its speaker steps forward. Another man—a "goon" if there ever was one—moves sideways in front of the door as it closes.

"Congratulations, Maxwell. Better to win by points than not at all, isn't that right?"

Mohawk bobs his head deferentially. "Yes, sir. Thank you, Mr. Gambarelli."

"I'm sure you made *someone* some money this evening." The man stops, hands deep in his long black overcoat's pockets and, with his eyes on Clay, says, "Can you give us a few minutes, please?"

"Sure, you bet." And without another word or a glance, Mohawk is out the door, the goon shutting it behind him.

The man comes closer but remains a respectful distance away, looking down on Clay looking back up at him. He's tall. Thick. And gives the impression of being sturdy, immoveable, as if built by cement blocks: a square head upon square shoulders upon a square torso, stone pillars for legs. Only his lips move in a face of granite when he rumbles, "I missed you at lunch today."

Clay blinks away the image of the Grim Reaper, a scythe blade curved over the man's shoulder. It takes a few seconds for him to find his voice. "Yeah. Uh . . . I had to go talk to somebody today."

There's a precarious silence. Clay's eyes flit to the leather-clad goon by the door, who looks to the floor and shakes his head, apparently suppressing a chuckle.

Gambarelli, unblinking, says, "Someone more important than me, I take it."

Clay doesn't know where his sudden nervousness is coming from. "Uh . . . it was about something really important."

Gambarelli's head swivels, and he and his partner share what is probably a very rare smile, before the head swivels slowly back. "I feel the need to remind you, Mr. Nehman, that it was *you* who asked *me* for help. Am I right?"

"Uh . . ." The man's cold, obsidian eyes bore into his.

"And what I am prepared to do is much more difficult, and much more risky, than what you have offered in return." The slightest dip of his chin. A piercing look . . . Then a shrug. "And yet, based on our first meeting, I trust you." The ends of his mouth turn up a fraction; the eyebrows barely twitch. "And I can certainly appreciate what you're doing. Even admire you for it, actually. Though I, myself, would have done it much sooner, you know . . . So I have gone ahead and honored our bargain—taken you for your *word*—in spite of your mysterious disappearance today."

The pause goes on much longer than is comfortable, before Gambarelli adds finally, stonily, "The wheels have been set into motion . . . There is no going back."

The man's gaze sharpens even further, in consternation, as Clay waits for the punch line. Mentally flinches as Gambarelli takes his hands from his coat's pockets.

"However, it still behooves me to ask you, Mr. Nehman . . ." The hands turn palm up. "Do we still have a deal?"

Clay doesn't believe in the Devil; but if there was one, this guy would sure fit the bill. Definitely. And though he has absolutely no idea what the man's talking about, or if he really is making a pact with the Devil himself, Clay feels himself slowly nodding his head.

"Good." A crevice of a smile forms, which is somehow even worse than blank stone. "Because I'm counting on you tonight. Just like you're counting on me." He continues to stare unnervingly. "Am I right?"

Clay nods dumbly, once again, not veering from the man's gaze. He feels strangely removed from the treacherous scene—and its consequences—as if it were somebody else's life, somebody else's responsibility. Which is exactly what it is—even if it is still a *part* of him at some level.

"Excellent. I'm glad to hear it." But with no hint of a smile this time. "Because any misunderstanding between us would cost you much, much more than you could ever afford."

Then after another successfully intimidating pause, Gambarelli makes his exit as abruptly as he arrived. The goon makes a gun out of his hand and shoots Clay with it. Says, laughing, "Knock 'em dead," before following his boss out the door.

Clay sits blank and unmoving, barefoot, in his trunks.

What just happened here? he wonders.

He casts his eyes about the empty room. Then slips on the fingerless gloves and punches his palm a few times. Tries on the mouthpiece for size. Gets up and stands before the full-length mirror on the wall and takes in his reflection, hardly believing what he sees. Hardly believing anything about this day. Or anything that happens to him anymore.

Since he left the tank, as Dr. Z called it, he's been seeing little bright lights of every color dancing over every surface; sparkling in the air, like a mist; making luminous auras around every thing—every person, especially. And now is no different, only amplified, perhaps, by the mirror, with tiny white lights flickering on and off and a silver-yellow glow surrounding his reflection.

But as much as he'd like to simply gawk in wonder at this strange phenomenon—no doubt an aftereffect of the drug—Clay knows he has more pressing concerns to consider. Like how to stay alive in the ring, or the "Octagon," as they call it. Not only has Clay never been a boxer, but Mixed Martial Arts is a sport unto itself. He's seen it on TV a few times but doesn't know the rules. He tries to remember what Reverend Z had said to his class.

Clay shadow-boxes for a while in front of the mirror, leaving black-and-beige whorls in the air. But the action triggers something within him and he's instantly on edge, keyed up, like a rodeo bull in its chute, waiting to be released. So he tries pacing, instead, trying to calm his nerves and clear his mind long enough to think about what he's going to say to the asshole when he sees him later. How he can possibly forgive him for what he did . . . If it will even make a difference, as he hopes.

But it's no use. His mind is too full of swirling images—of the possibilities—of what will happen in the next few hours. So he sits again and closes his eyes. *Deep breaths, deep breaths . . .* And watches the high-speed kaleidoscopic display of multicolored geometric shapes and designs on the back of his lids—some forming coherent pictures, still; most not.

And he waits.

THE RIOTOUS ROAR of the crowd. Flashing lights in every direction. People pushing and prodding and patting him down, shouting unheard instructions into his ear. It's almost a relief to finally enter the ring.

He does his best to tune out the announcer and other noises; hardly registers the sound of his own name and the cheers and catcalls from the stands; his sole intent to pick out the asshole amid the sea of shouting, gesticulating spectators immediately surrounding the eight-sided cage. His eyes pass over the brawny black figure of his opponent bouncing lightly on his toes, and Clay is reminded of Mohawk's final words of advice: "Use your feet; keep your distance. Don't wrestle with this guy; they don't call him 'The Python' for nothing."

Clay spots Mohawk now, his distinctive blue plume, excusing himself out of one of the rows and into the aisle. Clay tracks down the row—the fifth one back—and there he is: the asshole, in the center, in his sharp gray suit and burnt-orange tie, sitting between a voluptuous blonde and slinky brunette. Two seats down, Clay recognizes the sniveling sycophant from the restroom stabbing, back when all this started.

As always, the shock of seeing the asshole again in person, in spite of picturing him countless times in his mind, inexplicably ignites Clay's fury and sends his pulse pounding in his skull, a building crescendo that partially muffles the sound of the referee hollering his name.

In the center of the ring the referee has them bump fists, and the two fighters glare into each other's eyes. But whatever the guy is telling them is lost in the ruckus and to Clay's own internal chatter—*I am so screwed,* being the predominant theme.

Then, from opposite sides, the bell rings and the two men come together.

As much as Clay had thought at first about intentionally losing, while doing as little damage to himself as possible, the notion rankles his sense of sportsmanship and he'd finally discarded the idea. He'd also like to *win.* Not so much for himself but for *this* reality's version, who had earned the right to be here tonight. Plus, as somebody said earlier, everybody loves a winner; and getting the asshole to visit him in the dressing room, afterward, will be a lot more possible if he comes out the victor in this fight.

So, with the two circling, Clay takes the initiative and closes the gap, taking a swing as Rashad ducks and lunges for his legs, making Clay jump to the side and away. And after a second and third time of this, it's obvious his opponent wants to take this fight to the mat, just as Mohawk and Lonnie had warned. So Clay fakes a punch and kicks out with his leg instead as Rashad lunges, catching the man squarely in the chest. But Rashad is hardly fazed, and instantly the two are circling again as they were before.

Then, in a flash, Rashad has charged and has Clay wrapped around the middle, backpedalling, and Clay's driven hard against the heavy wire mesh of the cage. He brings an elbow down hard onto Rashad's back but at the same time feels one of his legs being caught up and lifted, and a second later Clay is crashing to his side on the mat, with Rashad on top, attempting to bend him into a pretzel.

In a panic, without thinking, Clay twists and lashes out, grabbing ahold of Rashad's arm and pulling, while also kicking and connecting and raising up on the other knee, then flipping Rashad over his shoulder as he stands, hunched, and kicks his foot out, then kicks again, spinning, breaking free of Rashad's grasp.

As he dances back, out of reach, Clay becomes dimly aware of the heightened commotion around him; and it registers that he'd just accomplished something pretty impressive, without knowing what the hell he was doing. A rush of confidence replaces the panic he'd felt only a moment before. *I can do this!* he thinks. He just has to trust his body—his years of training, his muscle memory—to know what to do.

But how to get his overactive mind out of the way?

However, he doesn't have much time to give it more thought as Rashad comes at him in a blur of kicks and punches that Clay can only partially block, most of them striking him with such power and such pain that he'd probably be on the ground if it wasn't for the side of the cage holding him up. He tries futilely to fight back, but it's all he can do to fend off the hammering blows—fists and knees both, coming at him relentlessly from above and below.

Then, almost mercifully, the pummeling stops, and Clay is suspended weightless for a moment, cradled in his opponent's arms, before being slammed onto the mat with such force that he's sure his back has just been broken. He struggles to take a breath, the wind knocked out of him, and rolls to his side, just in time to avoid a falling knee to the gut, but then immediately feels an arm looping around his neck, and a powerful pair of legs scissoring themselves around his waist.

Instinct makes Clay tuck his chin to his chest, keeping the muscled arm from his throat, but in the next instant he's being bent perilously backward as Rashad's legs and arms are flexed in opposite directions. Pain flares up Clay's spine. His hands flailing uselessly. His feet immobile.

Still on his side, Clay gasps and gulps as he tries impossibly to pull in some air, his eyes bulging painfully in their sockets. And it's at that precise moment he spies the asshole, five rows back, roaring with the rest of them, cheering-on his opponent, pointing, *laughing,* one arm slung possessively around the beauty in yellow by his side.

Charlene!

. . . her hand on the asshole's arm . . . standing close, looking up . . . laughing so brightly . . .

He knows it's not her—it can't be: the figure, the face are totally different—but as he watches in horror, the woman's features morph into the ones he loves and remembers so well . . . exactly as they were that auspicious, and portentous, night. Not years, but only days ago.

Their eyes lock amid a mass of jeering, howling faces. She stares imploringly as her mouth opens to speak. "Help me!" Clay hears her cry out in his mind.

The asshole's fingers grope her chest and pull her closer; and alarm bells, a klaxon, a whooping siren drown out any other noise. The red lights already flashing in Clay's peripheral vision fill his sight and bathe the world in blood.

Now, ignoring the crushing danger at his neck, Clay whips his head backward, extending the reach by curving his back even more, and connects with a satisfying crunch. Then, immediately, both his hands are reaching up and back over shoulders straining in their sockets, groping, grasping for purchase, before seizing his enemy's skull with furious fingers and gripping with the strength and rage of a man pushed beyond physical limits. His thumbs find the two spots they were searching for and dig in, with a squelch, past any resistance, as the arms and legs strangling him suddenly relax, and Clay is finally able to fill his lungs with air.

Then with a mighty roar, he lets it all out.

THE TRIP DOWN the wide hallway tunnel back to the dressing room is subdued this time around. There's none of the excited anticipation; no nervous chatter or shouts of encouragement. There isn't the ebullient entourage—only two other people—and no one is saying a word. Those they encounter on the way seem to press themselves closer to the walls and stare as the trio pass.

Up ahead, Clay spots Gambarelli's goon, in his expensive black leather jacket, waiting outside the door; and as Clay approaches, expecting the worse, the man pushes off and moves in their direction. But the gun he removes from his pocket is only the two-finger kind, and he smiles slyly as he shoots Clay with it, again, as he goes by.

Inside the large, empty room, the three men go in different directions—Clay to the metal bench by the lockers. The man called O'Brien takes a post leaning against the wall to the showers, while Lonnie stays pacing slowly in the center, a hand to his forehead, muttering, "I'm ruined . . . I'm ruined . . . I'll never be able to live this down." Then after a minute more, he stops and stares blankly into space. "They'll probably sue." He turns to Clay. "They'll probably sue the both of us."

And in the next moment, Lonnie is in his face. "You stupid, sorry, son of a bitch!" Quaking, red-faced with anger. "What did you *do?!* What the fuck happened to you out there?!" He holds up a clawed hand, inches away. "You don't just rip somebody's eyes out! There's *rules!* That's not fighting, that's fucking . . . *insane! . . .* Aaargh!" He tears himself away to pace again.

Clay keeps his gaze focused on his hands, their knuckles and palms still taped white but now stained pink with blood. They'd taken his gloves at the ring.

"Well, at least you'll go down in the history books," says O'Brien with a half smile. "This one has Tyson beat."

Lonnie turns and glares. "He's going down, period! He'll never fight again!" He throws up his hands. "And I'm probably going down with him!"

They remain in charged silence awhile; until Lonnie finally slows, then stops his pacing for good, his look defeated as he leans with one hand on the wall. The other he waves disgustedly in Clay's direction. "Get in the shower and get dressed." Covering his face. "Then get out of my sight."

There's a commotion from outside, in the hallway—sharp cracks, muffled shouts, raised voices, then stamping feet, as if from a herd of frightened cattle, growing louder. Soon the door flies open and in runs Mohawk, panting, the one open eye in his ruined face bugging out and searching, finding Clay.

"Dude!" he hollers, throwing his weight against the door as others try to follow him in. "Holy shit! Fuck! Your, your, your— your VIP, man!" he stammers. "The suit! Somebody shot him! Like, *four times!* Right here in the tunnel!"

This takes a moment to register. Clay had forgotten all about asking the asshole to meet him after the fight.

The image of Gambarelli's goon comes to mind; and the man's shooting gesture takes on a whole different meaning.

"I think he's dead, man!"

But Clay knows the asshole will *never* be dead. At least not for him.

There's a pounding at the door as the room contracts.

"That's okay," Clay hears himself utter numbly, succumbing to the day's events. "He's a hard person to forgive anyway."

A bright moon shimmering across the water. The hypnotic lap of waves upon the shore at his feet. He sits cradling his knees, a warm beer in his hand. A number of empty bottles by his side.

This wasn't the night he had planned—that they had planned—was it?

Was he wrong to be so jealous? Maybe it really was nothing.

But Charlene knows how he gets. He's told her a thousand times.

Still, he needs to find her. Apologize.

A shout, laughter. Come on! his friends call as they run into the water, naked, splashing each other gleefully. He recognizes the guys but not the girls—very shapely girls, he sees.

It looks like fun. And isn't that what he's supposed to be doing? Having fun? Celebrating?

He downs the last of the beer and stands, sways. Hesitates.

Then he's peeling off his shirt, kicking off his shoes. Wobbles and hops as he takes off his socks and jeans, his boxers.

Then, with a Whoop! he too is running waist deep, diving, coming up beside his buddy Neil, and splashing him, dunking him under.

Hands pull at his ankle and he kicks. There are hands on his legs, his butt, his back and shoulders. Then a burst of feminine laughter in his ears. Legs squeezing his waist. He turns to a shiny wet breast in his face.

Swimming, splashing. Playing, laughing. Playful hands . . .

A glimpse of movement on the shore—a flicker of yellow.

Flash

A bobbing head of wet, curly brown hair at his waist. The eager eyes of a strange girl. Teasing him with her tongue.

Familiar laughter nearby. Another half-naked girl holding out her phone, taking a picture.

Smile, she says.

DAY 13

CLAY WAKES to a telephone ringing on the bedside table. He ignores it at first, then reluctantly fumbles the receiver from its cradle. "Hello?"

"... your—six o'clock—wake-up call ... Good morning. This is your—six o'clock—wake-up call ... Good—"

He hangs up and nestles facedown into the cool, fluffy pillow and almost falls back to sleep, when the thought *Why do I need a wake-up call?* makes him raise his head, prop himself up on one elbow, look around to see where he is ...

And when he realizes that he doesn't know, it all comes back to him—the past many days of not knowing, of waking up in an alien environment each time, a different lifetime, a different *him*.

Ah ... shit.

He plops back down and pulls the ridiculously soft sheets over his head. He'll just sleep this one out, he thinks.

But he can only kid himself for so long before he's throwing back the covers and getting out of bed. He has to find out what kind of life he's found himself in today. And what his purpose is for being here. Hopefully he won't screw it up this time.

But it doesn't take much looking around for him to see that at least he's off to a good start. It's clearly a hotel room he's in, but a nice one—a *very* nice one, it seems. There's even a second room with a couch and coffee table, a big table and chairs, an even bigger TV, and a bar and fridge filled with all sorts of goodies. He helps himself to a bottle of grapefruit juice and takes a swig. Thinks about having some microwaved popcorn and a box of chocolates for breakfast. It's like a little apartment, he thinks, walking around.

Naked, Clay goes over to the expansive set of windows, their curtains pulled back to showcase a dark midnight-blue skyline with towering, sparsely lit buildings and the glittering white-and-red line of a crowded street far below. New York City. It has to be. But he doesn't recognize anything, and from this angle he can't be sure.

On the coffee table sits a brushed-aluminum laptop, open, with a power cord snaking to the wall somewhere. Leaning against the couch, on the floor, is a slim black leather briefcase. Over the back of the couch has been thrown a long wool coat so blue it could be black. And beside it, on the cushion, is a sleek silver cell phone. If he can access the devices, Clay knows, they're sure to hold some answers—perhaps set the day into motion.

But first things first: he needs a shower. He feels kinda sticky and like he needs to wash the previous day's calamity from his skin and start afresh. Today he's going to do everything right—he can sense it.

The bathroom is enormous, and on its marble counter lies a toiletry bag and some of its contents. In the mirror he's happy to see a healthy and well-built version of himself looking back. Nice haircut, even messed up. Good skin tone. No scars. He gives himself a smile and pats his not-so-bad stomach. He's going to guess he's about thirty—a few years older than yesterday.

Strangely, he thinks, he's getting used to all this. He has to laugh as he's getting into the shower.

THE BRIEFCASE ONLY compounds the puzzle. Within it, in the main compartment where the laptop also appears to go, are three thick folders: two plain manila and one in that distinctive burnt-orange-and-yellow with the now-familiar logo of Prospect Group. Inside this one are a number of inscrutable papers titled "Prospectus," "Financial Survey," "Outline of Services," "Agreement," and the like. All bearing an equally inscrutable signature and today's date—December 8, 2015—with the name Victor Suarez printed beneath. The other folders contain sheaves of financial documents—some on letterhead from an accounting firm, the others from a Grand Cayman National Bank. Again the paperwork refers to accounts and assets of a Victor Suarez, who, if the documents are legit, appears to be a very wealthy man.

The laptop had provided the first mysterious clues: The first, an e-mail from American Airlines, dated fifteen days ago, confirming a flight from New York to Miami, leaving today at 12:45 P.M. In his name. The second, another e-mail, from an Avianca Airlines, confirming a nine-hour flight from Miami to Montevideo, Uruguay (wherever that is), leaving tonight at 10:00. This one in the name of Ignacio Avila. Both e-mails had originally been encrypted and forwarded to a generic Hotmail account before being copied and forwarded again.

The next clue had come from the phone: a text message received at 8:41 yesterday morning, confirming a meeting for today at 9:00 A.M. The text was sent from an unknown number, according to the phone, but from what Clay now knows from the papers, belongs to Prospect Group. The log showed that he had responded "OK." And since then there have been no calls or texts, in or out. In fact, the only number ever called or received on the phone has been to or from the asshole's company—four in all.

He's still sitting with the towel wrapped around his waist as he begins going through the rest of the briefcase, looking for the gun or knife or whatever weapon he'd been planning on using to kill the asshole. He knows it has to be here somewhere . . . But all he finds, besides some miscellaneous odds and ends and a charger for the cell phone, is a navy-blue US passport bearing his name and photo, and an old brown leather wallet containing the usual and exactly $1,336 in cash.

No knife. No gun. What can this mean? How had he planned to do it, then?

Ah, the bag. He remembers, now, the black leather carry-on he'd spotted just inside the bedroom door. He goes to it and tosses it on the bed, unzips it, and begins taking out its contents. Which amounts to a single change of clothes, a pair of walking shoes, a thick paperback novel, two Snickers bars, and a water bottle. But no weapon of any kind.

The shoes . . . Why are his shoes in the bag? . . .

But the answer presents itself when he turns around. In the open closet area he hadn't paid any attention to earlier, hangs a single charcoal gray suit with a cream-colored dress shirt and snazzy purple tie. Beneath it, a pair of shiny black loafers.

Aha! But of course—for his meeting today. With the asshole.

He checks the suit's pockets but finds only a fat black pen with a white flower insignia on top, little silver rings around its middle, clipped into the jacket's inside pocket, which also holds half a roll of breath mints and a ticket stub for a movie or something. He checks for anything hidden within the jacket's seams, the pant cuffs, the shoes, but finds nothing else.

He rechecks the bag.

Oookay . . .

He returns to the other room and checks the overcoat for the second time, with the same results.

So he sits again on the couch, with the folders and papers spread out before him. Runs his hands through his now-dry hair. Thinks about what he's going to do.

Versus what he was certainly planning on doing.

He'd wanted to find whatever weapon there was in order to get rid of it. He doesn't want to go down that road anymore. He's seen what damage that kind of vengeful thinking can do, what it has caused him—in so many different ways, in so many different lives—and he's putting an end to it, in this one.

He's going to use this opportunity, this meeting today, he decides, to forgive the asshole instead.

And mean it.

Or at least try to.

At least try not to kill him, for a change.

A part of him wants to contact the professor, Reverend Z, and share the news of his decision. He thinks the Rev would approve, for sure, maybe even be proud of him. If this works, Clay promises himself—if by forgiving this asshole he can stop the insanity of visiting all of these probable lives—then he'll seek out Dzhelikhovsky, regardless of whatever role he's in, and share the entire story—but a *success* story—one last time, from the beginning. Whether the good doctor believes him or not, though he probably will.

And though Clay really doesn't see the point of going to Princeton (or wherever) again, he picks up the laptop and sets it before him. Goes online . . . Searches . . . Then selects the only result worth reading, it seems, from the paltry few shown:

PRINCETON STUDENT DIES IN AMAZON

The article is from 1999. Dzhelikhovsky was twenty-seven years old.

The cell phone buzzes and vibrates on the coffee table one second before both telephones in the "apartment" begin ringing. Clay answers the room's phone on the end table, beside the couch.

"Uh, hello?"

"Good morning, Mr. Suarez. I'm calling to let you know that your car is waiting for you downstairs, in front of the hotel."

"Oh, uh . . . thank you. Uh . . ." Clay looks to his bare wrist. "Could you tell me what time it is, please?"

"Of course. It's eight o'clock. Shall I tell the driver what time you'll be down?"

Shit. He isn't even dressed yet. He hasn't had time to think any of this through. "Uh . . . Yes, please. Uh . . . Tell him I'll be down in fifteen minutes, okay?"

"Yes, sir, I'll tell him."

It takes him only ten to get packed and dressed and out the door. He'd found an expensive-looking watch on the bedside table and another pair of boxers on the floor beside it. Along with three used condoms, which he really didn't have time to think about, right then.

Now, as he heads down in the elevator, hopelessly retying his tie, Clay reminds himself that today he's changing history. Whatever history it might have been.

HE'S CARRYING BOTH the briefcase and the small leather bag when he walks in, the lobby of 4 Financial Plaza tastefully festooned with strings of holly and bows and blinking white lights for the season. Clay shakes off the cold from his short walk from the limo and warily approaches the elevators.

There's a small group of people ahead of him, and when it's his turn he places both bags on the narrow wooden table beside the metal detector, as he'd seen another guy do.

"Traveling," he says to the security guard, with a smile, as he places his cell phone in the tray. Then he remembers his buckle and quickly removes his belt, for good measure. It feels good to be passing this way again with totally different intentions now. No worries.

The guard smiles back and pulls the bags toward him as Clay walks through. Then holds up a hand when the machine beeps loudly.

Shit! Clay freezes. He *does* have a weapon on him somewhere. He knew it! Still, he approaches slowly when the guard beckons. If he has to run, he'll need to at least grab the briefcase, for sure . . .

The guard's wand beeps and stops at a point over Clay's left side. Clay's pulse races as he pats himself, and through the heavy wool coat and suit jacket feels something solid there. His heart sinks. *Ah, shit.* How could he have missed this? With feigned coolness he reaches inside first one coat, then the other . . . and with a huge inner sigh of relief, pulls out the fancy, fat black pen.

He smiles and shows it to the guard, then holds it aloft as the guard wands him a final time.

The cursory search of his bags takes but a minute, as a couple of other people pass through the detector without a problem.

In the elevator Clay is to the back, his bags at his feet. A man and a woman, both dressed for the office, are standing in front of him, chatting companionably, when Clay twists the pen still in his hands and the ends separate and a long coil of dull brass-colored wire falls out to hang in a spiraling loop past his waist.

He's too surprised to make any sense of it, at first. Then—*Oh crap!*—he's doing his best to put the wire back inside the "pen." But within seconds the elevator stops and the doors open with a ding. So Clay swiftly transfers it all to his left hand and stuffs the tangle into the outer pocket of his coat as another young woman gets on. Then has to tuck in a portion of the wire still hanging out.

So, he thinks, chagrined: a garrote—right? He's managed to come with a weapon after all, despite his best efforts.

However, he's still determined not to use it. Unless . . .

No, he *won't* use it, he vows, no matter what happens. He'll get rid of it, the first chance he gets.

The doors ding again, on the twelfth floor, and Clay excuses his way out and into the same kind of reception area he remembers from before, only with a ruby row of poinsettias and a Christmas wreath at the front of the long, curving desk.

He announces himself as Mr. Suarez, then takes a seat after removing his coat and setting it on the couch, beside him. He's jittery, not at all sure exactly what he's going to do or say when he sees the asshole again—when he's faced with him this way.

He knows it's been over eleven years since graduation night, but it still feels like only a couple of weeks ago to him.

And, then, of course, he's killed the man (or had him killed) six or seven times already. It just feels *weird* to be forgiving him now.

He looks to his watch. He's early. He'll wait ten minutes, and then if—

"Mr. Suarez, hello!" It's the asshole himself striding forward, hand outstretched, wearing a near exact replica of the outfit Clay had first seen him in, outside in the Plaza, accompanied by his friends and The Gorilla.

Clay's too startled, at first, to speak or do anything but sit there, jaw clenched. His first instinct—to attack, to tackle this asshole and pummel the living shit out of him—is repressed only by the desire to resume a normal life again (whatever that is; he doesn't even know anymore). There are the faintest flickers of red in his peripheral vision, shooting stars; and he has to close his eyes and take a deep, calming breath. *Get a grip, get a grip.* Then another deep breath, willing his burning rage to ebb, to take a back seat to what he knows needs to be done instead.

He doesn't think he can do this.

"Are you all right?" The asshole has stopped a few feet away with a look of concern. He exchanges a glance with the receptionist, who picks up her phone.

Clay's forced smile becomes a grimace. "Yeah, yeah, I'm okay." He taps his chest. "Just a, uh, bad case of heartburn, is all. I'll be all right in a minute."

He stands and shakes the asshole's hand, repulsed and newly enraged. Looks him in the eye, but only for a moment, lest his true emotions become obvious. The man looks like a glorified used-car salesman, he thinks. All smiles. Not a hint of the rapist and killer within.

The blood rushing, roaring, in his ears, Clay misses entirely what the asshole's just said, but picks up his coat and bags and follows, taking one deep breath after another.

The asshole's office is halfway down the corridor, on the right, in the opposite direction of the restrooms. (Clay can't help but flash on the image of the man dead in a pool of blood, in front of the urinals.) The office is twice the size of this morning's hotel room, carpeted in the same plush beige as the hallway; the wall along half one side, closest to them, tall glass windows. There's a monolithic black desk at the other end, with a number of leather chairs facing it; a burgundy-colored couch and coffee table by the door; and a long, polished wooden table with chairs beside the floor-to-ceiling windows directly in front of them.

The asshole stops just inside. "May I take your coat?"

"Huh? Oh! No, no, that's all right. I'll, uh, I'll just hang on to it."

The asshole waves them over to the table by the windows, where they each take a seat only a few feet apart. There's a flat, high-tech phone in the center of the table, as well as two small writing tablets with pens.

"How about something to drink?" the asshole offers with that pasted-on grin. "Coffee? Tea? A soda?"

Clay's mouth has gone bone dry, and there's a throbbing, now, in his temples that he can't seem to rub away. "Do you got a Coke?"

"Of course." The asshole pushes a button on the phone. "A Coca-Cola for Mr. Suarez, please, Ashley . . . Thank you."

Clay's set the bag and briefcase behind him, the coat over the back of the chair within easy reach. He's wishing he still carried the garrote in his jacket pocket, and mentally kicks himself for the thought.

"So, Mr. Suarez, I take it you enjoyed your stay at the Carlyle? Did they treat you all right?"

It's as if the smile has been surgically implanted; along with that perfectly coiffed hair and fake tan; those bright blue eyes; that freakin' dimple on his chin. Clay wouldn't be surprised if the guy was wearing makeup. He sees the smile fade slightly and the asshole's eyes dart away and back, before Clay realizes he hasn't answered the man's question.

"Oh. Uh, yeah, the hotel was great. Thanks," he manages. "I coulda lived there forever."

The asshole laughs—more perfectly white teeth—says, "Good, good. And how 'bout Trish? Were you able to use those tickets to *The Book of Mormon?*"

There was a bit of a wink to that remark that Clay doesn't understand. He doesn't know if he did or didn't use any tickets. So he just shrugs and looks out the window, trying to figure out how he's going to do this—if he even *wants* to do this anymore. But does he even have a choice? . . . The table blocks his view of straight down, which he'd really like to see, but from so high up, he can spot the tail-end of a busy street in the distance, between many other impressive buildings, and the hint of water, way past it all, like maybe a piece of the ocean. The clouds hanging low over the city, like a cottony blanket. Seagulls, maybe, or pigeons.

He hears the asshole clear his throat, say less cheerfully, "So you've brought the papers, then, I take it?"

Clay turns back and, without meeting the asshole's eye, pulls the briefcase to himself and sets it in his lap. His stomach churning anxiously. He can sense the asshole perking right back up again as he takes out the three folders and sets them on the table between them, Clay's mind working furiously, trying to decide the right course of action to take, as the asshole pulls the papers toward him and begins slowly flipping through them. Does he follow through with his original plan, made before he got here, which is, of course, as always, to enact his revenge on this asshole who so richly deserves it, who so thoroughly ruined his life? Or does he try to put an end to the repetition of countless probable lives bent on revenge that he keeps finding himself experiencing day after freakin' day? . . .

What if it never stops? he wonders for the thousandth time.

No . . . No, it *has* to stop. Right here. Right now.

"Hey, uh . . ." He catches the asshole looking up from the papers (the ones from the accountant, it looks like). ". . . I'm not sure how to—"

The asshole's eyes are drawn away and Clay looks too, as an attractive older woman walks in carrying a small tray. "Please pardon the interruption, gentlemen." She sets down first a Coke in a tall glass with ice, upon a coaster, then another glass of something sparkling, closer to the her boss. "I'll be happy to get you anything else," smiling at Clay before she goes.

Clay takes a much-needed drink and licks his parched lips.

The asshole is waiting patiently, legs crossed at the knees, the open folder in his lap. "Yes, sir, you were going to say . . . ?"

Clay can't find a place to set his gaze. Part of him just wants to get up and leave, as if that act alone will be forgiveness enough. But he knows he has to say the words. And somehow mean them.

He takes a deep breath. Squeezes his eyes shut. "I'm here to forgive you," he exhales too loudly. Then after a pause, with the asshole staring back, his smile fading: "For what you did. For what you did to Charlene . . . And to me."

Lines appear upon the asshole's brow. A furrow between his eyes. "What? I don't—" He gives his head the smallest shake. "I don't understand."

"For what you did," Clay says. "At graduation. The party . . . You drove away with her."

The asshole just looks back, bewildered, his mouth open slightly, as if words are stuck there. "I don't . . ."

"I know what you did," Clay snaps, anger now fueling his confidence. "To Charlene." He'll forgive this asshole, but only after the man has admitted to his crimes.

The asshole's mouth closes to a stern line. He looks to the folder in his lap, then closes it, tosses it onto the table. Uncrosses his legs and sits up straighter in his chair. "How do you know Charlene?"

It's the way he said it that pisses Clay off, more. There's no denial to his voice, no apology. No remorse. As if he's above such things.

Through gritted teeth: "She's my girlfriend."

The asshole's eyes go wide at this, Clay's glad to see. *Now he's afraid,* he thinks with satisfaction. *As he should be.* The asshole has no idea how close he's come to death today.

"She's your . . . ?" The asshole stares. Slouches limply in his chair. Puts a hand to his forehead for a moment, then runs it slowly back through his hair. "No," he says, finally, with a shake of his head, "that's impossible." He sits up straight again. "Mr. Suarez . . ." His eyes go from Clay to the folders on the table, then back again. He reaches out and deliberately pulls all three of them toward him. "Why would you say that?" he asks.

Clay makes his voice cold. Deadly. "Because she *was* my girlfriend, you asshole. Before you raped her and left her in the woods. Before you probably freakin' killed her yourself."

The sudden panic in the asshole's expression is as clear as day. And as he quickly reaches his hand across the table, Clay slaps the phone away, causing it to hit the window and fall to the floor with a clatter.

Then the asshole is up and out of his chair, backing away. And Clay follows.

"Just admit it, asshole. That's all you gotta do." Clay stops and lifts his arms out to the sides. "Just tell me what happened, what you did. I already know y—" He has to take another deep breath and close his eyes momentarily as the memories of the past two weeks—his dreams—come back to him in a rush—a jumbled maze . . . Charlene dead in the grass; then alive, but in a wheelchair; brutally murdered; buried in the ground; raped; then disappeared . . . He needs to know what happened. He needs to make sense of what's been happening to him.

The asshole has made a dash for the desk at the far end of the room. He's reached the phone and is pushing a button by the time Clay comes striding up, the massive block of wood between them.

"I'm here to *forgive* you, damn it!" Clay practically shouts. "Just tell me what the hell you did to her." He's fuming, his anger getting the better of him, just barely controlled. Red specks dancing at the edges. "And *why*, for God's sake?"

"Sir?" A woman's voice.

In the doorway stands the asshole's assistant from earlier. But just as quickly as she appeared, she's gone. When Clay turns back to the desk, the asshole is replacing the phone's receiver.

"You're insane," is all the man says.

"Okay. Just tell me why, then. Why'd you do it?" It's taking every ounce of Clay's self-control not to leap over the desk and throttle this guy. His hands clench and unclench at his sides. "What'd she ever do to you, huh? Is it because she didn't want you? Because she fought you, is that it?"

The asshole's hand comes up. "Wait. Stop right there. Do you seriously believe for one second that I would ever hurt Charlene?" He scowls. "I don't know what the hell kind of stunt you're trying to pull here, Mr. *Suarez*, but—"

"You did! I know you did! I *saw* her! I'm the one who found her in the woods! I've seen her body! I've been to her freakin' funeral! I— She—" *She was pregnant with your baby!* But how can he say that? How would that make any sense?

"I'm sorry, but you are a very disturbed person." The asshole's eyes go to the door again, and Clay turns but misses whoever was there. When he turns back, the asshole has his hand in a drawer.

"Hey! What are you doing?" Clay moves quickly but the asshole moves with him, keeping the desk between them.

"Fuck!" the asshole shouts, both angry and scared. "You think Charlene is dead?" He makes a grab for something on the desk and holds it close to his chest. "You think she's *dead*, you sick fuck?"

"I know she is! It was on the freakin' news! They found her body in a—"

"Here!" The asshole holds out the object in his hand. "This was taken only three months ago. And as you can see, she is very much alive."

It's a framed five-by-seven photo of a family at the beach. The asshole standing shirtless in trunks with a small child—a boy—on his shoulders. The mother with her hands on the shoulders of their older daughter, smiling, laughing, her long blond hair lifted by the wind . . . that beautiful, beautiful face . . .

"What's going on?" A man's deep rumble this time. "Are you okay?"

The asshole holds up a staying hand to someone else who's entered. "Now, tell me," he says to Clay. "How do you know my wife?"

His wife . . .

Clay has to lean with his hands flat on the desk to keep from falling, his knees wobbly, all of a sudden. He can't tear his eyes away from the photo as the asshole sets it back down.

It's real . . . No! No, it can't be real . . . He reaches out but the photo is quickly snatched up again.

"Answer me!" the asshole yells. "What are you doing here? How do you know Charlene?"

Clay looks up into the asshole's furious face, gone bright red. He blinks. Looks to the two other suits in the room and wants to laugh. *Hey, it's The Gorilla.*

He looks to his coat and bags, far across the room.

Should have stuck with Plan A, he thinks ruefully.

He hangs his head for a moment and gives it a slow shake.

And as he lifts it and stands straight, sucking in a breath and looking around him, ready to meet his fate, for the beating that's sure to come, another image catches his eye—another framed photo, but much larger, on the wood-paneled wall off to the side of the desk: a wedding portrait of Charlene by herself, from the waist up . . . sitting, holding a bouquet of flowers . . . a tiara of crystals and tiny white blossoms in her hair, done up in a tousled bun, golden wisps curling around her face. That beautiful, beautiful face . . . It could have been taken just weeks ago, Clay thinks, at graduation. She looks just as he remembers, only better. She can't be any more than twenty-one—the age that *they* were going to get married, after college. The same age she was going to marry *him*.

He can't believe it. *How . . . ? Why . . . ?* What happened? What did he do wrong? Clay's throat constricts and burns . . . Charlene's image blurs.

No, don't go . . .

He holds out a hand and takes a shaky step, then another—

"Hey!" More angry voices.

—as the room begins to spin . . .

. . . and goes black.

Everyone excited for the start of summer. Those graduating excited for the start of the rest of their lives—the future, the possibilities.

The party's in full swing, the bonfire raging.

He'd been waylaid by his teammates earlier. Shamed into doing the obligatory beer bong, initiate the incoming seniors. A roaring burp explodes from his mouth.

Now he's looking for Charlene.

But she isn't with her friends. Or dancing by the fire. Or hanging out by the kegs.

He can't find her anywhere.

Where is she?

Where's Charlene?

Ah, there she is . . .

But who's that she's talking to? . . . Oh, yeah, the asshole from that fancy East-Coast college—Marni's cousin, the pretty boy. Big money. What are they laughing about? What's so funny?

He stalks over.

His finger in the asshole's face. Strong words. Staring him down.

Then Charlene, pulling at his arm—scolding him, at first, now coaxing, sweet-talking, making him feel like the asshole instead.

But . . . she'd had her hand on the asshole's arm . . . standing close, looking up . . . laughing so brightly . . .

Her worried face.

The asshole's smug grin.

Everybody's eyes upon him . . .

And now he's walking away—angry, proud—accepting the proffered joint. Making a show of it.

Don't go, she says. Don't go.

He stops and looks back. She hasn't moved from the asshole's side.

Let's go to the bluff, she says. Their spot. Where they can watch the sunrise, like they planned.

It hurts him, it kills him . . .

But he holds out his hand.

SUNDAY, JUNE 26, 2011   **DAY 14**

CLAY WAKES with a smile to the sound of a child's laughter. Soft sunny light, dappled shade, a swirling parade of dandelion seeds floating slowly by. A woman's laugh now, and a voice—one he would recognize anywhere.

Lying on his back, on a makeshift pillow, Clay turns his head; and there she is, sitting cross-legged on the ground, on a blanket, with a little baby in her lap, blowing softly on a dandelion pom held an inch from her lips. The baby kicks and giggles and reaches two-handed for the dancing puffs as they fly away. Charlene leans down to whisper into the baby's ear.

Charlene . . .

Now Clay knows he's dreaming. And though his heart swells, it hurts him to know that it can't be real. She can't be real. Alive.

He lays like this interminably, with his head at an awkward angle, not daring to move, or even blink, lest this magical moment disappear back into the ether, into the mists of sleep.

They're together on the same quilted blanket spread out in the grass, in a small clearing surrounded by tall, quivering trees.

Branches and leaves creating shimmering patterns of shadow and light over Charlene and the baby, who glimmer radiantly, like the beautiful, mythical beings they are.

Charlene holds up a fluffy yellow dandelion blossom now, and uses it to kiss the laughing baby's nose, chin, then each cheek, before letting greedy hands take it, which immediately put the flower in the baby's mouth. Making Charlene laugh, and Clay along with her.

"Oh, look, Daddy's awake!"

She holds the baby up and sets its dangling feet on the blanket, play-walks it toward him as she gets to her knees and moves closer, right up beside him. Smiling. Beaming. Luminescent in her white sundress.

"Guess who's been the perfect angel."

Charlene lifts and places the baby onto Clay's chest, so that they're practically face-to-face, tiny wet dandelion petals clinging to its lips and chin, huge round blue eyes looking into his own, unblinking, its little blond pink head bobbing almost imperceptibly. Clay lifts his hands and holds the baby carefully to him, in awe.

Is this our baby?

Their child . . . Just like they'd planned.

Still convinced that it's a dream, he remains silent, not wanting to break the spell. He looks up at Charlene, who's been watching his face and now blesses him with a tender smile so full of love that it makes Clay's heart do flips. Then she lays down and cuddles up beside him, resting her head upon his shoulder. Places one hand over his holding the baby.

Her touch, her presence, is like all he's ever wanted and more. The feel of her body pressing against him, her bare leg bent over his own, her full breasts upon his arm, fills him with such longing and completion both.

Can this be real?

But, no . . . He still has no memory of how he got here. The most he can remember, the past two weeks.

The tears of joy at the back of his eyes turn to ones of frustration.

One day! Just one day. That's all the time he has . . . But isn't that what he wanted, what he asked for—prayed for—just one more day to be with her again? To tell her how much he loves her, how much he's missed her? To tell her how sorry he is? . . . He's been given an amazing gift, he thinks now. And he's going to make the most of it he can.

Charlene's head stirs and he lifts his own a fraction to kiss her hair. *Oh, that smell!* The softness! And in a second he has to kiss it again. And again.

Charlene laughs quietly and turns her face to his. "Did you dream of me?"

Oh, you have no idea, he wants to say. The worst nightmares of his life. But of course he'd never tell her such a thing. Today is meant to be perfect.

He kisses her forehead, then the bridge of her nose. "You were wearing that pretty yellow dress you had at graduation, at the party. You remember?" Soon he'll be able to reach her lips.

"Mmm. Of course. How could I forget?" She moves her hand and places it on his chest, begins rubbing it in circles, as she's always done. "The first night of the rest of our lives."

Clay sighs contentedly. Gazes up at a sweet blue sky and popcorn clouds through the flickering leaves.

I'm home, he thinks. *I'm home.*

Please don't make me leave.

THIS IS A NICE treat," Charlene says. "We don't go out as much as we used to, that's for sure." She lifts the shawl draped over her shoulder to peek at the baby breast-feeding in her lap. "In a couple years, I guess, we can get a babysitter." She looks up and laughs. "Unless his little sister has arrived."

They're sitting at an outside table in the corner, at a small restaurant near the park. An umbrella shading them from the sun, which still manages to glint off the glass- and silverware upon the cloth. The remains of their lunches before them. Most of Clay's pasta dish sits still untouched; he'd been too nervous and preoccupied with staring at his beautiful wife and child—*his wife!*—to do more than pick at his food. Or make anything but the most rudimentary conversation. He doesn't know what to say without giving himself away. And as much as he wants to know about her and their life together, he wants more to simply hold her in his arms during this short time they have together.

"What about work?" he asks her casually. "Do you ever plan on going back?" He still doesn't know what she does, or if they even went to college, as planned.

"Of course," she says. "I can go back to the hospital anytime. But not until after Brandon's in school." She gives him a brief, funny look. "Why? You know I want to go back to work. Is something wrong? Is everything okay at Able? Is Reardon still upset about the Eagle City site? That wasn't your fault and he knows it."

Shit! "No, no, nothing like that. I was just wondering. Everything's totally fine."

So she probably did become a nurse after all, he thinks. Does that mean he's a construction manager?

It doesn't matter. He has to steer clear of such talk for the rest of the day.

"Are you okay, sweetie?" Charlene reaches a hand across the table. "You seem sort of depressed today. A little out of it. Are you coming down with something?"

It's the same thing Trudi had asked him at the campsite, and Clay grimaces inwardly at the pang of guilt he feels for cheating on her like that; and then chides himself for the memory of enjoying it so much.

"No," he says, taking her delicate hand in his and gazing into those sparkling green eyes he's lost himself in so many times before, "I'm just love sick, is all. Just loving this time I get to spend with you today." He stares transfixed at her beautiful, beautiful face, made even more so by however many years have passed. There's a maturity now, a seriousness, to her features that he's just now noticing and appreciating. "I've missed you," he says before he can catch himself.

He watches as her eyes turn moist, then look away, then eventually come back after a moment. A tight smile, which finally turns up at the corners.

She turns her hand over, palm up, and gives his a squeeze. "I've missed you too." It's said as a whisper.

They hold each other's eyes. And Clay's brim with joy. With gratitude. He feels himself grinning back at her; but still with that tinge of sadness he knows he can't hide.

He's never been able to hide anything from Charlene.

"I love you so much," he tells her as Charlene chokes out a sob and a laugh at the same time, casting her eyes down.

The baby stirs at her breast, its arms flailing, and lets out a soft cry.

Charlene flips back the shawl and lifts the baby up to her shoulder, begins patting its back gently, cooing into its ear as she sniffles and smiles and casts glances at Clay. Watches him staring in awe at her swollen, still-exposed breast.

She laughs. "What's gotten in to you today?"

He looks up at her face, at her flushed cheeks and bashful smile, and no longer cares what she may think of his strange behavior. He wants only to make love to her—to this woman of his dreams, his memories—while he still has the chance.

"Are we ready to go?" he says hoarsely. He hopes his expression conveys the intensity of his want, his need. He has the sudden urge to throw the table between them aside.

Charlene stares back at him for a long moment, then laughs softly, as if surprised, or embarrassed. She turns her face and kisses the baby's head, lifts it from her shoulder, holds the tiny infant out to him. "Here," she says. "You burp him, and I'll be right back. I'll tell the waiter."

Clay quickly stands and leans forward, taking the baby carefully by the middle, its big eyes wide and locked onto his, its tiny mouth in an *O* of wonder, its chubby little arms and legs flapping and kicking happily. Clay's unsure of what to do with it.

Charlene stands too as she slips her breast inside her dress. She steps around the table and drapes a cloth over Clay's shoulder. Gives a laugh as she guides his hands and the baby to rest against his chest.

She moves closer and, with one hand on the baby's back, the other on Clay's arm, lifts her face to his . . . and they kiss—tenderly, so tenderly—their lips lingering, brushing, coming together as if for the first time in years, then parting as their tongues begin to seek each other hungrily. Charlene reaches up and places her hand behind his neck, pulling him down, pressing herself against him, and Clay moans with desire. He wraps his free arm around the small of her back and begins moving his hand up and around, reveling in the feel of her through the thin dress, then down, where he can cup her ass, and squeeze.

"Oh, God," he says. "Charlene . . . If you only knew how—"

"Shhh." She puts a finger to his lips. Holds him with her eyes, meaningfully. Cheeks streaked with tears. Her smile happy or sad, he can't tell. "I love you too," she says softly. "That's all that matters."

The cell phone clipped to Clay's belt gives a low buzz and vibrates. Then again, and Charlene pulls away, motions to the baby. "You want me to . . . ?"

Clay shakes his head. "No, no, it's okay. I don't need to get it."

The kissing has left him in a daze. He longs to pull her to him again but she's already reaching for her purse slung over the back of the chair. "I'll be right back," she says with a look over her shoulder and a twinkle in her eye, a genuinely happy smile this time.

Clay retakes his seat and begins carefully patting the baby's back as he'd seen Charlene do. Its fuzzy little head bobs upon his shoulder; makes little jumping motions against him as it babbles quietly. Clay catches the eyes of a few other people at the surrounding tables and nods. He'd totally forgotten they weren't alone. He has to laugh when he thinks of how he was ready to bend Charlene over the table, right here, only a minute ago.

The cell phone at his waist had stopped buzzing after only four or five times, but now it starts up again. He ignores it at first, then curiosity makes him take it from his belt once it's stopped. The outside of its clam-shell case is beat-up and scratched, like it's seen a lot of heavy use outdoors. He flips it open.

On the small screen are two text messages. The first: **where r u?** Then: **call me**. The sender reads simply "**D**."

He snaps the phone shut and replaces it on his belt. Reaffirms his vow to ignore any and all calls that come through today.

He's eye to eye with the baby—Brandon—his son!—*their* son!—held up before him, the third in a series of giant bubbles upon its lips ("Ba," is all it really can say), when Charlene returns.

"You ready?" she asks, smiling.

His heart leaps. *More than you could ever know.*

CLAY STIFLES A YAWN. Opens his eyes and mouth wide, stretching his face. He'd slap it if he thought it would help. He needs to stay awake.

He's lying on his side, his head on the pillow, his body curled around Charlene's like two nesting spoons. Softly, he caresses her arms, the slope of her breast, her nipple. Then up over her neck and behind her ear. Runs his fingers through her long blond hair pooled beside him, tugging gently at her scalp, as he knows she likes.

"Hmmm," she murmurs, on the edge of sleep. "That's nice."

She presses against him and he can feel himself growing hard, once again, inside her.

They've made love half a dozen times already since they arrived home this afternoon, and still his desire for her isn't sated.

Two weeks ago, when they were both eighteen, in the reality he remembers living in so well, they'd had sex on so many occasions; but this is different. Slower, more relaxed, comfortable—though he'd at first been unable to control himself and had practically stripped the clothes off the both of them once the baby was in its crib.

This is *married* sex, he thinks. He had no idea anything could feel so good, so fulfilling at the deepest level. At times this evening, it seemed, Clay could sense their two souls bonding, becoming one, as they rocked in perfect rhythm, lips barely touching, breathing each other in.

They've stayed in bed, leaving only for a few minutes at a time, to the bathroom or the kitchen or the baby's room, bringing in little Brandon twice for a while, to suckle, then sleep in his mother's arms.

They'd played some music—a favorite CD from 2003—and sang along; but mostly they've stayed quiet and talked. And talked and talked and talked. Though he didn't have much to contribute to the conversation without sounding like an idiot, Clay had a lot of questions for her: about her memories of high school and college, her favorite things these days, her thoughts, her dreams and plans for the future . . . And he'd learned a lot this way, in the process.

They'd both gone to OU, as planned, and Charlene to nursing school at the same time. He'd had a stellar football career before barely graduating, apparently, with a few drunken run-ins with the law before then. And they were married as soon as they returned to Taloga, though they'd already moved in with each other, finally, the summer before their senior year. Then Charlene went straight to work at Children's Hospital, and Clay to work for Able Construction—though he's still not sure what he does there. Then, less than two years later, Charlene got pregnant. Their first baby turns six-months old next week, and they're hoping for two more, eventually. Charlene's sisters visit a lot, by the sound of it, and her brother, Conner, has moved to Dallas, not too far away. Both her parents are happy and healthy. Nothing was said about his own mom, so he figures it isn't good news and didn't ask. Charlene wants a couple of dogs, from the shelter, but not until Brandon is at least two. She can't wait to go to Yellowstone and Yosemite, and learn to play the piano, and see a real live Broadway musical, and travel to Europe with him someday—maybe in their old age.

Clay had almost described his recent visits to New York City, before stopping himself. Instead, he told her he'd take her around the world if that's what she wants. And that he'd be with her forever . . . If only he could.

Now, as a pair of scented candles flicker on the nightstand, he runs his palm across the top of Charlene's thigh, as far down her leg as he can reach, before bringing it up to rest on her belly, just above her thatch of curly blond hair.

Her body has filled out considerably since he last saw her, his last memories of her. Probably due to the pregnancy, he figures. She'd mentioned more than once, today, of being self-conscious of it, but for him, it's just more of her to love. He can't get enough of the feel of her—every generous curve and silken fallow. Her tantalizing scent. The taste of her skin, which he kisses now.

Fully erect, he moves slowly inside her, his fingers circling in front. But it soon becomes clear that she's drifted off to sleep, so he slows, then stops altogether, holding himself in a sensational limbo, his free hand now cupping a breast, rising and falling in easy rhythm, the steady beat of Charlene's heart in resonance with his own.

WITH A START, Clay catches himself as he drifts off to sleep—something he can't let happen. He needs to stay in this reality, this perfect version of himself with Charlene, for as long as possible. He'd rather die, he thinks, than have to live without her again.

Carefully, he eases out of bed. Goes across the hall to check on cute little Brandon, who's wide awake and gurgling softly to himself, gumming his little Poochie toy. Then together they go down the stairs and to the kitchen for another cup of coffee. The first pot of many sits hot and half full in the machine, waiting for him.

Only seconds after turning on the light, his cell phone buzzes yet again, skittering in place on the counter. He'd brought it down here hours ago. It'd been buzzing incessantly all evening and into the night, clipped onto the belt of his pants hastily discarded in the hallway upstairs; and once in a while he could hear it from their bedroom. He's been reluctant to turn it off, not wanting his regular self for this reality (lucky bastard!) to miss an important message from work or whoever else.

The phone's buzzing stops, as it always does, then almost immediately begins buzzing again as he pours his coffee, the baby sitting in the crook of his arm.

Shit! What if it's an emergency of some kind? he thinks for the umpteenth time . . . But, no, it doesn't make any difference. There's nothing more important than this time he gets to spend with Charlene again. He'll let nothing interfere.

Still, when the buzzing stops, Clay goes over and picks up the phone, flips it open. It won't hurt just to check.

31 UNHEARD MESSAGES, it reads across the top. The screen's filled with lines of texts—all from the same "**D**" as before—and the scroll bar, to the side, indicates there are many more. The most recent he can see:

> **why wont u call?**
> **what did i do?!**
> **I KNOW UR HOME!!**
> **WTF?!!!**

Clay pushes the POWER button and watches the screen clear, before closing the phone.

Tries to forget the words he's just seen. The implications.

He turns out the light and, with his cup of coffee in one hand, the phone in the other, the baby at his shoulder, goes back upstairs.

He tucks the now-silenced phone into one of his shoes, then places them, with his clothes, beside the bed.

He stands blowing on his coffee, holding the baby, as he watches Charlene sleeping, the candles still glowing beside her, softly illuminating her beautiful, beautiful face.

Her face. Charlene. The *only* woman he could ever love.

How could I? he thinks.

He gives his head a shake. No, how could *he?* rather.

Dumb-ass!

Clay mentally smacks his forehead. Begins to pace.

There has to be a simple explanation, he reasons. He's just jumping to conclusions. It's just some friend of his. A guy.

Oh why did I have to open that freakin' phone?

Clay goes to stand in front of the large pair of windows in the room, their slatted shades pulled up, to contemplate the view, this life, and his penchant for screwing up everything, no matter what probable version of himself he is.

He sips his coffee. Jostles the baby.

The moon lights up the street.

It's a nice home they have, in a nice neighborhood, on the north side of town, in a relatively new development—one his own company had played a large part in creating, Charlene had proudly alluded to earlier as she'd driven them home today. Up and down the block are big lawns and big two-story brick houses, wide sidewalks and small trees along a freshly paved street, a few cars parked in driveways—only one, he sees, parked on the street itself. Parked right in front of their house.

And as he watches, with a sinking feeling in his gut—his heart—the car's door opens and the inside light comes on. Giving him a glimpse of a white halter top and mop of curly brown hair.

Of the woman—the very young woman, the girl—who stands, now, beside it. Looking up at the very window he's looking out of. Who raises a hand, tentatively, then finally lowers it.

Who finally gets back into her car and drives away.

The trees glide by like ghosts, appearing then disappearing in the glow of his headlights. He's more than halfway around the circle of campsites, at the farthest point from the main road. And still no sign of the asshole's car.

They may not be here, either.

On the right: nothing there . . . On the left: nothing . . . On the right: Aha!

He slows and stops. Gets out. His mind buzzing like an angry nest of bees. Deep breaths, deep breaths, as he leans against the side of the truck . . . But it doesn't help.

He pushes off. Single-minded in his purpose, though what that purpose is isn't clear. More riled, more enraged, than he's ever felt himself to be.

The gravel crunches softly beneath his feet as he approaches the narrow entrance to the campsite. The shotgun Schaaschicks as he pumps a round into its chamber.

The Camaro glows a dull yellow in the moonlight, the far side illuminated, the back end toward him obscured by shadow.

He approaches steadily at an angle. From less than thirty feet away he can see the car subtly shaking, rocking from side to side on its struts. The sole of a small bare foot, flat against the backseat window.

He stops and stares—riveted, uncertain—as the foot slips away, leaving a smear in the condensation on the glass . . . then comes back.

Slips away again . . . comes back . . .

＊ ＊ ＊ ＊ ＊

DAY 15

CLAY WAKES from a fathomless depth, to the sound of clanking metal.

"Hey! Come get your tray!"

The space around him is murky dark. A pocked gray wall, less than a foot from his face.

He rolls over to a similar gray ceiling and an identical wall only a few feet away. Like he's in a box. What little light there is comes from the direction of his feet, and the noise.

"Hurry the hell up, goddammit!"

There, there's a wall of metal bars, placed vertically every few inches and horizontally about every foot. Behind it stands a fat man in a dark blue uniform wielding a club, which he again bangs against the bars.

"You want your fucking tray, or not?"

Standing stooped beside him is a smaller person, a black man, wearing a lighter, denim blue, holding something knee-high through a slot in the wall of bars.

Clay sits up groggily and swings his legs off the narrow bunk. He'd been sleeping under a single thin white sheet. Wearing plain white boxers.

It's a tray of food the smaller man holds, and Clay's able to reach it easily without having to scoot over. "Thanks," he says automatically.

A metal plate shuts over the slot, and the larger man in the uniform moves away.

"God bless you," says the black fellow, his grizzled face pressed close to the bars. "You gots you a Bible, son?"

Clay shakes his head. He doesn't know. Or care.

"Hurry the hell up!" comes the voice from down the hall.

"I'll try to get you one, all right?" The old man leaves, pushing the metal cart. "Be strong, brother. Give it all to God; he's gotcha."

Clay inspects the tray in his hands: a couple of rock-hard biscuits, some lumpy sort of slop that looks and smells like puke, a little section of applesauce. He sets it on the floor. Slides it under the slab of steel attached to the wall that is his bed. And looks around.

Against the back wall, close to where his head was lying a minute before, is a gleaming metal toilet. In the other corner, a tiny porcelain sink. Above both of these, a bare light bulb with a string, sticking sideways out of the wall. A rusted metal shelf bolted high on the wall opposite the bunk. A row of books on it. A plastic cup.

From outside comes more banging and slamming of metal. More yelling and cursing from a variety of voices. Then, finally, after a couple of minutes, silence. A toilet flushing somewhere nearby.

Ah . . . Okay . . . Clay thinks he's figured it out. Though it's become pretty obvious where he is.

He gets up and stretches his back. Steps to the bars and looks out, up and down the gloomy corridor. The bars cool in his hands. Nobody in sight. The wall across from him painted cement, flaking in many places, like his cell, and extending far in either direction. He appears to be right in the middle.

He sighs. What a way to have to end up.

He turns back to the dank, dark space.

Well, he obviously got caught for killing the asshole this time. It was bound to happen eventually, he figures. Or maybe it's for one of the other times—one of the other lives he's already visited. Maybe he's back again for "part two."

He tries to think, looking back. Was there ever a time when he got caught? . . . Yeah, that first time, when The Gorilla tackled him, probably. Yeah, for sure . . . Though he doesn't think there was any evidence linking him to the bathroom stabbing—except for fingerprints, and cameras, maybe . . . *Shit* . . . But he'd gotten away from the asshole's apartment without a problem . . . And there probably wasn't any way to link him to the prison hit, or the one at Madison Square Garden; but, who knows? . . . And then there's the— No, the captain and crew of that fishing boat had understood well enough, once he'd explained it to them— though he'd have to be let go, he was told, once they got to shore. However, he'd fallen asleep before then . . .

He wonders how he did it this time. If it *is* a new time. Though there's probably plenty of them, he figures. An unlimited number, according to Dr. Z.

Clay goes to lie back down on the bunk, on the pathetically thin mattress there. Puts his hands behind his head, to gaze up at the meager square of ceiling.

So, this is where he's come to visit, in this reality, huh? At least his purpose—his lesson to learn—is pretty clear: Revenge doesn't pay. Something he had to learn the hard way, this time around.

He feels sorry for the version of himself who has to live this way. He can't imagine a worser fate. He wonders if it's a long sentence. Or *life* . . . Regardless, he'd rather be dead than have to be locked up to rot away in a cage, like this—day in, day out. He's glad he only has to experience it for one.

He tells himself that, whatever life he finds himself in tomorrow, he's going to set himself straight. Apply everything he's learned. His new motto: Forgive and forget. No hard feelings.

Well, not *forget*, actually—that part sucks. He doesn't want to forget anything anymore. He'd give anything to have his memory—his old life—back.

If he could just relive that one night . . .

I get it, he tells himself—his Higher Self, his soul—*I understand now.*

Clay's sure that this whole experience these past couple weeks has been a way for him to see that too many of his soul's lives are being wasted on hatred and revenge, instead of embracing forgiveness. He wonders if this is how he's going to live from now on—experiencing all the possibilities, the probable outcomes, from that one night—from the decisions he made . . . affecting the decisions of everybody else involved: Charlene; the asshole; the real killer, if not him . . .

He's thankful that he was given a glimpse of at least one life where he'd made the right decision that night, where he hadn't set the whole sordid chain of events into motion. Even if he had made a mess of that one, too, it looks like, in the end.

Clay closes his eyes and brings up that wonderful day again. Of waking up beside Charlene and their beautiful baby. Of enjoying—truly enjoying—each and every moment he was able to spend with her. Holding her in his arms . . . Loving her . . .

He'll spend today doing nothing else, he decides—reliving his memories of Charlene when they were together, yesterday and before . . . Of his entire life—playing football, his friends, growing up . . .

After all, what else is there to do in a place like this?

CLAY WAKES FROM the golden vision of Charlene beckoning to him with open arms—her eyes, her smile, both so full of love and compassion. Understanding. Like an angel . . . Calling his name . . .

"Mr. Nehman . . ."

There's a soft metallic rapping at the foot of the bunk. Then again. "Mr. Nehman. Wake up, please."

Clay raises himself up on one elbow. Blinks. A man is standing just outside the cell, behind the bars. Balding, little round glasses, white shirt collar above a cardigan sweater, black windbreaker, tan slacks. Holding something to his chest.

"Hello, Mr. Nehman. I'm sorry to disturb you. I was hoping we might have a word."

Clay sits up. "Yeah, sure. Okay."

He stifles a yawn as he puts his feet on the cold cement floor, goes to stand, but the man motions for him to remain seated as he himself pulls up a small folding metal chair and sits down.

"But come a little closer," the guy says, "so we don't have to raise our voices and disturb the others." He's sitting almost sideways to the bars. A thin black folder and a thick black book with gold trim in his lap. "How are you?" he asks. "How do you feel?"

"Uh, all right, I guess. Considering."

The man slowly nods, chin tucked to his chest. "Yes. Considering." He looks up. "Have you made peace with yourself?"

Wow, this guy must be psychic, Clay thinks. "Well, yeah, partially. I've been thinking about it a lot lately. I know that I need to forgive and all that. Let it go. But it's hard to do."

The man's somber expression doesn't change. He doesn't blink. "And have you accepted Jesus Christ as your Lord and Savior?"

Or a preacher. "Uh, nooo . . ."

"Oh. Well, have you asked for the Lord's forgiveness, then?"

Clay brightens. "I've forgiven myself. I've forgiven everybody. Everything."

A beat. *"You've* forgiven your*self."*

"Yep. Uh-huh."

The preacher states, "It's only through the Lord that sins can be forgiven."

"The Lord? You mean, like, God or something?"

"Yes. Well, Jesus, actually, the son of God, but God, also. You can ask God if you prefer."

"Oh. Well, uh, I don't think either one would forgive me for what I did, because, well— I mean, it was pretty bad."

And I did it, like, a whole bunch of times, Clay mentally adds.

"You would be surprised at God's capacity to forgive," says the man.

"Plus, it's not like it was an accident or anything, you know. I meant it. I was pretty pissed, back then. But not anymore . . . I've changed . . . I don't think I'd do it again." He has to chuckle, picturing the asshole's face. "But, then again, you never know."

"What? You—?" The preacher's placid countenance becomes a shocked expression becomes a glare. Then, unexpectedly, something lights in the man's eyes. "Oh! So you remember, then. Finally! Excellent!" His hands go excitedly to the folder in his lap. He removes a typed sheet of paper. "Then you need to confess your sins to me now—to God—so that I can absolve you, so that you may enter the kingdom of Heaven."

"Uh . . . I think God already knows," Clay says.

"Yes. But have you repented?"

"Huh?"

"Are you truly sorry for what you did?"

"Oh. Yeah. I mean, I used to think he deserved it, but—well, even if he did . . . Now I know that killing him really didn't solve anything at all. It just ruined my own life, in the end," motioning to the tiny cell around him. "And every time, no matter what happened, I just made myself even more miserable by holding on to all that anger and hate." He shrugs, looking down at his hands. "Plus . . ." He hates to admit this, especially to himself. ". . . sometimes I'm not even really sure about what happened that night, you know? If he did it, or if it was somebody else."

The preacher just stares, his head held close to the bars, as if searching for something in Clay's face. "I see . . ."

Clay looks back and smiles sheepishly. Lifts a shoulder in a shrug.

The man straightens and goes back to his folder. Flips the first page. Then the next.

"It says here that you've refused psychiatric treatment for the past . . . nine years," he says. He looks up over his glasses. "Is this correct?"

Clay of course has no idea. But he's got shrugging down to an art form.

The man looks back to the folder. Reads further. "And that your appeal attorneys claimed you have no memory of the crime—"

. . . a small bare foot, sliding, leaving a smear on the glass . . .

"—and that you're not guilty by reason of insanity." Again that searching look, brows knitted, as if there's something fundamentally missing from Clay's soul. "So I have to ask you, Mr. Nehman: Do you persist—*even today*—to having no memory of the event?"

"Uh . . ."

. . . the foot coming back to the same spot on the glass . . . then sliding away . . . coming back again . . .

. . . the moonlit car rocking to some invisible beat . . .

"Mr. Nehman—" An exasperated sigh. "—are you aware of what is happening today?"

Clay slowly shakes his head. But by the man's dour expression, it can't be good. The name Clay puts to what he's suddenly feeling is "dread."

"Uh, no . . . What's happening?"

The man keeps staring. Angrily, it seems. Then, at last, his face softens, and he gives a little shake of his head. Sighs, but softer this time. He looks away for a moment, then back—with something almost like compassion. His voice is kind. "You are being executed today. By the state of Oklahoma."

It takes a few seconds for this to sink in. "What?!"

"But if you would only give yourself to Christ, and allow Him to—"

"For killing the asshole?!"

The preacher just looks at him hard again and shakes his head. Bends to the folder in his lap. Flips back to a previous page.

"Mr. Nehman, you are being executed for the murder of . . ." He lifts the folder, looking closely. ". . . Charlene Summers; on May 27th, of 2004."

The man's florid, bespeckled face balloons, warps, then fades . . . begins receding fast down a dark tunnel, taking the bars and the prison cell with him . . .

"Mr. Nehman? . . . Mr. Nehman!"

Everything is bathed *in red—dark around the edges. A dull drumming, a hammering, in his ears.*

There's the crunch of gravel as he steps toward the car, lifts the shotgun, and fires. BOOM! The back left tire explodes in shredded rubber, and the car's rear end sinks.

Schaaschick . . . *BOOM! The driver's-side front fender is peppered with shot, and the tire there begins hissing loudly.*

Schaaschick. *The Camaro's passenger-side door flies open as Clay walks around the back of the car, and a buck-naked asshole comes diving out, scrambles on the ground, goes running for the trees.*

BOOM! from the waist, and the asshole's ass and thighs bloom wet as he leaps into the brush.

Schaaschick.

A muffled cry from inside the car makes him stop and turn. Step to the open door.

Both front seats have been angled forward. Charlene sits naked in the back, one hand over her mouth—eyes huge, scared—the other between her legs. But it can't hide the deep flush of her skin, and the slick sheen of sweat covering her entire body. Her heavy breathing. Her matted hair. The guilt.

Her pretty yellow dress lies folded in the passenger seat, her bra and panties set neatly on top.

He stands staring in disbelief.

I'm sorry, she says, finally. Her voice quivers. I'm so sorry.

He can hear the asshole crying and moaning in the distance. Branches snapping as he tries to run or crawl away.

Charlene's eyes are pleading.

Please forgive me, she says.

His whole world implodes, goes from bright red to black. As he pulls the trigger.

HE REMEMBERS.

He remembers everything now.

All of it: everything that happened that night; and the next day; and the days since.

He remembers being picked up by the side of the road the following afternoon, miles away . . . covered in Charlene's blood, from when he'd held her, for hours. After.

He remembers the many months in jail. The trial. The asshole as a witness against him. The reaction from the people in town. His former friends and teammates.

And he can remember the past thirteen-plus years in prison— this living hell—on death row. In McAlester, the same place he'd "visited" eight days ago . . .

The irony isn't lost on him.

Of course, he can also remember the past insane two weeks, most vividly; but he doesn't appear to have missed a day of that time here, in *this* reality . . . Although he's certain those days weren't merely a dream . . . his imagination . . .

Pretty certain, at any rate.

However, he'd give anything for *this* day to be one—this fucked-up reality.

Perhaps they all are, he thinks.

Dreams.

What would Reverend Z have to say about that? Or the professor? Is each life but a dream within a dream—being dreamt by a mind much greater than that which we normally associate with ourselves? . . . A soul? A Higher Self? . . . Or is it a mishmash of quantum entanglements? . . . Random chaos? Or some kind of concealed order? . . . A "training machine"? A "game"? . . . Some grand experiment? . . . A school? . . .

Or is it all of these things?

The man who had strapped him down has returned and now fiddles again with the needle in Clay's arm. He's done everything with a cool efficiency and hasn't once looked Clay in the eye or said a word, not even to the other man in the room—the one in a cheap brown suit and tie, who receives the nod and solemnly steps forward.

"Do you have any last words?"

Last . . . Final . . .

"No," Clay says softly. He gives a slight shake of his head. What could he say, anyway? That he's sorry? That he's glad he's dying; that he could never live with the knowledge of what he's done? . . . And to who could he say anything to? . . .

"Wait," he says, more forcefully; and the suit holds up a hand.

Clay gives him a tight smile, in thanks. Stares up at the ceiling, his mouth suddenly dry, his throat constricted with emotion.

Says: "I'm really sorry . . . I'm sorry for the pain I've caused . . . I hope that whoever I've hurt, whoever's mad at me for what I've done, can forgive me . . . Not for my sake, but for their's." He waits for more to come, but . . . "I guess that's it."

He tries to ignore the actions all around him, all the eyes that he knows are watching hungrily from outside the tinted window, and instead tries to lose himself in the glaring light above his head—as an icy fire infuses his arm and chest, his entire body.

He recalls the vision—or was it a memory, an experience?— he'd had the other day of traveling to an infinitely more brilliant light than this, and wonders if that's where he'll be going now. Or if he'll wake again in yet another life, another version of himself, as if he's simply going to sleep.

He imagines there's at least one of him out there who's made all the right decisions, all the right choices, and he hopes he can visit there next. And stay, for a change.

From now on, he promises himself, he'll weigh every choice carefully—every thought!—and always try to do the right thing.

276 • *ERIC ARTISAN*

Because he can see now how only *one* bad decision can lead to so many more . . . And how the right one can make all the difference . . .

The hot summer sun wavers through the sparkling surface of the lake as Clay floats serenely below. His breathing suspended. His pulse slowing to a halt. His mind focused on one question . . .

He'd forgiven the asshole for killing Charlene (or at least tried to), he thinks. Now, can he forgive *himself?* . . . For *this?* . . . After all that he's learned? . . .

The urge to breathe—to live—is overwhelming; he's held it long enough. So he kicks to the surface. Breaks through with a gasp, his arms and legs treading water. Tosses his dripping bangs from his face.

Yes! is the one answer that repeats itself, over and over, as he takes in the life-giving air. Feels the warm rays of the sun. The cool breeze on his skin. As he looks to the pale blue sky and laughs, with abandon. As he sees Charlene waving happily to him from the shore.